After Dark with the Duke CH

"You're not completely right, either. In the world of the theater, most decisions are still made by men, and to survive and thrive in it, one must use the language men understand. And that language is flattery and flirtation. But it can be used to both keep people at a distance and to pull them in. When one is *not* a castle, one must use the tools at one's disposal. I cannot speak to the childish behavior, as that seems."

He was silent.

"We're that simple, are we," he said neutrally. "Men are."

"I'm afraid so." She offered him a tiny, pitying smile. "Well, that, and I like to flirt . . . some of the time."

"Very well. We have established I am a castle and you are in a fortress surrounded by free-roaming sheep. We have a sense of each other now, I believe."

By Julie Anne Long

JULIE ANNE LONG

After Dark with the Duke

THE PALACE OF ROGUES

AVONBOOKS

An Imprint of HarperCollinsPublishers

MIX
Paper from responsible sources
FSC® C021394
www.fsc.org

This is a work of fiction. Names, characters, places, and incidents are products of the author's imagination or are used fictitiously and are not to be construed as real. Any resemblance to actual events, locales, organizations, or persons, living or dead, is entirely coincidental.

First Avon Books mass market printing: December 2021

Print Edition ISBN: 978-0-06-304509-5
Digital Edition ISBN: 978-0-06-304415-9

Cover design by Guido Caroti
Cover illustration by Juliana Kolesova

Avon, Avon & logo, and Avon Books & logo are registered trademarks of HarperCollins Publishers in the United States of America and other countries.

HarperCollins is a registered trademark of HarperCollins Publishers in the United States of America and other countries.

FIRST EDITION

Printed in Lithuania

21 22 23 24 25 SB 10 9 8 7 6 5 4 3 2 1

*To the fabulous Read-Along hostesses of Instagram,
the Pied Pipers of Pennyroyal Green and
the Palace of Rogues, who have made
these past few months such a joy:
Natalie, Andrea, Sarah, Erin, Meg, and Laine*

*And to every one of you who participated by
sharing photos, wit, charm, and thoughtfulness.
I appreciate all of you so very much!*

Acknowledgments

❧❧❧

MY GRATITUDE to my darling editor, May Chen, and the brilliant people at Avon for their skillful work and beautiful covers; to my agent, Steve Axelrod, and his staff, Elsie Turoci and Lori Antonson, and to all the bloggers, reviewers, friends, and readers of Facebook and Instagram who so passionately share their love of my books.

After Dark with the Duke

Chapter One

ecco

$\mathcal{M}$ARIANA MADE a little show of scrabbling about in her reticule, but she already knew all too well how much she intended to pay the smiling hack driver who'd brought her all the way to the docks.

"I'm af-fraid I've only two p-p-pence."

She in truth had one pound, one shilling, and two pence.

But what was one more drop of shame in the ocean of it currently lapping around her conscience?

She couldn't see the hack driver's face anymore. The rain was sideways now. But she could feel his disappointment, like a light winking out.

Which made her feel lower than she already felt, low as a snake, which was low indeed.

He sighed. "Miss, if ye're here nigh on midnight in the rain at the docks in that rig"—he gestured to the fur-lined pelisse, her satin slippers—"you've need of it more than I do. I'll take one pence."

"B-bless you, sir." The unholy alliance of fear and cold and rain was making her teeth chatter.

"Oh, aye, it's *blessings* what puts food on me table," he said dryly.

He deposited her trunk with a thunk at her feet, and she paid him. His beneficence apparently did not extend to carrying the trunk over the threshold, and she could hardly blame him.

Should the door actually open for her when she knocked upon it, that was.

She couldn't entertain any other possibility.

"Your name, sir? If I can ever rep-pay you . . ."

He heaved himself back up into the driver's seat and took up the ribbons. "It's Malloy, madam, should that unlikely day occur. Good luck to ye and Godspeed."

He touched his hat and cracked the ribbons, and the horses lurched off into the wet night.

She was alone at the docks in dark interrupted only by the glow of the lamp on a hook, which illuminated a sign dancing on chains in the wind: THE GRAND PALACE ON THE THAMES. She squinted. Another word was very faintly visible behind them. Was it "rogue"?

One of the little gargoyles lining the roof drooled a rivulet of rain down her neck.

She cursed softly and bit her lip.

She took a breath, then seized the knocker and rapped.

She gave a start when the peep window in the door instantly flung open and an enormous, guileless, pale blue eye appeared.

"Well, good evening!" Mariana said brightly to it.

"Good evening," the voice belonging to the eye said by way of greeting, albeit somewhat suspiciously. "I'm afraid our curfew is eleven, which was two minutes ago. I was just about to bring in the lamp."

Mariana sensed room for negotiation.

"Oh, d-dear. I so apologize for the inconvenience and I shouldn't blame you if you'd like to lock up, but I wondered if you might have a r-room to let? It's a bit rough out here tonight, and I find myself in a bit of a p-pickle." She couldn't prevent her teeth from chattering, but she thought it best to keep her tone light and her accent posh. The one she'd learned from mimicking Madame Guillaume.

The blue eye narrowed thoughtfully.

And then the little peep window slammed shut.

Mariana crossed her fingers, closed her eyes, and prayed.

Suddenly the heavy door swung open, releasing a gust of warmth, and revealing a softly glowing marble foyer and a young woman wearing an apron and cap. "You'd best hurry, miss, or the rain will come in with you."

"Oh, thank you. You're *very* kind to trouble. Thank you! I've . . . I've a trunk. I hope that doesn't seem presumptuous. I couldn't leave it, you see, and I didn't know if you would have a room."

"I don't know, either," the young woman said cryptically, but she gamely pulled while Mariana pushed, and together they got it into the foyer. It left a glistening damp trail, and the dangling crystals of the chandelier above scattered little rainbows down upon it.

And then the maid, a fair-haired girl, ushered her into a pleasant parlor where a fire burned low.

Mariana turned to look back at the foyer, arrested by the little rainbows thrown down upon it by dangling crystals on the chandelier.

"Oh, my, isn't that the most *beautiful* chandelier?"

She was twenty-five years old and would never get over the enchantment of sparkling things.

The maid beamed at her as if she'd said magic words. And then she covered her mouth with her palm.

"Oh, ma'am, you're steaming!"

Steam was indeed rising from her. Mariana gave a startled laugh. "So I am! It's very chilly outside, and so wonderfully warm in here. Isn't that funny? You'd think I was the devil himself arriving. Or . . . an apparition!"

"Have you heard of a book called *The Ghost in the Attic*, miss?"

"Cor, I love *The Ghost in the Attic*!"

"It's my favorite!"

The maid and Mariana shared a moment of beaming accord.

Mariana's eyes began to droop. Oh, God, the warmth. It was like a hug, the room. She could not recall the last time she was hugged by someone whose main objective wasn't to shag her.

"Have you a room to let?" she prodded the maid gently.

"Well . . . it's not up to me, you see, miss. If you'll just wait here, I'll go fetch Mrs. Hardy and Mrs. Durand, and they'll want to speak to you for a bit. Our place is exclusive, like. And we've rules," she said proudly.

"Oh, my. Exclusive! How thrilling. Exclusive places are my favorite." They were now. "And that's very wise of them, of course. One never knows who might appear at the door in the middle of the night." She said this with only a little irony.

"I'll ask them if they'll come down. Whom shall I say is waiting?"

Mariana paused. Somehow she had not anticipated this question.

She was disinclined to lie, but the truth might get her chased out the door with a broom.

"I think it wisest," she said carefully, "if I tell Mrs. Hardy and Mrs. Durand myself who I am directly, if they are kind enough to meet me."

Mariana thought she'd succeeded in sounding the proper combination of genteel, confident, calm, amusing, and harmless—precisely the sort of person one wanted to let a room to in the dead of a rainy night by the docks.

The maid paused. Mariana held her breath.

"I'll go and tell them, then."

"SHE LOOKS FRIGHTENED," Dot stage-whispered. "And she's so cold she's *steaming*. And she's doing this." She clacked her teeth together noisily.

Delilah and Angelique reared back a little.

"Oh, dear," Delilah said.

Dot had found the proprietresses of The Grand Palace on the Thames in the sitting room at the top of the stairs, where they liked to conclude their evenings and talk about the day and plan the next one. Gordon, the striped and plump resident mouse and rat catcher, was curled up in his basket at their feet, and two warm husbands, Captain Tristan Hardy and Lucien Durand, Lord Bolt, were stretched out in respective beds in their respective rooms, waiting impatiently for them.

But there was much to discuss tonight. They'd just said farewell to the Earl and Countess of Vaughn and their family, and to Mr. Hugh Cassidy, and had begun to wonder whether they ought to advertise for more guests straightaway. Guests tended to come and go, but expenses tended to come and stay. There was also the matter of the newly finished ballroom in the Annex, the stage freshly hung with beautiful green velvet curtains, and the possibility, which seemed remote at the moment, of holding musical evenings there for which the public would buy tickets. It would be a marvelous source of income and good fun. There was also the little challenge of hiring a footman.

"She's young and has a very nice face, with one of these." Dot pressed her chin to make a dimple. "She has pale eyes and red hair, and she sounds like a lady . . . and she looks like a lady . . . and her pelisse is lined in fur, but . . ." Dot lowered her voice to a stage whisper ". . . I don't think she's a *lady*, if you take my meaning."

Angelique and Delilah exchanged a speaking glance.

Dot had once been the world's worst lady's maid, fired by a horrible duchess, then rescued and employed out of the stubborn, long-suffering goodness of Delilah's heart. She'd become a valued member of the household and a friend, after a fashion, even if they'd finally needed to firmly but gently admonish her about dropping yet another tea tray, this time because a fly had landed on her nose, and she'd sneezed, and closed her eyes, forgotten to open them again, and walked into a wall. They hadn't the heart to outright ban her from bringing tea. Opening the door to the surprise of new guests and bringing in the tea were her two favorite things to do.

And besides, she'd proven to be a veritable savant about describing the people who appeared.

"What makes you think she's not a lady?" Delilah asked.

Dot bit her lip. "Well, her dress is good wool and of the first stare of fashion, mind you, but I took her damp pelisse *from* her—she didn't hand it right off to me, like"—she made an imperious shoving motion—"and when I did, she said, 'Thank you, you're very kind.'"

Delilah and Angelique took this in ruefully. Dot knew most titled ladies didn't typically thank the servants any more than they would thank the settee for supporting their bums.

"Did you take her name?" Angelique asked her.

"She says it's better if she tells you directly."

"Well," Angelique said slowly, with another glance at Delilah.

Things had just gotten more interesting.

Dot clasped her hands in front of her. "Mrs. Hardy and Mrs. Durand, she . . . I do think she needs help. Will you go and see her?"

They both spared a thought for their husbands waiting for them.

And then Angelique and Delilah put aside their mending.

"Well, if there's anything we've expertise in, it's not-quite-ladies in distress," Angelique said blithely. "*Thank* you, Dot," she added pointedly.

Angelique was married to a formerly notorious, now (almost) entirely respectable bastard son of a duke, and Delilah was married to a famous former blockade captain who'd deservedly been *called* a bastard a time or two, but their unlikely friendship had been forged when Delilah's first husband—an earl—had up and died, leaving both of their lives in ruins. They had risen from the ashes.

They were both ladies to their marrows, and they both knew a title didn't make a lady.

"Do make some tea, Dot. And . . . perhaps bring in a snifter of brandy."

They stood at once and shook out their skirts, removed their aprons, patted and smoothed their hair into place to reassure their potential guest of their own respectability. They would discover soon enough what manner of lady the steaming woman downstairs might be.

Dot had only been wrong about a guest once. And if she was wrong about this one, well, they knew where the loaded pistol was hidden in the parlor. And they knew how to use it.

LIKE A MIRACLE, presently there appeared in the room two beautiful ladies who introduced themselves as Mrs. Durand, who was blonde, and Mrs. Hardy, who had very dark hair. Mrs. Durand held a knitted coverlet out to her.

Mariana accepted it with a sort of wordless peep of gratitude before lowering herself onto the settee. She closed her eyes briefly, savoring the comfort. Then snapped them open. It wouldn't do at all to nod off. Best not to lower her guard just yet.

"Thank you for coming down to speak to me. I know it is very late, so I should like to tell you two things straightaway. The first is that I currently have in my possession only one pound."

She inspected their faces for outrage or censure.

Delilah's and Angelique's expressions remained pleasantly interested.

Very slow, measured footfalls could now be heard on the marble of the foyer floor, accompanied by clinking and rattling sounds. It could easily have been a ghost in the attic dragging chains, but it was Dot bringing the tea.

"I'm *owed* more, mind you," she added hurriedly. "And I presently expect to have more. But that— that—*bounder* Giancarlo hasn't . . ." She pressed her lips together. "Forgive me. That is quite beside the point. The point is, I began the night with two pounds, but I needed one of them to bri—er, persuade my neighbor to spirit my trunk out through the back courtyard and over the fence."

There was a little beat of silence.

"May we ask why this spiriting was necessary?" Mrs. Hardy had lovely, patient brown eyes and one of the best game faces Mariana had ever seen.

"To avoid the little mob in front of my building who seemed eager to tear me limb from limb."

Through her slitted curtains, she'd looked down into upraised fists and furious, snarling faces shaping the word over and over: *harlot harlot harlot*. It hardly fit the circumstances, but it sounded clever when paired with "Haywood Street," so that's what the newspaper had printed. Three days in a row, as it so happened. There was a certain type of person who found that sort of thing delicious. It wasn't true.

Then again, truth didn't matter to those who feasted upon judgment like wolves on lamb.

"I found a hack right quickly, however," she added somewhat more brightly, into the silence.

Mariana was still rather pleased about this. She had chosen to take it as a sign that things might go her way. Poor Mr. Malloy.

Dot had made it across the foyer, and she now crossed the threshold of the room bearing the tea on a tray as though she were edging along the side of a cliff bearing the crown jewels on a satin pillow. The cause of the rattling and clinking was revealed to be the cups and saucers and sugar jostling against spoons and the china pot.

They all watched as she began to lower the tray to the table.

"Which brings me to the second thing I need to tell you," Mariana said. "Which is . . ."

It was somewhat gratifying to know that her audience was now on tenterhooks. Her mother had always claimed she'd had a flair for the dramatic.

". . . my name is Mariana Wylde."

Dot gasped, dropped the tea tray the final quarter of an inch to the table, and bolted from the room.

The rest of them watched, transfixed, while the single teacup spun and wobbled.

"I feel a bit as though I ought to put a half crown on black six," Mariana said brightly, finally.

Delilah reached out a hand and touched a finger to the cup. It stilled.

If only a celestial finger would reach down and touch her life just like that, Mariana thought.

"I jest, of course. I don't know a *thing* about gaming hells." She crossed her fingers in her lap.

"My husband thought he wanted to open a gaming hell once," Mrs. Durand said pleasantly and somewhat startlingly. "It's indeed a pleasure to meet you in person, Miss Wylde."

Mrs. Hardy nodded. "Indeed, it truly is."

Mariana exhaled. "Well, that is very kind of you, as it's hardly the consensus since the . . ."

Without warning, the last grains of her bravado trickled away.

She could not force her voice past that word; it was lodged in her throat like a bone.

She brought her hands up and tipped her face into them. She was shocked to find they were like ice, given how scalding the shame was.

She breathed into her hands. She heard only the tiny cracks and pops of the fire.

". . . duel?" Mrs. Hardy supplied gently, after a moment.

Mariana nodded slowly, resignedly, painfully.

She sighed, then pulled her hands away from her face.

To find that Mrs. Durand was holding out to her a snifter containing about one gulp of brandy.

Mariana took it. Sniffed it. Then mimed an ironic toast and bolted it.

"Oh, thank you," she gasped. "That's better."

Neither of their faces betrayed a flicker of judgment. Though she wasn't certain she detected undue sympathy, either.

Angelique poured the tea. "Sugar?"

"Yes, please. You're too kind," she said, amazed, near to tears now. "You're being so kind." She looked out toward the foyer. "I fear I frightened your maid. Will she be . . ."

"Oh, I expect Dot is more thrilled than scandalized. She reads the gossip to the maids in the kitchen every morning, and you are a particular favorite," Angelique said. "We have followed the trajectory of your career since your role alongside Madame LeCroix last year."

"A bit like the tea tray, the trajectory of my career," Mariana said ruefully.

At first it had been *thrilling* to see her name in the gossip columns—she'd been compared to Angelica Catalani—the great Catalani!—for her pureness and depth of tone and her pretty face. She hadn't known she was only skeet. That it was society's hobby to launch a person skyward, and then aim and fire and shatter them into smithereens just for the joy of watching them fall.

"We've actually had the pleasure of hearing you

sing, Miss Wylde," Mrs. Durand said. "We didn't recognize you without that magnificent wig and the beauty patches. You died very beautifully on-stage. Nearly everyone in the theater had a hand-kerchief out."

Mariana was thrilled. "Oh, then you saw the afternoon performance? I was meant to go in Madame Wilhelm's place for the remainder of the run. Until things . . . took a turn." Two nights later, as it so happened.

"My husband, Captain Hardy, was offered use of a box owned by an esteemed acquaintance. And while normally he would have needed to be press-ganged into attending an opera, he wanted to please me. So we went. As did Mrs. Durand and her husband, Lord Bolt."

"It was the aria from Giancarlo Giannini's new opera. Isn't it an exquisite piece?" Mariana said wistfully. "He's gifted . . . the knave," she added darkly.

Dot had made a somewhat sidling return to the foyer, trailing three other sidling maids. They'd brought a ladder, which they propped up. They began to mill about the chandelier.

"Funny. It usually only requires one maid to douse the chandelier lights," Delilah murmured acerbically.

"I can't remember the last time I heard any-thing so beautiful," Angelique told Mariana. "I can truthfully say it was an *honor* to hear you sing, Miss Wylde."

Mariana did not think compliments and tributes would ever lose their gloss, even though she had come to realize she deserved them. But taking a compliment was always that moment a bit like a curtain being whipped aside in a dark room to reveal a brilliantly sunny day: a certain inner bracing was required to accommodate their full splendor.

"Well. That was better than brandy for warming my cockles, Mrs. Durand. Thank you."

Delilah got up and closed the door to the room against the shamelessly eavesdropping maids.

Mariana had experienced good luck and bad luck often enough in her life to know that one could easily masquerade as the other. She wasn't certain what tonight's events would turn out to be, but given the turn the conversation was taking, she was starting to like her chances of at least getting a room.

Still, she thought she'd better settle that part straightaway.

"You have been very kind to me, so I shall be straight with you. I've no other place to go at the moment. I've enough to pay for a room for a . . . night or two?" she hazarded.

They had the *best* game faces, she thought admiringly. They said nothing at all, pleasantly.

"If you can spare a room—any little closet that would fit me would suit, the scullery, this lovely room—and should you not wish to keep me for a guest, I shall set about finding a place on the morrow. If I attempt to return to my own room on Haywood Street, I think the crowd outside would tear me to pieces. And as of now . . ." She drew in a breath. "I'm worried I won't be allowed to sing in England again."

"Both would be tragedies," Angelique said sweetly.

It might have been the brandy, but Mariana laughed. Something about the very dark *dryness* of that was fortifying.

In fact, something about the place, these women, and this little room, made her feel certain she was safe. That she'd done the right thing at last after a series of inadvertently doing quite the wrong things.

Although this sensation could also be the brandy.

"We sometimes negotiate fees based on special circumstances, Miss Wylde," Delilah added.

Angelique darted a look at Delilah.

"Here's a question I've been mulling, Miss Wylde. What brings you to The Grand Palace on the Thames? It's hardly on the beaten path, so it's unlikely one would stumble across it as they fled. It would have been your specific destination."

Good heavens, these were clever women.

She took a breath. Then reached beneath the coverlet she was gripping closed, found her reticule, and retrieved the folded scrap of newspaper.

"This was wrapped around a little drinking glass I purchased in a shop some weeks ago. I know you are not quite like me . . . but I kept it, because when I read it I thought . . . here is another woman who has had a complicated life. Who is more than the newspapers would have her seem. And now she's married to Lord Bolt, because it's something everyone seems to know now. They had the name of your establishment wrong, but my hack driver, Mr. Malloy, somehow knew how to find it anyway."

Delilah glanced at Angelique worriedly. She already knew what it was. They both did. It was another of the hateful gossip sheets.

But Angelique, after a brief hesitation, took it from her.

"You must believe me when I say that I hope this does not stir painful memories for you, Mrs. Durand," Mariana said.

For Angelique, this little paragraph had indeed been shocking. Painful. Terrifying, even.

Now, reading it, she realized that it had become a source of strength. Because it had exposed to the light an old, shameful wound, and in so doing, the wound had finally healed.

Lord Bolt was bound to blow and blow he did at White's! Seems his devil's blood got stirred when Lord Hallworth dared to reminisce about a certain Mrs. Angelique Breedlove, dead Derring's former mistress and current mistress of a boardinghouse called The Rogue's Palace on the Thames. Hallworth was pinned against the wall with his own cravat for the trouble. No duel was fought and Hallworth croaked out an apology. But there is one doxie in the world who can rest easy knowing Bolt will rush to her defense. Probably because he took Derring's place.

Angelique looked up at Miss Wylde, wordlessly, and she waited for any hint of the sensations she'd felt when she'd first read it—the shock, the horror, the shame.

She found, oddly, that she felt nothing at all but gratitude. Revisiting the moment reminded her of how far she'd come; it was a bit like reading a page from an old diary about someone she used to be. It was a reminder that she, Lucien, and The Grand Palace on the Thames had survived such casual ugliness because they were all surrounded by such love.

But Miss Wylde had worriedly sunk her teeth into her bottom lip.

"I . . . I thought . . . this Mrs. Breedlove is a woman who knows that life takes many twists and turns. And while I don't believe you were *ever* a doxie—because, regardless of a few, er, decisions I have made, *I* am not—I thought that if any part of this is true, you might be inclined to . . ." she gulped a breath ". . . believe me when I say that things are *not* as the gossip sheets would have you believe. What they wrote isn't true. Even if I can appreciate how the saucy little pairing of 'Harlot' and 'Haywood Street' is so very, very tempting for a gossip writer." She said this tautly.

Delilah and Angelique were quiet for a few pensive moments.

Angelique quirked the corner of her mouth. "Your insight is uncanny, Miss Wylde. It's convenient to blame the woman for things, especially when a man of power is involved."

"I am not claiming to be utterly blameless. But I am not to blame, if that makes sense. You look happy now, and that . . . gives me hope. And this place is just so *beautiful*," she said wistfully. She turned her head this way and that to take in the worn but pretty settees in shades of rose, the flowers on the mantel.

This was precisely the right thing to say to these women.

"I will understand if you prefer not to keep me here in light of the scandal. But if I've a roof over my head for a day or two"—she was already negotiating—"I can perhaps get word to Signor Giannini, in the hopes that he can pay me the balance of what he owes me for my performances so far, and then I can head for Scotland, where my mother has gone to live with a cousin." This had been deemed more practical than Mariana and her mother attempting to squeeze into the tiny room on Haywood Street that Mariana could afford.

Her poor mother. *You're destined for greatness, Mariana*, she'd always predicted. How on earth would she ever be able to tell her what had happened?

There was a little silence.

"Well, Miss Wylde," Mrs. Hardy said. "We do thank you for your candor. It is our custom to take a few minutes to privately discuss whether we ought to admit a potential new guest, as the safety and comfort of all of our current guests is paramount, and we like to make certain the atmosphere here remains congenial for all. If you'd like to review our rules to see if you have any objection to them while we have a chat, do feel free." She handed Miss Wylde a little card printed with the rules of The Grand Palace on the Thames. "Meanwhile, please drink more tea. We suspect you need it."

DELILAH AND ANGELIQUE opened the door of the reception room to the frantic scuffle of slippers on marble, then the thunder of footsteps retreating up the stairs. Fleeing maids.

Delilah sighed. Eavesdropping maids could be dealt with in the morning. At least the foyer was empty now and the chandelier doused.

As was their habit, they crossed into the main sitting room, the site of much merriment, familial joy, knitting, spillikins, secret lust, a pantomime pirate battle, and on at least two occasions, vigorous sex.

The fire was still burning but was scarcely more than a glow. They both pulled their shawls tightly about them, thinking wistfully of the warm husbands waiting for them in their snug rooms.

"I like her," Delilah said at once, in a whisper. "And I believe her."

"So do I. Furthermore I think I know what *else* you're thinking, Delilah . . ."

"And?" Delilah's breath seemed to be held.

Angelique bit her lip. "It could work," she said.

Delilah gave a little hop. "Oh, Angelique! She landed on our doorstep like a *gift*! Well, she would have been more of a coup before two fools decided to shoot each other over her, but now we can *afford* her. We can ask her to sing for one night in exchange for her board. We'll send out invitations . . . sell tickets . . ."

"But the *costs* involved."

"And the fun involved!" Delilah brought her hands together in a little clasp as she thought of something. "Angelique . . . we can decorate the ballroom with bunting! And *flowers*!"

"Bunting, yes. But flowers are an outrageous expense. And we can't completely denude the blossoms in our little park outside."

Delilah thought furiously.

"Tissue flowers?" she ventured on a whisper. "Can you see it?"

Angelique was silent. She pressed her lips together. "Delilah, I think my pulse is racing."

They both muffled laughs.

"We'll have a program printed. We'll call it . . ." Delilah swept a hand out dramatically ". . . the Night of the Nightingale."

"Sublime! But the cost of printing tickets and programs and ads in the newspaper . . ."

"Well. We'll do the usual."

The usual was to beg, borrow, trade, barter, charm, and occasionally gracefully coerce to get the things they needed for The Grand Palace on the Thames. Partially out of thrift, as their fortunes did tend to fluctuate, and partially out of the pure joy of the sport. They could make quite a bit of what they needed by hand. Actually purchasing something besides food was usually for when all else failed.

"But a mob wanted to kill her tonight, she says. Will we make a target of her if she's onstage?"

"Well, they'll have to buy expensive tickets to kill her," Angelique said.

"Angelique!" Delilah pretended to be scandalized.

"In all seriousness, my sense is that many aristocrats like to get a good look at those they're judging so they can feel superior," Angelique added.

Delilah had once been married to an earl, which made her a countess, and she knew this was true. "Will they *pay* to experience that particular delicious sensation?"

"They should be so lucky! She's extraordinarily talented. But we shall sell some tickets at a lower price, too, and perhaps give a few away, because *everyone* deserves to hear her, not just the rich."

"Oh, yes. That is, if she agrees to do it."

"If she agrees."

"And besides, no one will be able to lay a finger on her, especially with Captain Hardy and his former regiment in attendance."

"Oh, are they coming, too?" Angelique asked.

Delilah laughed softly.

"It's a gamble," Angelique said.

"Literally every moment of our lives, from the moment I hired Dot to this place, to Tristan, to Lucien, has been a gamble. And yet here we are."

They looked across the foyer, where poor Miss Wylde's head was drooping into her chest.

"Let's get her tucked into a room for the evening and tell her our idea in the morning before we get carried away," Delilah said.

"Oh, Delilah, you may be forgetting about something. Or rather . . . someone."

Delilah went still. "Oh. The duke."

"The duke."

They fell silent.

"Well, perhaps she won't even notice he's here."

They stifled laughs at that.

And with fingers crossed, they went to tell Miss Wylde the good news.

Chapter Two

❦

"IT'S POSSIBLE you'll hardly notice I'm here," was, in fact, what General James Duncan Blackmore, the Duke of Valkirk, had said to Delilah and Angelique a fortnight ago, at the conclusion of his interview.

Later, this had struck them as funny. After all, even when the moon isn't visible in the sky, everyone knows it's still up there. Valkirk's influence was immense, and shone on every part of England.

Five years had passed since the war that had made him a general, a legend, and subsequently a duke. A huge handsome statue of him was erected in Hyde Park and was now perpetually topped with a modest crown of bird shite; in the British Museum hung a painting depicting him wearing a scarlet dress uniform and a triumphant sneer. Some years earlier he'd written a slim book called *Honor* that had become a sacred text for earnest young men hoping to live noble lives of bravery and distinction. No doubt he would be interred in Westminster Abbey when the day arrived, provided they could cram another dignitary into the place.

The actual man proved almost alarmingly vital in person.

Yet there was a sort of impenetrable certainty to him, and a grandeur that had nothing to do with pomp. Delilah and Angelique thought this certainty seemed actually to be a sort of completeness, as though, having done what no other human could do, and seen things no other human had seen, he'd nothing left to accomplish, and nothing could possibly impress him.

Roughly the same, of course, might almost be said of a cliff.

He took up a good deal of room on the settee and, it seemed, most of the available oxygen in the room. It was as though his history crowded in with him like an invisible entourage.

"I'm writing another book, you see," he told them. "My autobiography. And I need a place to stay while I finish it, as my London townhouse is undergoing renovations."

Ah. This, apparently, was what there was left for a man like Valkirk to do: record the story of his life so that young men all over England could pore over it to learn the secret of greatness.

They could sense in him a tendency to briskness straining against his faultless manners; he took care to speak gently. No doubt he assumed, rightly, that Delilah and Angelique were awed into speechlessness upon meeting him. Everybody was.

When he'd admired and approved their list of rules (not even a duke was exempt from their rules), he'd endeared himself to them forever. Because who knew more about rules and the right thing to do than the Duke of Valkirk?

He was a man. They hadn't yet met one who couldn't be domesticated with a warm fire, some drinking chocolate, Helga's scones, and kindness, which was a bit how wolves had become dogs. They were confident they could make him comfortable.

But they'd needed to break the news to Mr. Delacorte, whose sentimental heart had taken a buffeting when Mr. Hugh Cassidy had improbably married the daughter of an earl staying at The Grand Palace on the Thames and ferried her off to his home in the wilds of New York. While he was happy for Mr. Cassidy, Mr. Delacorte missed having a friend who was game to go to a donkey race or to a festival featuring men attempting to grasp fleeing greased pigs, or any of the other entertainments available to thrifty men who eschewed gaming hells.

He didn't miss having an earl and countess about the place. The strain of reining in his natural exuberance sawed at him.

"We all miss Mr. Cassidy," Delilah began.

"He is a prince among men," Delacorte said, forgetting that he'd have enjoyed Cassidy a good deal less if he'd been an actual prince.

"Well, we think you'll be pleased to know that we're getting a new gentleman guest!"

Mr. Delacorte smiled expectantly, his blue eyes shining as they shifted between Angelique and Delilah.

They realized they might have overplayed their bright, encouraging expressions when he narrowed his eyes. "How might a bloke address this new guest in conversation?"

Their silence was a beat too long.

"Your Grace," Angelique finally admitted.

"He's a *duke*?" Delacorte croaked incredulously.

"He was a general, first, mind."

"How is that *better*? Hold on. You can't mean Valkirk? Valorous *Valkirk*? Holy sh . . ."

When he'd first arrived at The Grand Palace on the Thames, he would have lost a pence then and there to the epithet jar in the sitting room. One of the reasons he was happy at The Grand Palace on the Thames was that he felt the ladies would "knock the rough corners from him." He *wanted* a bit of civilizing. He liked to think he was getting more civilized by the day.

"We won't be calling him 'Valorous Valkirk' in the sitting room, of course," Angelique said.

"He was *made* a duke because he was brave in the war," Delilah tried. "He wasn't born one, like Lucien's father. Perhaps think of him as a bit like Captain Hardy! His beginnings were likewise rather modest. Only . . . he's now a bit grander than Captain Hardy. And perhaps . . . ah, quieter."

Mr. Delacorte often congratulated himself on bringing the taciturn Captain Hardy out of his shell (a notion that would have greatly surprised Captain Hardy), but he'd found it no mean feat. They were now business partners and friends, but Hardy was never going to be as voluble as Delacorte preferred. Notably: Hardy hadn't seen fit to tell him that he'd talked a duke into staying here.

Because Captain Hardy had indeed been the one who'd enticed the Duke of Valkirk to take a suite of rooms at The Grand Palace on the Thames. He'd presented this coup to Delilah and Angelique with much the same pride and fanfare as Gordon, their striped cat, presented them with dead mice. After all, the suites ought not to sit empty. And it was the duke who had loaned them his opera box; he owned one, perhaps because it seemed like something a duke ought to own, and while his son made good use of it, the duke never attended.

"So . . . a bit like Captain Hardy," Delacorte guessed. "With a dash of Bolt thrown in, perhaps?"

"Ah—a bit like Captain Hardy. Not at *all* like Bolt." While it was generally acknowledged that Lucien was quite reformed, predictably good company, responsible, successful, and besotted with his new wife, he'd begun life as the bastard son of a duke and had sown every oat conceivable when he was a young man. His youthful exploits had been gleefully documented by the broadsheets and would likely be recalled for decades.

Whereas Valkirk's entire allegedly blameless life ensured he was spoken of only in hushed, reverent tones, and the details of his life had been reported as national news, safely on the front page of the newspaper. Never on the gossip pages.

"Why does he need to stay here?"

"He's writing his memoirs, and he thought a change of scene would help, as there are apparently too many distractions in his townhouse with builders and whatnot. And he needed to stay in London in case he's required for a parliamentary vote."

Mr. Delacorte was quiet.

"Does he at least play chess?" he asked hopefully.

"Probably," Delilah told him.

Such delightfully improbable things happened with such startling frequency at The Grand Palace on the Thames that one would likely need a crowbar and a good deal of prying to get Mr. Delacorte to leave, and truthfully, they would be happy to have him stay forever.

The duke was due to move into his suite in three days.

***

Dear Mama,
  I hope this finds you well.

MARIANA HAD WRITTEN those words, and only those words, when she'd first arrived at The Grand Palace on the Thames three days ago.

They'd glared up at her accusingly from the foolscap on the little desk in her room ever since.

She wrote to her mother at least once a fortnight without fail. The very *idea* of her mother worrying about her, along with the remote but distinct possibility that the London papers might have already traveled down the secluded, muddy lane in

Scotland where her mother had been compelled to live with her grim cousin Edith and her cousin's husband, George, was yet another fine stratum of torment laid down over all the others papering her soul at the moment.

Even if the newspapers had reached her, it's possible her mother would not have ventured past page one and the article about how the Valorous Duke of Valkirk had donated a hundred pounds to a charity run by the Marquess Champlin. "What a fine person he is!" her mother had marveled more than once over the years, a refrain echoed all over England every day.

Perhaps that was how she'd ease her mother into the news. She could write:

> *Dear Mama,*
> *I hope this finds you well. You might be excited to hear that I was mentioned in the paper on the same day as the Duke of Valkirk!*

She'd also contemplated taking a "let's rewrite history" approach:

> *Dear Mama,*
> *I hope this finds you well. You may have heard something concerning by now, but I should like to tell you it's all a very funny misunderstanding. The newspapers got it wrong. "Harlot of Haywood Street" is the name of the new opera by Giancarlo Giannini, and I*

play the starring role! And Lord K. and
Lord R. are merely characters in the story, not
my lovers. Can you imagine! Lord K. wasn't
really shot, and he isn't really at death's door,
so you needn't worry about that, either.

But she, of course, wouldn't lie to her mother.

And she could still hear that gunshot. Her body still jerked every time a door slammed.

And she didn't feel insouciant at all about it.

Her stomach knotted.

"Lord K." and "Lord R." was how they'd referred to the men in the papers, to protect them, of course, because they had titles. They always printed her full name, however. Otherwise how would everyone know who to blame?

At least Kilhone was still alive, last she'd heard.

Her mother was so proud of her. Still was, no doubt, in her likely current blessed state of ignorance.

Her indecision about what to write after those first few words was also rooted in thrift. Foolscap was expensive. She, like all the other guests at The Grand Palace on the Thames, had been provided with two sheets. For a pence she would be supplied with more. Given that she needed to squeeze her pence until they begged for mercy, she was going to need to make this particular piece count.

She'd slept like the dead the night of her arrival, exhausted from a fortnight's worth of ricocheting from circumstance to circumstance like a billiard ball. The following morning, Mrs. Hardy and Mrs.

Durand had presented her with their idea for a musical evening, which amounted to Mariana singing for her supper and board, as well as a percentage of any earnings after her bill was satisfied. She'd immediately agreed, of course, even before she'd seen the lovely new ballroom. They fixed a date for the event for a little over a month hence.

"What if I'm still a pariah by then, and nobody comes?" she'd asked them. "What if I cannot properly repay you?" She'd said this matter-of-factly, rather than beseechingly. They were doing business, after all.

"We'll foist some tickets on our friends. But the *ton* will have moved on to persecuting someone else, surely. We'll get Captain Hardy and Lord Bolt to stage a duel, if not," Angelique said.

"We jest, of course," Delilah added, hurriedly.

And then she bravely asked the thing that worried her most, given how kind these ladies had been. "What if the very *notion* of me turns everyone away from The Grand Palace on the Thames, forever?"

"We've withstood worse," Mrs. Hardy said calmly. "And survived."

"We've discussed all of this and weighed the odds, Miss Wylde, and we have decided to bet on you," Mrs. Durand told her, firmly. "We thought you could sing for forty-five minutes, with a break between, and—"

"Forty," Mariana countered. "With an intermission to meet the guests." Mainly because she liked to negotiate.

"Done—we thought surely you can *break* their cold black hearts during the show, and then win them during the intermission?"

She smiled slowly. Mariana frankly thought she could do exactly that. A few light ballads, then a hanky-soaker of a popular ballad, an aria from Giancarlo's opera, *The Glass Rose*, the one that would simply *scour* their souls, and leave the more tender-hearted members of the audience *prostrate* with emotion, then perhaps a Rossini aria . . .

And then, during the intermission, by God, she would enchant them. She would unleash all of her native charm, well-seasoned with a little skillful acting and flattery. She would be so genteel and gracious and witty and so clearly noble of spirit that they would all depart thinking, *There's no way that angelic creature is capable of a single indiscretion, let alone shagging her way through the House of Lords. The newspapers must have gotten it wrong.*

Because it was all she had in the world. That was it: she was pretty, she had charm, she could sing. It seemed a rather thin layer of protection between her and the abyss, but it would have to be enough.

Even before the duel, her career had begun to seem like an endless plow through a thicket—her path would clear a bit, and then she'd come across another dangling, tangling vine. She was growing weary of brazening her way through conversations she only partly understood, because they were a meld of English and Italian, a language she'd never learned, which meant the only way she could perform arias was by imitation. And she was weary of managing men as skillfully as a conductor directs an orchestra: dodging their hands while flattering them, keeping them at bay while still keeping them interested. She was *very* good at flirting, but it seemed terribly unfair that it had become something of a grim chore.

All she wanted to do was sing. And maybe make one thousand pounds per season, like Madame Catalani, who could make her own rules. And make sure her mother was safe and happy and comfortable in her own house. Entertaining *any* desire beyond those things was a sheer luxury.

So they all shook hands on it, she and Mrs. Hardy and Mrs. Durand. She liked their confidence; it was bolstering and contagious, and somehow, she knew it was built from experience, which was the best kind of confidence.

She'd needed to agree to The Grand Palace on the Thames rules, too, in order to stay here, and so far she'd found every one of them delightful. She had never lived in a place so exclusive it came with a list of requirements for guests printed on a little card. This thrilled her, rather, and she kept it on the desk so she could look at it.

All guests will eat dinner together at least four times per week.

The food here was *heavenly*. It was all she could do not to seize her plate and lick it after every dinner. Helga, the cook, was a genius. One had to be quick, however, to keep up with Mr. Delacorte, who created foodscapes, mountains of potatoes and rivers of gravy, on his plate, which he then swiftly, cleanly demolished the way a vengeful God might with a tornado. It was an awe-inspiring thing to witness.

All guests must gather in the drawing room after dinner for at least an hour at least four times per week. We feel it fosters a sense of friendship and the warm, familial, congenial atmosphere we strive to create here at The Grand Palace on the Thames.

She would *not* be flirting with anyone's husbands, though when she got a look at Captain Hardy and Lord Bolt, she had cause to be grateful indeed for their sheer decorative appeal. But there was a sort of sealed, inviolable contentment to people deeply in love; she'd recognized the same quality in her parents. It made her wistful and restless. The whirlwind world in which she found herself now was full of the window dressings of it, the flirting and sex and flattery and drama. When all of that was cleared away—say, by a gunshot— emptiness remained. She wasn't certain whether it was a mercy or not that she knew this.

All guests should be quietly respectful and courteous of other guests at all times, though spirited discourse is welcome.

So far the spirited discourse involved how they intended to decorate the ballroom for the Night of the Nightingale and whether they ought to play Whist or read aloud from *The Ghost in the Attic*.

Mr. Delacorte was jolly and pleasant, and his lovely blue eyes were twinklingly appreciative of Mariana's feminine charms, but she got the sense he preferred a cozier sort of female, rather than the more sparkly sort, which she was. They recognized in each other a fellow card, and became fast friends. He imported remedies from the Orient and India, which he then sold to surgeons and apothecaries up and down England, and he'd shown her the samples in his case, little pills, vials, teas, and powders. "Ground-up herbs and animal whatnot!" he'd said. "Most of 'em work a treat." He'd entered a business partnership with Captain Hardy, who owned a ship, and Lord Bolt, who already had a successful enterprise importing goods from the Orient. He resembled a sturdy, well-fed Welsh pony, and laughed a good deal.

Mrs. Pariseau, a dashing widow with snapping dark eyes and wonderful silver stripes in her dark hair, was clever and worldly but quick with a laugh and a wink. She'd played Faro with Mariana last night; they'd placed wagers using buttons, and Mrs. Pariseau had lost nearly all of them. And now Mariana was learning to play chess from Dot, who had learned it from Delacorte.

She'd learned that Dot was a collector of vocabulary words, too, another person who was compelled to learn by listening.

They all got on famously. No one seemed to mind that she had been in the gossip columns. After all, Lord Bolt lived here, too.

There was also, unfortunately, an epithet jar, however. It always seemed to hover accusingly on the periphery of her vision, as if it knew how often she wanted to let fly with a "bloody," which would cost her a pence. She couldn't risk it.

Guests may entertain other guests in the drawing room.

Which was the genteelest possible way of saying that bedrooms were for sleeping, not for orgies.

Curfew is at 11:00 p.m. The front door will be securely locked then. You will need to wait until morning to be admitted if you miss curfew.

She quite liked knowing she was securely locked in at night. Dot might have opened the door to one gently pleading woman, but surely she wouldn't be tempted to allow in a mob howling for her blood? She amused herself briefly by imagining the proprietresses calmly conducting interviews with people holding torches and pitchforks, one at a time.

If the proprietresses collectively decide that a transgression or series of transgressions warrants your eviction from The Grand Palace on the Thames, you will find your belongings neatly packed and placed near

*the front door. You will not be refunded the
balance of your rent.*

She could not *imagine* doing a thing to jeopardize
those rules, in light of the kindness of the ladies of
The Grand Palace on the Thames. She could well
understand why Mr. Delacorte and Mrs. Pariseau
never wanted to leave, if their rooms were anything
like hers.

Against the wall was shoved a narrow, soft bed
heaped in layers of coverlets, topped with a quilt,
and crowned with a plump pillow. Alongside it lay
a braided rug in shades of rose and green; it was
a pleasure to press her feet into it first thing in the
morning. A mirror the size of her face was hung on
the wall above a basin and a water pitcher painted
in little pink flowers. Across from the wardrobe was
a desk, and on it perched a tiny vase from which
a sprig of white blossoms peeped. It made the entire room smell like spring. She'd carefully tied her
cherished pink satin ribbon, the one her parents had
given her on her tenth birthday, around the vase, to
make the room feel a little more like home.

Her window offered a view of another building,
all brick, and an alley in which she'd seen two cats
making love.

She rehearsed in her head another approach to
the letter.

*Dear Mama,
    I hope this letter finds you well. I've some
wonderful news. I've moved into a lovely new*

*room at an exclusive boardinghouse. You must
pass an interview to be admitted. If you're
found wanting they won't let you in! I've made
many fine new friends and the food is very good.
I'm to sing at an event featuring only me at
the end of the month, and lords and ladies will
be invited. Right now, there is a little blossom
in a vase on my writing table, and the smell of
it reminds me of the first trip you and Papa
and I made to the seashore so many years ago.
Do you remember the green hills on the way?
Sometimes I picture them when I can't sleep.*

It was neither untrue, nor entirely true. Much
like the gossip written about her, the difference
was in what was omitted and what was included.

Was it dishonest?

It left out the part where she'd awakened with a
start last time, from a dream in which she plum-
meted out her window into the gaping maw of
someone screeching the word *harlot harlot harlot.*

She suspected *those* dreams would be her lot for
a while.

But she'd be fed and housed at least through the
month.

At any rate, she didn't write the letter.

She would try again tomorrow. It was time to go
downstairs to the sitting room to join in the cozy
familial atmosphere and spirited discussions, and
revel in the fact that for now, she was safe from
anyone in the *ton* who might judge her, even if she
wasn't quite safe from the epithet jar.

Chapter Three

☙❧

SHE CAME to an abrupt halt when she noticed a man standing between Mrs. Durand and Mrs. Hardy.

Something about him seemed immediately as stark and strange as if an obelisk had been dropped into the sitting room. The lines of him—the span of his shoulders, the incline between them and his waist, his jaw—were as elegant, severe, and clean as if his maker had trimmed them out with the tip of a rapier. The top of her head, she suspected, would just about reach the knot in his cravat.

She was a cobbler's daughter and she always looked down. His boots—Hoby, if she had to guess—were black mirrors.

Mrs. Hardy saw her, and her face lit in welcome. "Your Grace—"

Your *Grace*? Holy Mother of—!

"—we should like to introduce Miss Mariana Wylde. Miss Wylde, His Grace, the Duke of Valkirk."

Thusly the first legend she'd ever met in the flesh turned to face her directly.

She didn't know whether she would call him

handsome. Only that his presence worked on her senses like the clash of a gong.

His nose seemed to have been broken at least once, but the result suited the terrain of his face, and intriguingly suggested he'd come up against violence and walked away the victor. His mouth was long and rather fine. Beneath thick, straight brows, his gaze was deep-set and uncomfortably penetrating, as though he was forever searching for enemies on the far horizon. He could probably frisk a soul for sins and, once discovered, keep the knowledge of them to himself, for strategic use at a later date.

The stark colors he wore implied he thought he needed no embellishment. She was inclined to agree. But she knew one would need to pay a tailor dizzying fortunes for that fit and that fabric, not to mention the staff to keep it jet black and snow white.

She was instinctively certain there wasn't a soft place on the man.

When she wrote to her mother about this later, she would leave out the part where she stared up at him, mutely, like a looby, for a full three seconds, and go right into the part where she curtsied.

Because her curtsy was a thing of beauty. She knew, because it had gotten rave notices when she'd played a perfidious courtier in *The Glass Rose*, before she'd been promoted to queen for a night, which was more or less immediately before two men decided to shoot at each other over her. She had not been born genteel, but damned if she couldn't convince anybody that she was.

"Your Grace . . ." Nerves had made her voice go a little too seductively breathy. "Meeting you is an honor I never dreamed I'd have in this lifetime."

When she was upright, she thought it best to appear simultaneously devastating and virtuous. This meant lowering her gaze shyly at least a second or two. This was a brutal sacrifice, because her entire being wanted to continue studying his face to decide how she felt about it.

She raised her head what seemed like a vast distance to meet his eyes.

Only to discover that a screen of faint but unmistakable bored cynicism had moved across his features.

This was so disorienting, she nearly brought a hand up to touch her face to make sure it was still there.

"How do you do, Miss Wylde." His voice was a wonder. All bass she could feel right in her chest. She noticed his dark hair was a bit longer than fashionable, and unlike the rest of him, hinted at a disinclination to remain in formation. A shock of it dropped over one brow, and in this a few silver threads glinted.

They regarded each other in silence. Hers purely dumbstruck.

His unmoved.

No pupil flare, no twinkle, no slow lowering of eyelids to appreciative slits. Nothing remotely akin to the things she was accustomed to seeing in the faces of men the moment they got a look at her. Instead: hard, speculative, and cynical.

The backs of her arms went cold.

She had a terrible feeling that the Duke of Valkirk read the entire paper. Even the gossip columns.

"Miss Wylde," he said politely, in that voice. "I apologize if this is a presumption, but you've the same name as someone who has lately made an appearance in the *London Times* with reference to a duel."

Her heart slowly, slowly contracted into an icy fist.

He wasn't one bit sorry for that "presumption."

And did he *ever* blink?

He seemed to be, in an entirely dispassionate way, merely curious about how she'd respond. As though he couldn't care one way or the other, but he might as well prod with a stick at a small, flat animal to see whether it was sleeping or dead.

He already knew that her only options were to lie or to admit to being at the center of a sordid scandal.

Or: to turn tail and run out of the room.

She understood instantly that he was a terrifying man.

> *Dear Mama—I regret to inform you that the Duke of Valkirk is a right bastard.*

Then again, he was still a man. Wasn't he? Even if he was orders of magnitude more potent in real life than other men? She had not yet met one she couldn't ultimately decipher. They'd *all* thus far regrettably proved the same beneath the skin, even if this one's skin was made of battered steel plate, granite, and meanness.

She would need to be very careful. Most of her instincts had been clubbed senseless, but pride and flirtation, both possibly stronger than they ought to be, formed a hopeful team.

"Everything I know about you I've learned from the newspaper as well, Your Grace," she said lightly. "There's something we have in common."

"That, and having the misfortune to be present when young men were shot. Of course I considered it my duty to prevent it, if I could." He said this mildly.

She went still, as winded as though she'd slammed into an invisible wall.

The subtle implication being that she'd all but stood there and cheered on two men aiming pistols at each other as though it were a horse race. After, no doubt, untangling her naked limbs from the pile they'd all formed during their sexual debauch.

"Since you've evidently found shelter here, Miss Wylde, you may yet be ignorant of the fact that Lord Kilhone continues to cling to life," he added.

How could anyone say such brutally direct things and make them sound like casual conversation?

"I'm happy to hear it. It wasn't for lack of trying to get himself killed," she said, mimicking his lightness. Because she owed her survival to the fact that she was a quick learner.

Contempt would have been better than whatever it was he directed at her from beneath those thick brows now. It wasn't even indifference, precisely. His seen-everything eyes—she could imagine they'd gazed upon shattered bodies on the battlefield, down the barrels of rifles and cannons, at kings and lords and enlisted men and doubtless every imaginable type of female, naked and clothed—burned through her as though she were scarcely worth the effort of keeping them open.

She'd once seen a flaming scrap of newspaper cartwheeling through the air on a breeze. That's precisely how she felt.

And now he was just toying with her. As though this, not spillikins, was *his* idea of a game.

A stray thought meandered through her focus: no *wonder* we won the war. For God's sake.

"I believe they're out dragging the Thames for you," he told her. "The current theory as to your disappearance is that you cast yourself in out of a fit of remorse."

Who was she if he'd burned her down to nothing? Pride struggled through again. Of a certainty there were more beautiful women in the world. But she doubted there were any more bloody-minded.

"I suppose I'm touched that I've been missed at all," she said lightly, self-deprecatingly. "I understand some of the rooms here even have a view of the Thames."

"My rooms do."

Rooms. Plural. Because of course a single room could never possibly contain his big, fat duke head.

"Well, only think, Your Grace. If this were a game of blindman's buff, they'd find me in no time as the river is not more than, oh, fifty yards from where we stand now."

Behind her, her best audience, Mr. Delacorte, chuckled softly. Bless him.

"Ah. So you're saying what happened was a game to you?"

His tone was mild, curious. His voice was baritone silk.

His eyes were mercilessly negating.

She could imagine the testicles of a thousand enemy soldiers shriveling at the tone.

She would be damned if she would give him the satisfaction of watching her prostrate herself for his absolution. She'd done nothing wrong.

If only she truly believed this, in her heart of hearts.

If only she knew for certain there was nothing she could have done differently.

"No doubt a man of your stature seldom has time for games, so perhaps you've forgotten the meaning of the word, Your Grace," she soothed. "You ought to play a few games with us." She raised her voice a little. "But I must warn you, Mrs. Pariseau is to spillikins what Gentleman Jackson is to boxing."

Mrs. Pariseau, who *did* like her and *could* be charmed, laughed. "And Miss Wylde will win your estate in Faro, Your Grace, if you aren't careful." She winked.

Mariana froze. Oh, for God's sake.

"I shall *always* be careful around Miss Wylde," the duke said, and winked back at Mrs. Pariseau, winning her devotion for life.

He settled in with a pen and a sheet of foolscap, and, Mariana was certain, forgot her promptly.

THE DUKE DIDN'T forget Mariana.

Or rather, one would have to be first remembered to be forgotten. She'd simply disappeared from his thoughts, the way the tables and chairs in the parlor had now that he was no longer in it.

She was right. To him, she did not signify.

He'd gone with some relief to the smoking room after about an hour of sitting in the drawing room, per the rules. And now he was thinking about his late wife, Eliza. Sometime during the seventeenth century, well before he'd bought his London townhouse to please her, the twenty-foot-high ceilings had been painted with blue skies and clouds, among which cherubs swathed in gossamer scarves cavorted. If one must have cherubs in the house, the ceiling was the best place for them, he'd thought grimly. He did not often look up. He'd always thought painting a sky on a ceiling confusingly suggested one would rather be outside. Which, for him, was generally true, so that's where he went.

Metaphorically speaking, he'd been the smoking room in his marriage, and his wife had been the parlor just outside. They'd lived adjacent lives, with an invisible impermeable wall between.

His taste in art was more prosaic: he favored

good paintings of horses and dogs and ships, preferably hung where he could see them, at eye-level. And quality in all things, damn the expense, and he'd been able to damn expenses for nigh on a decade. He'd slept rough on muddy ground as an ensign and on the finest four-poster beds in rooms so vast and marbled-clad one could hear the soft "tick" of a dropped crumb. He appreciated comfort. He preferred comfort.

But he frankly thought he might still love small, smoky rooms the best.

This one was kitted out in all the colors of a snug den: various shades of browns and mahoganies and creams, heavy curtains and a good rug scrolled in stain-hiding colors, on the premise that men are essentially animals once let out of sight of women, and it was of no use to fight it.

Big, sturdy chairs, a battered table perfect for propping up booted feet. Brandy in the snifter and cigars in the humidor. A cloud of smoke, and three other men leaning against the walls, in that reverie caused by the first suck on a good cheroot. He knew and liked and, more importantly, profoundly respected Hardy. He'd heard of Bolt, because everybody had. Hardy had attempted to describe Mr. Delacorte to him but, apparently at a loss for words, stopped himself. "You'll see," was all he'd said.

Mr. Delacorte was the first to break the silence. "We had an earl here some weeks ago," he volunteered, hopefully. "His whole family. They felt right at home."

"That's a relief to know, Mr. Delacorte," he said gravely, ironically. "Thank you."

"Right nice bloke," Mr. Delacorte added.

There was a little silence.

". . . for an earl?" the duke suggested mildly.

This was, in fact, true. But Mr. Delacorte, who at the best of times was often a bit like an exuberant pet struggling to remain on its best behavior, was nobody's fool. His smile was tentative. He was not willing to believe the duke was funny yet, lest his hopes be crushed.

"Put your trousers on one leg at a time, though, Your Grace, like the rest of us blokes, I imagine. Ha."

The duke exhaled smoke. "I've a staff of a dozen who gently lift me with a series of pulleys and then lower me into them, lest I'm abraded unduly."

"HA!" Delacorte bellowed happily and slapped his own thigh.

The duke gave a start.

From within their individual veils of smoke, Hardy and Bolt suppressed smiles.

"Some mornings I need to do a little dance to get into mine," Delacorte said.

"I've gathered we're fed well here. As dancing is not one of my talents, I shall have to exercise restraint at the dinner table," the duke said.

Delacorte smiled broadly, as if the duke just kept exceeding his expectations. "They mend us well, here, too." Delacorte gave a pat to the egg-like curve of his belly. "Shirts, waistcoats. Should you find things need letting out or fastening back on."

"Very good to know." He had an expensive tailor now and a fastidious, underutilized valet. He knew how to sew his own buttons, mend his clothes, black his boots, and knit, thanks to the army. He didn't particularly want to do any of that anymore, but at forty-three years old, there was almost nothing he could not only survive, but shape into a triumph.

Except for his bloody book.

He looked across at Lucien Durand, Viscount Bolt, another former denizen of the gossip columns. No youth had been wilder or angrier. He'd been assumed drowned after a night at gaming hells a decade ago. Precisely the sort of man the duke had raised his own son not to be. Bolt had allegedly returned from the dead harder, wiser, and much reformed, so reformed that Hardy had gone into business with him.

Much more like the man Valkirk wished his son would become.

Sometimes Valkirk thought it was the only way anyone *could* transform: a death, metaphorical or otherwise.

"I'm acquainted with your father, Bolt."

"I imagine your paths would have crossed," Bolt said idly. "Given that there are only a handful of dukes in the world, the temptation to congregate must stir now and again."

"Brexford," the duke mused. "He's a bit . . ."

There was a small, fraught silence.

". . . of a bastard?" Lucien supplied. Ironically, given that *he* was a literal bastard.

The duke blew a languid smoke ring. "I was going to say he's not very interesting, is he?"

It was such a scathingly perfect indictment of the man who had cut Lucien so callously out of his life that everyone else in the room went motionless with awe.

Brexford was dull, wealthy, shallow, smug, and content. He possessed no qualities a man like Valkirk could catch hold of or relate to.

"I suppose he isn't." Lucien was both amused and somewhat touched. "Faultless, though, one might say."

It was a little dig, his own way of exercising Valkirk's sense of humor.

Valkirk rewarded him with a small, patient smile.

There was his reputation as a sort of national saint. And then there was the man he truly was, which was a good deal more complicated. No one got through war with an unstained soul, especially not a brilliant, effective general. And everyone in this room, save Delacorte, had served in some way.

"I'm not related to *any* dukes," Delacorte volunteered. "I've a brother, mind, and relatives scattered about Scotland and Ireland. But I've sold remedies to apothecaries in London who've sold them to dukes."

Both Lucien and Captain Hardy had privately discussed how they both longed to meet and dreaded one day meeting Mr. Delacorte's brother, not to mention his other relatives.

"Speaking of other people who allegedly wound up in the drink, but remain among us," the duke said to Bolt, "I must say I did wonder at the inclusion of Miss Mariana Wylde among the guests, given the rigorous interview process."

There was a sudden, wary silence and a swift glance exchanged between Bolt and Hardy.

Captain Hardy apparently lost the mute coin toss, so he spoke.

"My wife and Mrs. Durand are kind people possessed of excellent judgment," Hardy began evenly, "and Miss Wylde was in immediate need of shelter when she came to us as she felt her life was in peril in her own home. They could not find it in their hearts to refuse her. We have so far found her to be a fine and amiable guest. You have my word of honor that our wives and everyone who lives here exercise the utmost care in protecting the privacy of our guests. And should Miss Wylde somehow manage to instigate a duel in the parlor, she'll be promptly evicted."

Hardy's word of honor was worth gold.

But the duke was a little skeptical on one point. "Has anyone ever been evicted?"

"I was," Captain Hardy said.

". . . before we were married," Captain Hardy expounded, faced with Valkirk's incredulous silence and single arched brow.

"It's a long story," Hardy finally muttered.

The silence stretched.

"Wives," the duke said, finally. Thoroughly, sardonically amused.

Both Lucien and Captain Hardy offered careful smiles.

As a blockade captain, Hardy had run notorious smugglers to ground. He and his men had set fire to all the boats in a village known to have abetted criminals. He was as ruthless and rigidly disciplined a man as Valkirk had ever met.

And he'd gone and married himself an Achilles' heel.

Valkirk had been the son of a farmer and was a twenty-year-old soldier when he'd wed the youngest daughter of a viscount who'd been over-blessed with five of them. And while it was generally considered that Valkirk, then James Duncan Blackmore, had married well above his station, she was much later congratulated on her foresight to marry a man clearly destined for greatness. Perhaps she'd known. James hadn't known. He'd only known that when one began life at the base of a mountain, the only option was to conquer the bloody hell out of the mountain. The safest view, the best air, were at the very top.

And so that's what he'd done.

He knew a sort of steely, immutable pride that his grandchildren, and all who came after, would be safe from harm or struggle or the sort of upheaval and poverty he'd known as a child. He'd made certain of it. From up there, as a sort of lookout, he could keep all of them safe.

It was why, in large part, the presence of Mariana Wylde, of all people, set his teeth on edge. She, and the young men who congregated in the dressing rooms of opera singers, and those that milled about them, were shallow and volatile and reckless, an affront to his life's work, destined for bad ends and, like people who were drowning, they pulled others in with them. She was pretty, he supposed, in an ordinary way. It was hard to imagine a man shooting anyone over her. Reputations like hers rubbed off on others like newsprint.

"The on dit is that *you* might be looking for a new one," Lucien said.

"A new wife?" Delacorte perked up.

"There's always on dit," Valkirk said, taking pains to sound bored. "This is nothing new."

There was a short silence.

"But the *acceptance* of invitations to dine . . . that's a *little* new?" Lucien suggested slyly.

Hardy stared a warning at Lucien.

But Valkirk just shot Lucien a balefully amused glance. "I forgot that at least one of you was a member of White's."

Men liked to complain the women were gossips, but men, in his experience, were almost worse. Though he'd found listening to it at White's had been useful more than once.

Lucien gave a low whistle. "Titled mamas must be all but shot-putting their daughters at you."

Valkirk handed his empty brandy glass to Hardy, who had gestured questioningly with the decanter in his direction. "It's really more of an underfoot type of thing. And an every-time-I-turn-around type of thing. And an 'oh my goodness, I didn't know you intended to visit the

National Gallery today, Your Grace, have you met my daughter, Prudence?' type of thing."

He wasn't unsympathetic. The mating games of the aristocracy were ridiculous on the surface and serious as a guillotine beneath.

He was a mere generation removed from peasants. He wanted a legacy that would withstand the test of centuries, an edifice of extraordinary wealth and power that could not be broken or breached, built from powerful ancient names entwined and intermarried. So if he married again, he'd marry damn well.

It just seemed ironic that he could choose any pretty thing with a title now when his first marriage had been built on gratitude (his) and ambition (mutual). Still, beneath—far, far beneath—the thick armor of cynicism and glory the years had layered on him, there remained something of that twenty-year-old soldier who could not believe a woman had said yes to him when he'd asked.

He didn't know what he would base a new marriage on.

He didn't hate the idea of more children.

Or a woman in his bed.

He'd never kept a mistress. That sort of arrangement had always struck him as impractical, improvident, an invitation to chaos. And not only that, dishonorable, if one was married. So few wives were truly ignorant of a husband's mistress, and even fewer were happy about it if they knew. They merely endured the indignity. This struck him as unjust. Just because a man could get away with something didn't mean he should.

He had not been a saint throughout his marriage. But he could not have done that to his wife.

And he definitely wouldn't do it now, when the nation, still somewhat reeling from a bloody, brutal war, looked to him as their hero, the example of all that was right and good. They needed him to be the man they believed him to be, honorable, decent, brave, a beacon they could point to and say, "Be like him, son."

"So *that's* why you're hiding here to write your memoirs," Delacorte mused shrewdly.

Bolt's and Captain Hardy's eyes went huge at the word "hiding" directed at, of all people, Valkirk.

With the vision born of decades of peering into the souls of men, Valkirk inspected Delacorte and found not a shred of guile; besides, his own pride was woven into his fiber. In other words, one couldn't insult *him* into shooting anyone simply over a feckless soprano who juggled one too many lovers.

"I find The Grand Palace on the Thames, on the whole, a handsome and congenial place, and I expect to accomplish a good deal of work," he said pleasantly.

In other words: yes.

"In other words, yes," Delacorte said.

The duke couldn't help it: he grinned at him.

"I expect it's like a buffet, all those young ladies. Like when Helga sets out kippers, bacon, ham, and sausage on Sundays," Delacorte suggested wist-fully.

"If that's what happens, I'm looking forward to Sunday," the duke said.

"Too much choice can be a little dangerous, Your Grace," Delacorte told him. "On my last trip to India—I've been importer for some years of remedies from the Orient and the like, you see, and I sell them to apothecaries here in England—I met a bloke who worked for the governor. Had a little headache and was offered a choice of about ten different headache powders, and he couldn't decide, so he finally closed his eyes and chose one. He woke up three days later naked in the jungle next to a Bengal tiger who was sniffing his geni-tals. He had no idea how he got there."

The three other men froze, drinks and cigars halfway to their mouths.

"The whiskers tickled him, you see," Delacorte explained. "That's why he woke up."

"Friends to this day, he and the tiger," he added into the elongating dumbstruck silence.

"Thank God for whiskers, I suppose," the duke finally said.

Hardy and Bolt grinned.

"Perhaps it's better to just let the wife come to you, Your Grace," said Delacorte. "Sometimes they just show up, like, out of the blue."

"I think that's how you get a cat, Delacorte," Captain Hardy said. "Not a wife."

* * *

Dear Mama,

MARIANA STARED AT the foolscap and mulled. The quill was in her hand, but she wasn't yet prepared to write. She imagined saying:

> *Plans for the Night of the Nightingale are going splendidly! The ballroom has wonderful acoustics, and I think I know just what I'll sing. We are going to decorate the ballroom like a garden in the moonlight, with flowers, trees, stars, and the moon! We are going to place handbills all over the city! And sell tickets for the show—for four shillings. Almost the cost of an opera box. It will be very exclusive.*
>
> *Now, I fear I have some disappointing news: the Duke of Valkirk is a dull and unpleasant person. He only speaks a few words at a time and won't join in any of the games in the sitting room at night. Perhaps because he's getting old and tired. He has a fine line right across his forehead.*

She wouldn't, of course, write any of that to her mother, who was not free of lines, fine or otherwise, and she had no illusions about escaping that fate herself.

She in fact still hadn't written anything at all to her mother, and her letter was now nearly a week late.

It was another example of a truth that wasn't a truth. She wished the duke was anything so benign as dull. He had only to be himself to be considered interesting, and in merely being himself, he had somehow all but eliminated her, the way an ocean engulfs a drop of water.

But Mariana yearned for a confidante. Her circumstances remained roughly as secure as a lifeboat on a sea that could turn stormy at any time. She was very aware she was here on the gentle sufferance of the ladies of The Grand Palace on the Thames until the time came for her to sing, and she was unaccustomed to charity. She'd need to get a message to Giancarlo somehow to let him know to where she'd fled. He might be a bit of a rogue, but as a composer and director, he knew talented sopranos were not so thick on the vine that he could afford losing one to tar and feathers. Or starvation.

And before the ladies went through the trouble of printing handbills and placing them in the finest establishments on Bond Street, in Grosvenor Square and St. James's Square, and all about the Italian Opera House, there was a little matter of reputation repair. Otherwise the little audience that had been underneath her window the other night might show up at The Grand Palace on the Thames.

"Have you anyone who might be willing to speak on your behalf? Someone the newspapers might find newsworthy? Perhaps someone with a title, or, er . . . a certain stature?"

Lord Bolt had asked this during the planning meeting they'd held yesterday afternoon, before the arrival of the duke. He'd had more than a little experience with renovating a reputation.

A number of titled men liked to congregate backstage after performances, but she personally knew only four of them. Two of them had shot at each other, ostensibly because of her, the third was Lord Bolt, and the fourth was the Duke of Valkirk, who had already court-martialed her in the tribunal of self-righteousness.

"Madame LeCroix?" she suggested, tentatively. "I sang alongside her in a production last year, and we got on well. She was kind to me." Madame LeCroix had since retired from the stage, but was still much admired and respected in London for her charitable works. How charitable the retired diva might be toward a young one caught up in a scandal was anyone's guess.

"I shall send a message to Madame LeCroix," Lord Bolt said.

How had it come to this?

She longed to unburden her heart to someone, to anyone. But she could not think of anyone quite like her, and that was the problem. Society did tend to like its categories and labels, and there was no place into which she comfortably notched. One couldn't be "a bit of a whore," for instance, any more than one could be "a little bit pregnant." One either was, or one wasn't.

She was a singularity. She was feeling her way in the dark, and the dark was littered with pitfalls that looked like delights and delights that turned out to be terrible pitfalls.

She stared at the foolscap and daydreamed words onto it.

Dear Mama,

I hope this letter finds you well.

It's partly true, what they said in the newspaper. I felt I ought to tell you.

I have always tried very hard to be good. But he was very handsome, and a lord, and he said to me things like "beautiful" and "bewitching." I think lords learn those words at Eton because they think they'll work on women like me, and as it turns out, they're right.

Sometimes, I wish I didn't remember how our family used to be in our rooms over the shop, because that life was the aria, and everything since feels like just its echo. I suppose I felt very alone, which is why it all happened. I like to think I have learned a lot about men, but I worry I only know how to manage them. Perhaps that's all I'll ever need to know. I don't suppose I will ever get a glimpse inside a man's heart. I think I would know if I had. Wouldn't I know? How do you know?

I also sometimes wish I didn't now know how much I enjoy kissing and—well, everything else. But I do. (Moreover, I'm good at it.) But it's like a duel, I suppose. Not something one ought to do without a good reason. Ha. At least I now know.

It did not make anything better.

I did not understand that pride, temper, and champagne could make men so apt to shoot each other.

It all happened so quickly.

And I swear to you on Papa's grave that I only went to a gaming hell once, and the pelisse was a gift, not a payment.

She sighed and put the quill pen down. She wouldn't be writing the letter tonight, either. That much was clear.

Had the Duke of Valkirk learned words like "bewitched" and "beautiful" and used them to seduce women? It seemed nearly impossible to imagine him in the throes of anything other than self-importance.

If she were being more truthful, it was also impossible to imagine him needing to *try* to seduce women. He was possessed of unfair charisma and the kind of body that, when considered apart from his odious personality, might tempt a woman to slide right underneath.

It shouldn't matter to her, given all of her current concerns. But his instant judgment felt like an injustice layered upon an injustice, which was somehow, finally, an injustice too far.

But it was revelatory, too. It was useful to know that it took only one person to make her feel small, when she had tried so hard for so long to be seen. This would never do.

She would make him see her. And the best way to do that was to somehow best him in a way he couldn't possibly ignore.

Chapter Four

❦

"Brrr. Oh, goodness. Does anyone else feel a chill?" Miss Wylde murmured, with a little shudder, as the duke entered the sitting room after dinner the following day. "I aver the temperature just dropped five degrees."

As barbs went, it was unsurprisingly unoriginal. Miss Mariana Wylde was no doubt accustomed to ceaseless doses of attention and would try any number of things to get it. He'd felt it, a very little. But she'd no hope of leaving a mark.

He settled in at the table just behind where Dot and Miss Wylde sat at the chessboard and laid out the things he'd brought down from his suite—a newspaper and foolscap, ink and pen. The room was unpretentious and comfortable, which also described his suite in the Annex, with its surprisingly excellent bed and the little flower in a vase on the mantel and another next to his bed.

The duke had no objection, really, to the boardinghouse rules requiring "familial gathering" in the sitting room. There were worse things than being surrounded by handsome, chattering, contented women who were unlikely to bother him overmuch; it was a bit like having a view of a garden out of the corner of his eye.

He liked having people about, even if he didn't necessarily want to talk to them. Strangers were often too deferential or too fawning or too mutely rapt. His own tendency to abbreviation—some might call it *abruptness*—born of being accustomed to barking orders, and a sense that time and life were so precious one ought not spend them listening to nattering—didn't help. He often felt a bit like his own statue in Hyde Park, at the center of everything and yet entirely removed, as though he existed now only to awe. The sort of thing parents would bring young children to gaze upon for educational purposes.

Dot glanced quizzically at the fire, which was leaping healthily, then back at Miss Wylde.

The room in fact was quite adequately warm and cozily lit with lamps and candles. "Would you like another shawl, Miss Wylde?"

"Oh, no, thank you. The chill seems to have passed us by for now," she said easily.

He cast what was meant to be a swift, baleful look across at her, only to intercept her cool one. She demonstrated that he was not the only one who could lift a single brow. Hers were a shade darker than her hair, feathery mahogany arcs. The shape was echoed in the full curve of her lower lip. Hers was a symmetrical, unexceptional sort of prettiness.

He suspected her previous popularity was all due to trying very, very hard.

He wrote,

Dear Arthur,

He didn't know what he wanted to say to his son yet. He'd genuinely thought starting the letter would help him understand how he wanted to finish it. He ought to have learned his lesson about that by now. He stared at it.

Dot liked to make little clopping sounds with her mouth when she moved the knight, as though he were galloping across the board. Also, because she claimed it helped her think.

A lot of clopping was going on now.

It seemed to be quite a long journey across the board.

He could and had slept through nearly everything, gunfire, drunken fistfights, lashing storms . . . but it seemed the clopping was the thing that would finally twang his nerves. Something about the utter pointlessness of it.

Hardy and Bolt had been spending the evenings attending to arrangements for a new warehouse as they expected their ship to reach port in little over a fortnight. Delacorte was engaged in a game on the other side of the room. Valkirk could not retreat to smoke just yet, per the rules.

"Why, good evening, sir!"

The knight had apparently finally arrived at its destination and was now being greeted by a pawn.

"Chess is typically a rather quiet game, isn't it?"

the duke said with the deceptive mildness that usually reduced ensigns to stammers.

"It was. It *was* a quiet game," Delacorte concurred over his shoulder, somewhat sadly. It had ceased to be the game he recognized once he'd taught it to Dot, who had made what could only be described as embellishments.

He had joined Mrs. Pariseau, Mrs. Hardy, and Mrs. Durand in a game of Whist while Dot explained the intricacies of chess, as she understood them, because the strain of teaching Dot chess had finally shown Mr. Delacorte the boundaries of his goodwill.

Although he fully expected she would one day win a game.

"Oh look, Dot! What *is* the bishop getting up to with the *queen*?" Miss Wylde said. "The scandal of it all!"

They both giggled.

"What if the knight catches them at it? Oh *ho*!" Miss Wylde continued.

"I expect there will be a duel," the duke drawled beneath his breath.

Mariana fixed him with a stare that he could *feel*. He did not look up from his foolscap.

Dot propped her chin in her hand as she perused the chessboard. "Knights, queen, king, bishops . . . why are no pieces named for dukes?"

"It *does* seem an oversight," Mariana mused. "I think because dukes would ruin the fun for all the other pieces. You see, dukes could only go in very straight, narrow lines, so they would disapprove greatly of the bishop for having the *nerve* to do anything so original as move diagonally."

Dot laughed. "What else?"

"And then . . . the duke would be able to tell all the pieces on the board what to do, because only the duke would know, of course. And no one would *ever* win a game. Let alone enjoy one."

"Cor! It's a good thing dukes aren't included with chess sets," Dot said in all innocence.

"A good thing, indeed," Mariana concurred.

"Oh my, it suddenly got *colder* in here, didn't it, Dot? Did you feel a chill?"

Did his jaw set a little as he made his way to the table? Unless it was a trick of the light, she thought it had. Mariana allowed herself the tiniest surge of triumph.

The duke had settled in at the table with the same kit he'd brought down last night. This time, he'd snapped open the newspaper and begun to read. Perhaps looking for a fresh batch of people to judge.

Today Lord Bolt had received a message in response to the one he'd sent to Madame LeCroix, and it seemed she was amenable to saying a kind thing or two about Mariana, which could then be printed in the newspaper. Then Mariana had sung for fifteen minutes today in the ballroom and thought she was in fine voice, all in all, though she dearly missed a quartet or a good pianist to accompany her. Every time she sang on a stage, she was entirely in the world of the song, and it was a welcome escape from everything else.

On the whole, today was an improvement over yesterday, and she was willing to believe it was the beginning of a trend.

"Your Grace, we're given to understand that you're writing another book," Mrs. Pariseau said deferentially. She was intrepidly social, Mrs. Pariseau was.

"Yes."

"How goes your work?" Mrs. Pariseau pressed.

"It goes apace," he told her, politely. He flicked a glance up from his newspaper.

"*Another* book?" Mariana took this up, boldly.

"Oh, Miss Wylde," Mrs. Pariseau said, "perhaps you already know this, but he's written a very famous book on honor!"

"What was your book called, pray tell, Your Grace?" Mariana ventured.

He stared at her. "*Honor.*"

She dug her nails into her palm in a vain attempt to keep her face from heating to pink.

"It's very generous of you to share your expertise, Your Grace. How would anyone know the proper way to behave if we hadn't a book on the topic?"

He regarded her coolly a moment. "Your question goes some way toward explaining your appearance in the gossip columns, Miss Wylde."

A little silence ensued.

"I've another question, Your Grace."

He fixed her with those eyes. She met them.

"What does one have to do in order to be dishonorable?"

"If we are adhering strictly to the definition of dishonor . . . it is knowingly behaving in such a way that impugns the dignity of another, or otherwise brings harm. To knowingly and without shame behave without regard for consequences that may bring someone else to harm. In so doing, to violate the rules of polite society."

She found that she was gripping the table surreptitiously, as if to maintain her grip against the onslaught of *certainty*. What must it feel like to be so briskly, insufferably certain of oneself? He said things as though they were inalienable truths.

And what the hell did "impugn" mean?

"Who decides what those rules are?"

"Society as a whole in a given era dictates the mores of that era."

"And then they write about it in the newspaper, I suppose."

"So it would seem," he said idly, and returned to his reading.

Her temper began to simmer.

"Will you be addressing *all* of the virtues in a series of books, then? Is that the book you're writing now?"

"Why? Have you need of a review of them, Miss Wylde?" he said mildly. "Or perhaps an introduction?"

"I know there are seven. I also can tell you firsthand their application seems rather flexible among the aristocracy."

"I'm certain you can," he said with a sort of hateful detachment.

"But it seems to me, Your Grace," she pressed, "that an intimate knowledge of all the vices would be necessary in order to convincingly write about virtues. Such as *honor*, for instance."

He lowered the newspaper, and his dark eyes appeared again.

That momentary flicker in them made her wonder if she was about to be challenged to a duel.

"How do you mean, Miss Wylde?" Mrs. Pariseau piped up.

"How does one describe the day without knowledge of the night? How does one describe honor without a knowledge of dishonor?"

She had his attention. Which was a bit like holding a hot horseshoe freshly forged on an anvil.

"And for that matter, how does one describe, oh, chastity, perhaps, without an intimate knowledge of lust?"

That screen of cynicism moved across his face again, and he eyed her the way he might an ensign he was about to order flogged.

She'd just put the duke in the position of declaiming about chastity and lust. She had no idea if either was considered an official virtue or vice, but she was pretty sure they were considered opposites, and one was considered a sin. She'd done a good deal of soul-searching about both.

She'd take making him uncomfortable as a win.

"May I refer you to prudence and temperance, Miss Wylde, then, if you're looking for an introduction to virtues," he said politely. "Although the expression 'closing the stable door after the horse has bolted' comes to mind, for some reason." The last words drifted, and with the tiniest of self-amused smiles, as he returned his attention to the newspaper again.

She was grateful she didn't have a knitting needle to hand, because she had a fleeting fantasy of hurling one, javelin style, into his forehead.

Dot, listening closely, was puzzled. "Wait. *Is* chastity a *virtue*, or just something you call it when you don't—"

"It's a virtue, a fine one," Mrs. Hardy assured her hastily. For the time being, she thought it was probably best not to encourage Dot to entertain complex notions about the permeability between vices and virtues, because she might explain them to the maids. It would lead to more dropped tea trays. Or pregnant maids.

"Your Grace, I apologize for pressing the point"— Mariana of course wasn't at all sorry—"but have you, then, some experience of dishonor?"

"Given your fascination with contrasts, it sounds to me as though you're a scholar of Aristotle's writings on the virtues then, Miss Wylde," the duke said.

She went silent and fixed him with a cool stare. Because she didn't quite know who Aristotle was, and she was an actual scholar of nothing apart from how to survive.

He didn't blink, and neither did she, and this wasn't easy. Something perverse in her was determined to meet his eyes again and again until she didn't feel a thing. Certainly not the jolt she felt now, from her forehead to her toes.

"Oh, my mate Aristotle and I regularly have a pint or two together at the pub," she said finally.

Mr. Delacorte, bless him, chuckled behind her.

"Having only a drink or two with a mate would be the virtue of temperance, Miss Wylde, and having six or seven and getting well and truly foxed would be a vice," Mrs. Pariseau chimed in. "I know which side I land on."

Mariana frankly thought it would be rather fun to one day get well and truly foxed with Mrs. Pariseau.

"But I *think* what His Grace is saying," Mrs. Pariseau continued diplomatically, "is that you are making quite the Aristotelian argument. Aristotle maintained that virtues are really a sort of . . . oh, how did he put it, Your Grace?"

"A golden mean," he said at once, because of course he knew everything. "Aristotle defines a virtue as the sort of perfect average between a vice of excess and a vice of deficiency. So it *is*, after a fashion, a study in contrasts."

Mariana furrowed her brow. "I *think* I understand. What you're saying is, for instance, that an excess of *self-righteousness* would then be a vice? Because wouldn't the—what was that again, Mrs. Pariseau?"

"The golden mean," Mrs. Pariseau replied approvingly.

"—be humility? Or is that on the excess end of the scale, too?"

He studied her, lips slightly pressed together. She'd never known any man who could say so much without changing his expression.

She didn't even precisely know what she wanted from him. Apart, perhaps, from being seen. This would likely be impossible. Her pride—which wasn't a particularly useful quality at this point in her life—refused to attempt to ingratiate herself to him, and her instincts told her it was useless. He had sealed her into the little glass jar of his scathing indifference, and she could get no purchase on the slick, unyielding sides of it in order to escape.

She supposed she would at least like to punish him a little. To introduce a little discomfort and uncertainty into his world as revenge for introducing a *lot* into hers. If someone like him thought her only bulwarks against the world—beauty and charm and talent—were paltry and common and tedious, how was she to survive? She might as well go into battle naked.

Though she suspected she looked very well naked, truthfully. She hadn't heard one complaint.

"Aristotle described the virtues as courage, temperance, liberality, magnificence, magnanimity, ambition, patience, and friendliness." The duke enunciated this emotionlessly and tersely and managed to make them sound like the names of soldiers he was ordering before a firing squad.

The net effect was that everyone present silently and somewhat uneasily reviewed their souls for these virtues, and decided they might be missing a few.

Mariana wasn't certain she knew what "magnanimity" or "liberality" meant, but she wasn't about to ask him.

"Magnificence," regrettably, fitted him the way his beautifully tailored suits did.

"Then is chastity a virtue by that definition, or a vice?" she pressed. "Isn't it an excess of chastity *not* getting enough—"

Mrs. Hardy cleared her throat noisily.

"And I suppose one can be an expert in *one* virtue and a failure at another? For instance, excelling at magnificence and failing at friendliness? Or do they all necessarily come as a set, like chess pieces?"

She noted a flicker of irritation, and somehow this was absurdly satisfying as if she'd been trying for hours to strike a spark from a flint.

"And who gets to decide what the virtues are? Why should Aristotle get to decide?" Mr. Delacorte was skeptical. "Do we elect new virtues as one does an MP? And if not, why not? We ought to have a vote."

"Oh, I do love to vote!" Dot enthused.

"Excellent point, Mr. Delacorte," Mariana said stoutly. "Who decides?"

Delilah and Angelique exchanged glances. Rumblings of a rebellion were underway. Before they knew it, a guillotine would be erected for the epithet jar.

"For that matter, who decides what the *vices* are?" Mariana pressed. One admonishing jar in the room was tyranny enough.

"I should think you would want to ease your way into the notion of virtue, Miss Wylde, as one does with new topics of study," the duke said. "Aristotle has identified more than seven, and Thomas Aquinas identifies even more of them."

"St. Thomas Aquinas!" Mrs. Pariseau clasped her hands in bliss. "Your Grace, oh, I do so appreciate a *learned* man."

Mrs. Pariseau liked to flirt, and that's precisely what she was doing now, but she'd made it clear she wasn't about to saddle herself with another husband, as the last one had left her reasonably financially comfortable.

"We haven't yet played charades here in the sitting room," said Mrs. Durand suddenly, thinking it might be time to change the topic. "Charades would be rather amusing to try one of these nights."

"We pantomimed a pirate battle once, Valkirk." Mr. Delacorte liked to catch new guests up on the history of the entertainments in the sitting room. "Bolt was once almost killed by pirates, and so we all pretended to be pirates, even Captain Hardy."

"Was he, indeed?" the duke said idly. "It does seem like something you'd want to relive again and again."

"He killed the pirate instead," Delacorte reassured him.

"That seems the best route to take when a pirate is trying to kill you."

Like a child with a new toy, Delacorte always looked delightedly about the room with a "did you hear that?" expression every time the duke said something dry.

"Have you killed any pirates?" Delacorte asked.

"Eleven only yesterday," the duke replied, to Delacorte's beaming approval.

"I would *love* to play charades," Dot exclaimed. "Is that where we all pretend to be other things?"

"Only while we're not working, Dot," Angelique hastened to remind her, imagining Dot pretending to be a bunny, for instance, and hopping with a tea tray.

"And perhaps another evening!" said Delilah hurriedly, noticing a certain grim set to the duke's expression. "A . . . month from now. We've so much preparation to do for the Night of the Nightingale. Perhaps we'll celebrate with charades or a pantomime when it's over!"

"Perhaps we ought to have a charade of all the vices," Mariana suggested.

"I'm certain you'll be able to more than credit-ably perform any vice, Miss Wylde," the duke said charitably.

He returned to his newspaper and therefore missed her cold stare.

"I'm certain I *could*," she muttered after a moment, which was about as clever a rejoinder as she could muster.

Frankly, she thought it might be fun.

"I call gluttony!" Mr. Delacorte said after a moment.

"We *do* have the most delightfully spirited dis-course in this room," Mrs. Pariseau said with a happy sigh. "All credit to Mrs. Durand and Mrs. Hardy, who seem to know precisely who ought to stay here."

"IT'S A CONUNDRUM," Mr. Delacorte mused two days later, aiming a stream of smoke upward in the smoking room one night, when Captain Hardy and Lord Bolt were present and the duke was out at an engagement. "Miss Wylde in the sitting room feels like . . . when you open up a window on a spring day, and in comes a breeze and birds tra-la-la'ing their heads off. And the duke . . . I suppose he's like the first frost, ain't he? And the first frost ain't a bad thing. It's just a very *different* thing. So I don't know *what* kind of weather we have in the sitting room at night."

It was always warm in the room, though. Even though Miss Wylde unfailingly gave a little shiver, drew her shawl more tightly around her and said something to the effect of, "Goodness, a little chill just ran through me. It was like winter in my very soul," when the duke passed her table to settle in.

And each night his jaw clamped just a little more tightly.

ON THE FOURTH evening after the duke's arrival, Mrs. Hardy and Mrs. Durand thought music would be a welcome change of pace from philosophical discussions, idiosyncratic chess, spillikins, and subtle but palpable tension. On the theory that music soothes the savage breast, they thought they'd give that a go.

"Why don't we have singing? Oh, Miss Wylde . . . we hesitate to call upon you, as we know you've sung for audiences at Drury Lane and the King's Theater . . . but we did wonder if you'd favor us with a song," Mrs. Hardy said.

"Oh, my goodness, Miss Wylde, we would all be so grateful!" Mrs. Pariseau breathed.

"But please do not feel obliged," Mrs. Durand added hastily.

They were so very kind. They were offering her free room and board! She couldn't and wouldn't disoblige them, and she'd love to take center of attention over the man behind the newspaper.

She'd availed herself of the ballroom for about fifteen minutes again today, running through scales and exercises, enjoying the surprisingly fine acoustics of the place and the luxurious velvet curtains. It would be pure recreation to sing a light ditty or two.

"I'd be delighted to! I wouldn't want to sing an aria—I'm very loud, you see, when I sing in full voice. It's more pleasant to be at a bit of a distance from me."

"You'll get no argument here," the duke murmured, from behind his newspaper.

She ignored him and sat down at the pianoforte. "But . . ." Inspiration struck. "One can turn anything into a song. For instance, I could sing a song about . . ." She glanced about the room. "Oh, I've a jolly idea! Would you play a C and G and E for me, Mrs. Durand? Make it a bit jaunty? Like this, perhaps."

She demonstrated at the pianoforte, tapping out the keys. Angelique skillfully obliged her.

And as Angelique played a few bars, everyone save one person leaned forward in breathless anticipation. Her impulse was *always* to win over audiences no matter how large or small, and she knew just how to do it.

She clasped her hands, tapped her foot, then launched into her song:

> In Mr. Delacorte's case is quite an array
> Of lotions and potions to make aches go away!
> But if you take the wrong one
> Or perhaps a too strong one
> You might wake up next to a tiger one day!

Delighted shouts of laughter and applause erupted.

"COR!" Mr. Delacorte smacked the table over and over delightedly. Each time he did, the duke twitched. "I've never been a song before!" He was dazzled.

Mariana performed whimsical shallow curtsies to the room at large.

"We could write even more verses one day! Just like *The Ballad of Colin Eversea*! The story of Stanton Delacorte."

Everyone beamed at her. What a pleasure it was to be beamed upon approvingly, and how perverse it was that she craved one particular smile in the room and she wasn't going to get it.

The duke hadn't even lowered his newspaper.

"Your voice is so pretty Miss Wylde," Dot said shyly.

"You're very kind, Dot," Mariana said. "Thank you. I feel as though I'm simply fortunate."

"Would that the rest of us were fortunate." The duke scarcely spoke above a murmur, but she heard him as surely as if he were right next to her ear.

"But it's what I do for a living," Mariana added. "I should be pleased if everyone else would take a turn. I should like to be entertained, too! Mrs. Hardy, do you play?"

Delilah hesitated. "Yes . . . I've no gift, mind . . ."

Everyone good-naturedly protested.

She laughed. "Very well! I'd be delighted. Angelique, will you join me in this?" Delilah stood.

"Oh, why not!" Angelique agreed cheerfully.

They murmured together over the pianoforte, deciding upon a tune.

And then Angelique began to play.

"Oh, I *love* 'Black-eyed Susan,'" Mariana sighed.

Delilah and Angelique did lovely justice to the long and aching song of a sailor and his woman saying goodbye to each other.

Oh Susan, Susan, lovely dear,
My heart shall ever true remain.
Let me kiss off that falling tear,
We only part to meet again.
Change as you list she wins, my heart shall be
A faithful compass that still points to thee.

And while Angelique and Delilah made eyes misty all over the room with their rendition, and even the duke seemed rather still, Mariana used the cover of John Gay's many, many verses to compose in her head another little tune. The lyrics, born of pure simmering anger and raw inspiration and wicked, wicked, desperate mischief came to her so swiftly, so wholly, surely the angels must have been on her side. Or perhaps it was devils. At this point she thought she'd take any help she could get.

She applauded happily along with everyone else when Delilah and Angelique brought the song to an end, and waited a respectful moment.

Then she suggested: "Perhaps something lighter now? Another song has just come to me, and I believe we can all sing this one together! Would you like to hear it?"

"Oh, indeed!" Enthusiasm was unanimous, minus one.

Mariana went to the pianoforte again to pick out the tune, while Delilah watched to learn it.

"I think . . . C, G, and E . . . then C D F D E C D C, like so . . . yes, *precisely*."

"Oh, that's delightful." Delilah was pleased as she tried it. "Quite sprightly!"

"Wonderful! Now when I bring my hands together like this"—Mariana clapped them—"I'd like you all to give a clap, too. So watch carefully. You'll know why in a moment. Mrs. Hardy, shall we?"

Delilah launched into the tune, and Mariana

waited two bars before she turned to the room full of happy, expectant faces and sang:

"Oh, I'm a lord of great valor and honor."
At least that's what he told her before he climbed on 'er . . .
. . . *stairs* to the *ball*room to partake in a ball
But to the occasion he could not rise, only fall!
"What's taking so long?" cried the maiden fair.
"Have pity," he said, "and patience, I pray.
"I've a stick up me CLAP and gray in me hair!
"I've a stick up me CLAP and gray in me hair!"

Delilah's delighted face slowly devolved into wide-eyed alarm while her fingers, seemingly independent of her horror, continued to move over the keyboard. Angelique had frozen, astounded, staring at Mariana.

Everyone else—save one person, of course—was *thrilled*. They cried out in delight. Mr. Delacorte slapped the table and hooted.

"Are you ready to sing with me?" Mariana enthused. "Everyone now!"

Mr. Delacorte, Dot, and Mrs. Pariseau joined her in such full voice that they didn't notice Delilah stopped playing the pianoforte midway through.

"Oh, I'm a lord of great valor and honor."
At least that's what he told her before he climbed on 'er . . .
Stairs to the ballroom to partake in a ball

But to the occasion he could not rise, only fall!
"What's taking so long?" cried the maiden fair.
"Have pity," he said, "and patience, I pray.
"I've a stick up me CLAP and gray in me hair!
"I've a stick up me CLAP and gray in me hair!
"I've a stick up me CLAP and gray in me hair!"

Most of her audience fell about laughing and applauding.

Two of them were cautiously gauging the temperature of the room to see if everyone understood what had really just happened.

One of them was as still as if he'd been driven into the ground with a hammer, and he was studying her speculatively.

It felt *wonderful*. So wrong, and so wonderful. It was sex. It was the ball landing on your number on a roulette wheel after you'd wagered just a little too high, which she'd done only once in her life. She wouldn't do it again, but she was *glad* she had done it.

What virtue had she just annihilated?

"Oh, Miss Wylde, that song is a *delight*! I shall be singing it whilst I go about my day," Mrs. Pariseau said.

"*What* a happy song about dancing," Dot said, wiping tears of laughter.

"Yes, there are so few happy songs about 'dancing,' Miss Wylde," Mrs. Durand said dryly, rather pointedly. "So generous of you to add to the canon."

She deserved more than a little scolding. But she thought it was *just* subtle enough that she could feign innocence, and she was going to bask in the champagne bubbles of her cleverness. She'd had so few wins, recently. She felt positively fulsome with triumph.

"I suspect you have a wonderful singing voice, Your Grace," Mrs. Pariseau said, emboldened and aglow with the happiness of good music. "You ought to sing a tune. We'd be so honored."

"Yes, why *don't* you join in the singing, Your Grace?" Mariana felt emboldened, too. "I'm certain Mrs. Pariseau is right. You excel at so many things, it would doubtless be yet another triumph to add to the chapter called 'Triumphs' in your memoirs."

He didn't reply. He regarded her with something very like genuine interest. In fact, speculatively.

"Most operas are performed in Italian, are they not, Miss Wylde?" He was very polite.

Unusually polite.

Almost deferential.

"It is my opinion that the best of them are, indeed, Your Grace." It was lovely to know something definitively that he seemed not to know. The evening was getting better and better.

"Such a lyrical language. So expressive and *vibrant*."

"Oh, yes," she agreed. A little more cautiously now. She wasn't used to hearing two relatively pleasant sentences in a row from the duke.

"There's a beautiful Italian expression . . . it's a favorite of mine. Perhaps you know it? I should be pleased indeed if you could turn it into a little tune, with perhaps a poignant melody."

"It would be *my* honor, Your Grace." Perhaps, the general that he was, he'd decided to call a truce, knowing the battle would go on and that she could, in fact, draw blood.

"It's this . . ." he said, slowly and beautifully. "'Non smetto mai di strillare come un orribile pappagallo.' Isn't that beautiful and profound?"

"'Non smetto mai di strillare come un orribile pappagallo.'" She flawlessly, slowly, imitated the way he'd savored the words. She hadn't the faintest idea what they meant.

Mrs. Pariseau cleared her throat. "Miss Wylde . . . ?" she said quietly.

But Mariana didn't hear her. She only knew she could not hesitate for long without looking like an absolute fool in front of him. So she nodded.

Later she was to remember the duke's immediate little smile.

A snippet of an aria she loved possessed a similar rhythm to those words. With a tweak or two, she could adapt the duke's phrase to it.

The room was utterly silent as she lowered her head and took a breath.

And then she slowly lifted her head, closed her eyes, and soulfully released the words with full power, trilling the *L*'s for all she was worth, hands over her heart.

"Non smetto mai di strillare come un orribile pappagallllllo!"

A resounding silence ensued.

She frankly thought it was a creditable, if not tour de force, performance.

There ought to have been applause, or at least a sigh or two.

Something was terribly wrong.

Mr. Delacorte did pat his hands together tentatively. But he tapered off at the sight of Mrs. Pariseau with her hands over her mouth, her eyes wide and fixed on Mariana with what looked like shock and—more horrifying—sympathy.

A cold dread traced Mariana's spine.

Mrs. Hardy and Mrs. Durand were similarly wide-eyed and very still.

That bastard had walked her into a trap. That much was suddenly horrifyingly clear.

Dot and Mr. Delacorte had picked up the mood of the room and were somber, if confused.

"*Thank* you, Miss Wylde," the duke said, sounding bored. But his eyes glinted dangerously. "That was even better than I expected."

She saw then how he'd done it. He'd used her flaws against her. He thought her an ignorant peasant, all instinct and nerve, and he'd extrapolated from there. He had trapped her neatly with her own pride, and he'd played a hunch that she wouldn't be able to resist lying about it.

She knew at once there was no winning against this man. Ever. She would not ever signify.

She supposed she was glad he'd been the one standing between the English and the French. But she was also glad there was bird shite all over his statue in Hyde Park.

She stood in the middle of the room, her palms damp, a cold knot in her stomach, and wished this was in fact an opera stage and that a trapdoor would open beneath her and she would topple in and perhaps die.

She wondered who would be brave enough to tell her what it meant.

It turned out to be Mrs. Durand.

She cleared her throat and said, with an exaggerated sort of politeness, "'I never stop squawking like a hideous parrot' *is* indeed an unusual expression, Your Grace."

"And now it's also a song," the duke said placidly, and lifted the newspaper again to read.

Chapter Five

❧❧❧

"WE CAN'T let this stand. We need to have a word with the duke."

"You mean . . . reprimand him?" Delilah whispered.

Angelique hesitated. Then nodded slowly, with deep regret.

Neither of them knew why they were whispering. They were in the sitting room at the top of the stairs; everyone else had gone to sleep. It seemed that a crime terrible and magnificent in its subtlety had been committed. Miss Wylde had retreated to her rooms immediately thereafter and had not returned for the rest of the evening.

It had been devastating.

The bawdy little song she'd delivered earlier had been veiled enough that it could be explained away, and yet they both knew what—and who—it had been about. And so did the duke.

He'd been provoked.

Nevertheless.

Delilah considered this. "It will be a shame to celebrate my first wedding anniversary with a divorce."

Angelique stifled a laugh. "In all seriousness, do you think Tristan would ever forgive you if we evicted Valkirk? Not that we're going to take it quite that far," she added hurriedly. "Although . . . imagine the publicity. It could go either way, really. People love exclusivity, and would be awfully curious to learn that not even Valkirk could meet our standards."

"That might be an amusing exercise to imagine once we settle this little problem. It's just . . . do you suppose he'll take kindly to it?"

Angelique had no answer for her. "No matter. We must do it. And we must do it tomorrow. The air was positively humid with reproach in the sitting room, and I shouldn't like Mr. Delacorte or Mrs. Pariseau or Dot to think we'd allow them—or anyone—to be treated that way. And I shouldn't like them to feel free to *behave* that way."

And so, an hour later, in their cozy bedroom, Delilah broke the news of their intentions to her husband.

She'd gotten into her night rail. She brushed her hair a hundred strokes then plaited it.

She waited for him to be half-undressed before she told him, in case, she thought mordantly, it was the last time she was able to feast her eyes on that view of his stunning torso. When he twisted slightly, there was a slight gap between his taut waist and his trousers, and it made her head go light. She always wanted to slip her hand into it. She could now, anytime she pleased. One of the millions of benefits of being a wife.

And that's when she told him about what had just happened and what she and Angelique planned to do.

He stood, shirt dangling in one hand, and listened. His jaw dropped. "Bloody hell, Delilah. It's *Valkirk*. How can you even . . . I just . . . he must have been sorely provoked."

"He was indeed a little provoked."

"There you have it."

"Even so."

That "even so" contained "she's just an opera singer on the rise and he's a bloody national treasure and should know better."

And Tristan knew it. He mulled this. "That man won a battle when he was wounded and had only two hundred men and the French had . . ."

"I know."

"And he's never asked for anything in return, and yet he . . ."

He trailed off at her limpidly sympathetic gaze. Of course. Everyone knew this about the duke.

He sighed heavily and dropped his chin to his chest. "Damnation. I think you and Angelique are right. I think he ought to apologize to Miss Wylde."

"I'm sorry to have to scold a hero, Tristan." Her husband was a hero to many, too. She knew the men he truly admired could be counted on the fingers of one hand, and he needed those.

He sat down on the edge of their bed. "Speaking as someone who transgressed here at The Grand Palace on the Thames and nearly paid the ultimate price . . . I am just so grateful I never have to leave. Perhaps he'll feel the same way."

"Ah, but you have *incentives* to behave," she murmured, looping her arms around his neck.

He kissed her, and he spent the next two hours thoroughly appreciating those incentives.

VALKIRK HAD REGRETTED it at once. He'd felt as though he'd stood up in the parlor, pulled out a pistol, and gratuitously shot a sparrow from the sky.

For the remainder of the evening, the room had been silent, dense with reproach and wondering amazement. Some of that wondering amazement was his own, directed at himself. He knew what he'd done was beyond the pale. He'd won a certain quiet respite. And no one could truly argue he hadn't been provoked.

But it didn't justify what he'd done.

Miss Wylde was never to know it, but in so losing to him she had, in fact, done something that very few people would in a lifetime: bested him at something. Even if it was the stupidest contest of wills ever conducted.

Because it wasn't so much the ridiculously competent little song that had somehow sprung from her brain while everyone sat there, misty-eyed in the throes of a ballad. He begrudgingly admitted that this was true talent.

It was the cumulative effects of every night walking into that pleasant, familial room and being told he was cold.

Nevertheless, he knew he was going to need to apologize.

The following morning, as he crossed the foyer intent on a brisk walk, he was stopped by Mrs. Hardy and Mrs. Durand, who were standing together in the reception room.

"We'd like a brief word, if you would, Your Grace. If you would be so kind as to join us in here?"

He'd no compelling reason to say no.

"Please do have a seat," Mrs. Durand said pleasantly.

Warily, he lowered himself to the settee opposite them.

There was a little silence. Then Mrs. Hardy took a breath. "As you're a man who appreciates the value of time, we'll come right to the point. We feel you have been . . ."

She turned to Mrs. Durand.

"Churlish," Mrs. Durand said gently.

Mrs. Hardy nodded, her eyes soft with tender, yet unyielding, regret.

The duke was stunned.

"Churlish," he mused, as though his tongue could scarcely shape the word.

"The rules of our establishment require our guests to be, at the minimum, civil to each other, if they cannot be kind. We value Miss Wylde's custom every bit as much as we value yours. And while your objective may not have directly been to hurt Miss Wylde's feelings, we do believe your objective was to *win*, whatever the cost. Which you did. The consequence was that you hurt her feelings. And embarrassed her." This was Mrs. Durand.

"We are *genuinely* fond of our guests, including you, and so grateful for their custom that it pains us greatly when any of them do not take to each other. As our entire aim is to create a congenial, if not familial, environment for our guests," Mrs. Hardy added.

He was speechless.

"But she . . ."

He couldn't do it. He couldn't bring himself to say to these two women, *But she led the room in a cheerful sing-along about my alleged impotence.*

And they likely knew it.

They had him, and it was almost funny.

He pressed his lips together. He slowly leaned back and studied them.

"I can offer you no argument. Everything you've said is correct. It was unworthy of me."

They were sympathetically quiet.

Mrs. Durand raised her eyebrows, as if she knew he could do even better.

He sighed. "One gets in the habit of ruthlessness, you see, when winning is a matter of life or death."

"We're familiar with that quality in men." Little smiles here.

"I saw how to achieve my ends and so . . . I fear I did what I needed to do, reflexively."

Their silence remained politely interested and gently, immovably damning.

"We can see how that would be a useful, even heroic, quality in . . . warfare," Mrs. Hardy allowed. The telling pause intimated, *But not in the parlor.*

"It was not only an unworthy reflex," he expounded. "Perhaps worse than that, it was ungentlemanly." Hell's teeth. It really was.

"And we strongly feel it is *unlike* you, as you are all that is graceful and genteel. Then again, one might be more irritable if, for instance, the writing of one's memoirs wasn't going well."

He leveled a cool stare at her and admitted to nothing.

"Please accept my apology. And I shall of course apologize to Miss Wylde," he said after a moment. "And to the other guests."

"That would be most gracious of you. And we would be very grateful," Mrs. Hardy said.

"She might not possess the kind of education or upbringing you've had the privilege to experience, but she's clever and a delightful person, all in all, and we do believe she has been hard done by in the newspapers," added Mrs. Durand.

He let this last bit lie. It was *clearly* not the time to debate that particular point.

There was a little silence.

"So what happens now? Am I to be ejected from my comfortable suite, then, like Lucifer from this heavenly realm?"

"Well, that depends."

There was another silence.

"That . . . depends?"

Surely this wasn't happening.

"We so hope you prefer to stay, Your Grace. We've *loved* having you here, and we enjoy making you comfortable. We think, however, in addition to your apology, you might offer to assist Miss Wylde in learning to speak Italian. She is clever and has expressed regret that she doesn't speak it when she sings it so magnificently. She learned it by listening and mimicking, and we admire her pluck. Perhaps you can offer her a few hours of your time to tutor her in the language."

"Give her *more* of my time? I'm to do penance as well?"

He was accustomed to incinerating others with a censorious gaze.

He'd never reckoned with the power of a pair of brown eyes and a pair of hazel eyes, both aimed at him with a sort of implacable, feminine sympathy.

"It's one suggestion, Your Grace. Perhaps you've another gracious gesture in mind," Mrs. Hardy said.

Oh, she was good. How petulant it would be if he'd said, *How about no gesture?*

It was the modifier of "gracious" that rather fenced him in.

"We will also have a word with Miss Wylde, about ways in which she can feel comfortable to be herself without . . ."

". . . working my last nerve?" he said grimly.

"We're so sorry that's how you experience it. Perhaps she's merely trying to impress you," Mrs. Durand suggested brightly.

"No doubt," he muttered. This seemed likely.

He knew Miss Wylde wanted his attention. But most females did try to impress him. He wished they would not *try*. It was like being flogged with little satin ribbons, repeatedly. He supposed there were men who might enjoy and even pay for ribbon-flogging, but he found it confounding and pointless. A bit like shadowboxing.

He sighed. "Very well, Mrs. Hardy. Mrs. Durand. I shall apologize to Miss Wylde and offer her Italian lessons. Do send her in, if you would."

They stood, and he stood.

". . . and then I shall congratulate Hardy and Bolt on having the good fortune to marry such diabolical females."

They departed, wearing smiles, to send Miss Wylde, while he was left to wait for Miss Wylde like a damned suitor.

PRESENTLY, SHE APPEARED.

"Ah, good morning, Miss Wylde. Thank you for agreeing to meet me here in the reception room."

"You're welcome, Your Grace," she said pleasantly.

He didn't ask her to sit. Which was all to the good. Mariana didn't want to spend any more time in his company than absolutely necessary, and she supposed it was a signal that he intended to get this over with quickly.

"I've something I'd like to say," he continued.

"Very well."

There ensued a pause that grew comical in duration.

"Take your time, Your Grace," she said gently. "When you've never said those particular words aloud before, you might be a little uncertain about their pronunciation. I'll be happy to assist you if you stumble. I excel at parroting things."

She could literally see the muscle in his jaw flex when his teeth clamped down.

"I apologize for hurting your feelings." He said it rather quickly and tersely.

". . . and embarrassing me," she prompted generously, as if he were a novice actor and they were learning a script together.

"And I apologize for embarrassing you. It was unkind and unworthy of me. I should not have done it."

She waited, almost leaning forward.

He raised his brows. "Well?"

"It was very nicely said. It's just that I can hear the word 'but . . .' fair echoing at the end of the sentence. I think you ought to say all you wish to say, Your Grace. Rather the way one ought to like to pull all of the splinter out, rather than leave just that pesky little bit in."

He studied her and then produced a speculative almost-smile that immediately made her want to retract her suggestion and leave the room with her apology, and at a great clip.

"But . . . I think you hurl flirtation and childish behavior like boiling oil over a castle wall. Who are you without it? Anything? Anyone?"

She felt the scalding, astounding, all-fired nerve of the man! Duke or no duke. The *injustice*!

And it finally snapped, the tether on her temper. "Have you ever paused in front of a mirror? You *are* a bloody castle." She nearly hissed it, then raised a hand abruptly. "Yes. I know. I oughtn't say 'bloody.' You don't know how the epithet jar vexes me. It's diabolically effective given that I haven't a sou to spare. I cannot afford to be as expressive as I like."

"Indeed it is a shame you've felt so repressed," he said tersely.

"I don't suppose you've given any thought to why I feel obliged to . . . how did you so elegantly put it? Hurl things from a castle rather than roaming about outside of it, free as a . . ." Hell's teeth. She could not for the life of her think of what might roam the grounds of a castle freely. And then a memory inconveniently sparked and it was out of her mouth before she could stop it. She said, ". . . a sheep."

He stared at her for a time. Lips pressed together.

"As free as a sheep," he repeated flatly.

"Yes," she said firmly, raising her chin, committing to her metaphor. When in doubt and backed into a corner of her own making, embrace bravado for all it was worth: that was her credo.

"So you're saying I'm not wrong about the hurling boiling oil bit."

"That's not what I said at all."

"But—"

"You're not completely right, either. In the world of the theater, most decisions are still made by men, and to survive and thrive in it, one must use the language men understand. And that language is flattery and flirtation. But it can be used to both keep people at a distance and to pull them in. When one is *not* a castle, one must use the tools at one's disposal. I cannot speak to the childish behavior, as that seems an entirely new inspiration. I've a new muse."

He was silent.

"We're that simple, are we," he said neutrally.

"Men are."

"I'm afraid so." She offered him a tiny, pitying smile. "Well, that, and I like to flirt . . . some of the time."

"Very well. We have established I am a castle and you are in a fortress surrounded by free-roaming sheep. We have a sense of each other now, I believe."

"Are you conceding my point, then, regarding castles, boiling oil, and the lot?"

"Miss Wylde, 'concede' is perilously close to the word 'surrender,' and the entire point of castles is to prevent one from ever needing to do that."

"Oh, of course, Your Grace. Your reputation for not surrendering was once featured on page one of the *London Times*. I believe it was the day I appeared on page six."

"I assume you learned Italian phonetically, then."

"If you mean by parroting it, why, yes, I did."

He paused.

"Rather impressive." He sounded a little surprised.

"You don't *know* how much that praise means to me, Your Grace."

He took a breath. "I wondered if I might also make amends for my unkindness by . . ." he took yet another resolute breath ". . . offering you lessons in Italian. I speak and write it fluently."

"So I surmised."

They regarded each other from across the room, their eyes very slightly narrowed.

She'd increasingly felt as though little by little he was dialing her into focus with a spyglass. She imagined all of his thoughts in his unnerving brain, lining up like pieces on a chessboard.

"Why sheep?" he said suddenly.

She gave a little start and was instantly cagey. There was a little silence.

"I do not want to tell you," she said.

His eyebrows went up. He had not expected this.

His silence was not the conceding sort. He was going to be silent until words were compelled from her, like a soldier ordered into formation.

"Very well, Your Grace. I will tell you, if you will answer a question of my choosing, when I choose."

"Are you negotiating with me, Miss Wylde?" He sounded less incredulous and displeased than she'd anticipated.

"Yes."

He mulled this. "Very well. I am allowed three refusals."

"You're suggesting that you're allowed to refuse to answer a question three times before you'll agree to answer one?"

"Yes."

"One refusal."

He considered this. "Done."

She drew in a breath. "When I was a very little girl, my family and I—my mother and father and me—traveled to the seashore. We did this only twice. We lived and breathed our little patch of London, you see, which we quite loved. We knew everybody! But we'd neighbors all on top of and next to us and cobblestones on the ground outside, and—"

"What sort of work did your father do?"

"He was a cobbler, like his father and grand-father."

He nodded crisply for her to continue.

"He had a little shop on Tully Street near Hay-market, and we lived above it. Cor, we were busy. I still remember all the customers by name and . . . it was lively. And a great deal of work all day. We weren't rich, but we never wanted for a thing, mind. Anyhow, I was eight years old and my fa-ther decided we ought to take a trip to the seashore in Brighton. He'd traded a pair of shoes to a friend who drove a hack, and so we had a carriage to our-selves. I tried very hard to stay awake to see all the new things, but I fell asleep straightaway . . . When I woke up, everywhere there was so much velvety green. Like blankets heaped up in piles. And the sky was so blue and empty, it was like a china plate. And on this green were sheep, and they looked like clouds in a green sky. It was like waking up in a dream. I thought I was suddenly in a fairy world. What's more free than a cloud? To drift this way and that. To take on new shapes and colors. To see the whole world."

He was silent. But it was clear he was listening closely.

"It was a very pretty sight. It was the first thing that came to mind—sheep and clouds. I've always wondered who owned those sheep."

He was quiet a moment. And then he said:

"*Mi chiedo chi sia il proprietario di queste pecore.* I wonder who owns these sheep."

She was instantly intrigued.

"*Queste pecore mi appartengono.* These sheep belong to me," he continued.

"*Queste pecore sembrano piccole nuvole.* These sheep look like little clouds."

"*Queste pecore sembrano piccole nuvole,*" she breathed slowly, each word phonetically, rhythmically flawless. Like she'd been given a magic spell. "It's lovely when you say it that way, isn't it? It sounds like the beginning of an aria. The curtain rises on green fields made all out of heaps of green velvet, and there are little sheep among them, perhaps fashioned out of felt and cotton wool, and the shepherdess in the most adorable frock strolls onstage—"

"—and her flock is eaten by wolves because the daft woman is busy singing about how they look like little clouds instead of watching them."

"Operas do not need to make sense," she said

with tolerant placidity. "They only need to make the audience feel things. Like a lovely dream. For how often do dreams make sense? Dreams of the sort you have when you go to sleep at night."

"Why on earth is that necessary? Why is any of that necessary?" His patience sounded uncommonly frayed.

He might mean dreaming. He might mean this conversation. He might mean The Grand Palace on the Thames.

She wrinkled her nose in mock sympathy and tipped her head. "Feelings are not your forte, Your Grace?"

"I should think life is operatic enough without introducing an additional element of absurd drama, let alone a drama one pays to see. I keep a box at the opera but I do not use it. My son does."

"Fair point, Your Grace. It's just that one person's absurd drama, as you put it, might be another person's matter of life or death. And not everyone prefers their waking lives to their dreams."

"Are feelings your forte, then, Miss Wylde?"

"Good God, no. Feelings are like a stiff wind. They can blow you right off the jetty."

He pressed his lips together for a long moment while he studied her.

"Blow you off the jetty?" he said finally.

"Another time," she said, with an airy lift of her hand.

"I am all anticipation."

"I will admit I enjoy knowing I've the power to make others feel things with my voice. To transport them to another place. To lift them up out of themselves."

"A power, is it?"

"Oh, yes."

They regarded each other fixedly. She noticed that his posture, which heretofore had always looked as though he had a long rifle for a spine, had relaxed a very little. She imagined that "a very little" was all this man ever relaxed.

"Very well, then, Miss Wylde. I will attempt to impart the rudiments of conversational Italian over a series of hours. I suggest three o'clock to four o'clock each afternoon for the duration of my stay. Would you like to avail yourself of lessons?"

"Yes, please. Thank you. I've permission to use 'bloody'?"

"Miss Wylde, I was a soldier. Epithets are practically a second language for military men. My sensibilities cannot be violated with mere words."

"Even when uttered by a woman?"

"Even when uttered by a woman."

There was a little pause during which she rather loudly thought but did not mention the words she'd sung the night before, which had violated his sensibilities, which had arguably led to the two of them standing here today.

"I anticipate the hours I'll be spending in your company will necessitate its use once or twice."

"I should feel I have failed in my duty as a tutor if you are not so inspired."

There was a silence.

He sighed. "I sense a 'but,' Miss Wylde."

"Not so much a 'but' as . . . an 'and,' Your Grace. I've a list of things I've heard many times over the years in Italian, and I should like to know at last what they truly mean. And I should like to learn the meanings of some of the lyrics that I've been singing. If you would be so kind."

"Yes. Of course. I'd be pleased to do that. Tomorrow, three o'clock in the afternoon in the antechamber of my suite. Do not be late. Now, if you would be so kind as to excuse me?"

"I would be so kind," she said on a grave hush, and curtsied to him as he bowed, and the two so kind people parted.

Chapter Six

❧❧❧

*H*ER HEART was beating absurdly quickly as she made her way up the stairs and down the hall the following day to the duke's chambers. She was escorted by Dot, who was thrilled to be charged with the errand.

They paused in the hall and peered down it.

At the end of it was an anteroom attached to the duke's room, fronted by heavy double doors, both sides open. They could see the man himself at a great table, illuminated by the sunlight from the large arched window as if he were onstage.

"I'm fine from here. Thank you, Dot."

"Good luck!" Dot said. And then, touchingly, she gave her elbow a little squeeze. "I shall return at four, Miss Wylde. It's when he likes a bit of tea."

It was an anteroom of sorts that must have been a library a century or so ago, when the building was new. Shelves were built into the wall.

He glanced up and saw her framed in the doorway.

"*Buonasera*, Miss Wylde. I commend you on your punctuality. You are, in fact, a few minutes early. I am just replying to some correspondence from my solicitor."

Behind him sat a handsome brass and wood clock about a foot tall. Its face was pale, and black roman numerals marched around it. A brass pendulum swung back and forth inside it.

"*Buonasera*, Your Grace. *Grazie*. I wasn't certain how long the journey from the house to this suite would take. I shouldn't like to be flogged for tardiness."

"You'll be grateful to learn that we no longer flog for tardiness in the military." He sounded abstracted. He didn't look up from the sentence he was inscribing. "We put men on the rack. Or tell their mothers."

She smiled cautiously.

He swept one hand out without looking at her. "If you'll take the seat opposite me, I shall just be a moment."

She settled in, gingerly.

Folded her hands, primly.

She watched his quill fly across the page like a living thing, darting and leaping to make letters. She was a little sleepy from her midday meal and it was soothing, almost mesmeric, to watch. Two miniatures were propped on stands in frames on his table, a pretty dark-haired woman and a young man who looked like a precise blend of the duke and the pretty, dark-haired woman. She wondered whether he had ever taken his family to the seashore, or if he had always been off fighting.

It seemed odd and possibly a little dangerous

to be so close to him. He was something better appreciated from a distance, like a gryphon. If he turned, his shoulders would all but block the sun from the window.

Next to him was a stack of foolscap. She peered at it. Across the page on top were the words "Chapter Two." It thus far seemed to be comprised of about three sentences, several scratched out words, and small drawings.

"I see you've drawn . . . a little horse, and a flower of some sort. And is that . . . is that meant to be a dog?"

He smacked his left hand lightly down on the foolscap and pushed it aside, all the while continuing to write. He hadn't even looked up.

"The horse and dog looked rather similar. Perhaps if you made the horse's tail a bit fluffier?"

He cast a swift but potently baleful glance upward at her, then re-dipped his quill and continued his correspondence.

"Three sentences only. Chapter Two must be the one where you reminisce about all your pleasurable pursuits."

She wondered just how much piss-taking she could get away with when it came to a duke.

He ignored this while he sprinkled sand on the letter and pushed it aside, too.

And then sat back and directed the whole of his attention to her, one eyebrow arched as though he was assessing how to handle a recalcitrant subaltern.

Everything he did was brisk and precise. She

was reminded of the time she'd witnessed a man loading a rifle, the sharp, swift, finite, methodical steps. She wondered if life was like that for the duke: he knew precisely each step to take, and when, and what the result would be.

How must that feel?

"So, Miss Wylde . . . how much Italian do you in truth speak or write, if any?"

She cleared her throat. "Ah . . . very little."

"If you would kindly share a few words with me." It wasn't a question. It was a command. She supposed she'd better get used to that.

"*Buonasera. Grazie. Prego.* I know the meanings of those words. *Aria. Aria di sorbetto. Cadenza.* Mostly musical words of that nature. Man, woman. You, me. Some pronouns."

"So far during your career . . ." She didn't care for the slight ironic lilt he'd given to the word "career"—it rather suggested the words "of vice" ought to follow it. ". . . you've learned *all* your singing roles, and the lyrics to arias, by ear?"

"By parroting, if you would, Your Grace."

There ensued a pause during which she could almost hear him meticulously re-looming his fraying patience.

"I apologized, Miss Wylde," he reminded her heavily. "Might I suggest we move on?"

"What fun would that be?"

He pressed his lips together.

"You are a . . . cobbler's daughter, you said?"

"Yes."

"And have you had any formal education?"

"By formal—"

"A tutor. A governess. That sort of thing. To teach you languages and maths."

"Not . . . as such."

His little confirming nod indicated both that he took that as a no, and that it was precisely what he'd thought. "Yet you're fairly well-spoken."

Well. She was almost amused. Her pride took that as a glancing blow. "Fairly," she repeated, musingly. "Damned with faint praise. May I say 'damned' in here?"

"Do you see a jar?" he said. He gestured broadly.

He was studying her again, a little thoughtful shadow between his brows, as though she were a map to an unpromising territory. His forehead indeed featured a faint line, and there were a few more of those raying from the corners of his eyes. She wished his shoulders weren't so admirably vast.

"If you learn the arias well by listening, what do you hope to gain from Italian lessons?"

She hesitated, her pride and impulse toward sarcasm warring with the genuine desire to *know*. The blessed relief that would bring. Here, for the first time in her life, was someone, an *intelligent* someone even if he was rather a bastard, who could teach her. And she could endure a bastard if there were some return on the investment of endurance.

And so she told him the truth.

"Well, it's like trying to see through a dirty window, isn't it? It can be done, but you never see all you *want* to see, only bits of it. And the effort is so . . . it's ultimately exhausting. I can glean quite a bit from context, but am always at a slight disadvantage, and I want to never be at a disadvantage again."

His expression shifted subtly. It could not precisely be said that it softened. It became interested, she would have said.

"How much money do you have?" she asked kindly.

"Refuse," he said smoothly without so much as an eyebrow twitch. "How was it you came by your facility—ease—with speech?"

"I know 'facility,'" she said calmly. "You needn't translate every word longer than two syllables."

"Very well," he said with equanimity. "Why don't you just tell me when you'd like something defined? Two people who have survived insulting each other without fighting a duel should not stand on ceremony."

It was the oddest sensation to be yanked between seething resentment and the impulse to like him, the latter of which she felt he did not quite deserve. But he was difficult in an interesting way, and one could so seldom say that about men.

"Well, my mother taught me to read and write. She made sure of it from the moment I could walk. Of course, it helped in the shop, to do accounts and take orders and the like. Our shop was near the theater, and we had quite a variety of customers. Actors and actresses and singers, and lords and ladies and everyday folks. It was Madame Elaine Guillaume—"

"The opera singer?"

"You've heard of her."

"One can hardly be British without having heard of Madame Guillaume, Miss Wylde. Rest her soul."

Mariana nodded. "Yes. Well, she used to come into our shop. She heard me singing one day and was quite taken by it. She said I had genuine talent." It was still a magical moment to Mariana, and one she never tired of reliving in her mind. "She offered to give me voice lessons in exchange for bits and bobs to do with her shoes. She did so love her shoes, but she loved gambling even better, and she was often a bit short."

"How serendipitous. Lucky," he clarified.

She sucked in a breath. She *hadn't* known that word. He was effortlessly astute. She found it both bracing and unsettling. Lord, how he must have frightened the soldiers into behaving.

"She was kind, and I do miss her. She was so *sophisticated* and good fun—Mrs. Pariseau reminds me a bit of her—and I suppose I learned diction from her. Copied her, like. Cadences, accents, little habits and fancier manners, that sort of thing. From the people I met who came to visit her in her flat, too. Later, in the theater, when I began getting roles, some of the patrons were very well-spoken."

"Yes. Both Lord Kilhone and Lord Revell, for instance, went to Eton and Oxford, where one is nothing if not well-spoken," he said pointedly.

She thought of "bewitching" and "beautiful." Did that count as being "well-spoken"?

She stared at him coolly. "In short, one might

say I owe my career entirely to gambling. One never knows what sort of luck a vice will lead to, Your Grace."

He was still for a moment. Then offered her a slow, sardonic nod. Conceding a point to her.

Dear Mama—the duke's face is a bit long, and so sculpted it was like he had no choice to go on to be something insufferably important just so they could carve a marble bust of him and install it somewhere public, where it could sit in judgment of all the passersby. I could lay my hands against the hollows beneath his cheekbones, but I might cut my palms on the corners of his jaw if I did. He is regal, but I'm not certain he is handsome. His eyes are very fierce. It's only just after three o'clock and I think his beard is about to make itself known.

She gave a start when he suddenly dipped his quill and began writing words in a column.

"Who are the woman and the boy in the miniatures?"

It was what she'd *really* wanted to know from the beginning.

He went still. His eyes flared in surprise.

He leaned back in his chair slowly.

Then studied her with a little speculative scowl that transformed into reluctant and amused respect.

"Do feel free to go on underestimating me, Your Grace."

He studied her like she'd been studying him. She wondered if her face yielded up anything new or interesting. If it did, he didn't of course reveal it.

"Very well," he said quietly. "As I'm a man of my word, I will tell you. My wife, Eliza, who passed away five years ago."

"Thank you for telling me." She paused. "And I'm sorry for your loss."

It was what one said. He'd doubtless heard it thousands of times.

But she was suddenly held motionless by a realization. The war had ended five years ago. His wife had died five years ago.

The things that had formed the foundation walls of his life, in one fell swoop, had disappeared five years ago. She wondered if a man like him had ever felt off balance.

He nodded his thanks. "The boy is my son, Arthur, who is twenty-two. Probably about your age," he hazarded.

It was pretty risky to guess a woman's age, but at least he'd come in with a low number.

"I'm twenty-five." She could not see a reason to be coy about it, as it could be of no interest to the duke.

"Ah," was all he said. Because that was exactly how much it interested him.

"She was pretty. Your wife."

"She was," he said shortly. He'd taken to writing again.

"She must have been a saint."

"She'd have to be to endure me. Is that the very

original point you're making?" he said dryly. He paused, and then his expression reflected that he'd had another inspiration.

"It's just that you seem rather intolerant of flaws, and surely only a saint possesses none."

"Intolerant of *some* flaws," he said abstractedly after a moment, with a little smile. He dipped the quill again.

"And I possess the full complement of the objectionable flaws."

He paused to look at her. "We can use our hour to discuss useful Italian vocabulary, or itemize flaws."

"Oh, let's do both."

His mouth curved slightly. The column of words he was writing was growing lengthy.

"It might *not* break, you know," she mused softly, speculatively.

"I beg your pardon?" he muttered.

"Your face. If you *really* smile. You've done it before."

He paused to, ironically, reward her with a scowl.

She smiled beatifically at him. "I *can* be amusing, you know."

"Are you in the habit of writing your own notices for the newspaper, Miss Wylde?" He did, at least, sound mildly amused.

"If only that were an option. You've clearly read the last thing written about me, and you and all of London have decided it might as well be my epitaph."

He ignored this, unless one counted the single twitch of a brow. He dipped the quill again.

"Epitaph has *three* syllables," she pointed out. "Good word, that."

His quill continued moving.

"Your Grace, if I may be so bold . . . what *are* you writing?"

"I will share it with you in one moment, if you would be so kind as to be patient and perhaps not prate, which I suspect you do when you're nervous."

So she was quiet. She tried not to jiggle her foot.

He paused and looked across at her. He seemed lost in thought.

"She wasn't quite a saint. She had a bit of temper," he said suddenly. Surprising her. "My wife." He said this with a sort of rueful affection. One corner of his mouth dented.

She wondered what it would be like to ever be mentioned with rueful affection by a man, who would dent one corner of his mouth.

"Surely this temper was never directed at you, as you've no flaws."

"It bodes well for your success as a pupil, Miss Wylde, that you're so observant." His mouth curved at his own joke as he returned to writing.

"You've no *notion* how much I notice."

"Oh, I've some notion," he said grimly.

He finally stopped writing. He regarded her from across the table, absently tapping his quill.

"I'm curious how you know how to . . . shall we say . . . interpret a song if you don't speak the language. Aren't most operas in Italian? Perhaps because Italians are often profligate with their emotions. *Excessive* with their emotions," he said suddenly.

"Thank you. I didn't know 'profligate.' "

He smiled swiftly.

"Perhaps they are profligate." She liked having a new word. "Compared to the English. But we ought to be grateful for it, because it results in the most thrilling and glorious music. Perhaps that's why we have opera. All that excess must go somewhere, and it spills over into beauty."

"Whereas the truly great English opera has yet to be written," he said. "Because feelings are not the forte of the English."

"Oh, but we must not discount Mr. Thomas Arne, and *Artaxerxes!* Lots of murder and romance. Then there's Mr. John Gay and *The Beggar's Opera* . . . I should so love to play Polly Peachum one day. Who knows, Your Grace? Perhaps one day an opera will be written about your memoirs. Although I imagine it would be difficult for even me to sing over the sound of the cannon firing."

His eyes crinkled.

And then something alarming happened: they lit with true amusement, and in lighting somehow revealed themselves to be filled with subtle little amber and russet lights.

Oh, dear God. They were beautiful.

She did not like knowing this.

It seemed terribly unfair that he should have yet another advantage.

Two tiny curves appeared at either side of his mouth. Dimples.

She stared at him.

She really ought to smile back, but suddenly she was dumbstruck and wary of this evidence of charm.

"Aren't opera singers on the whole famously temperamental?" he asked. "Buffeted about by great winds of emotion. No choice but to throw vases and tantrums. Laughing one moment. Sobbing the next. Threats and exhortations. That sort of thing?"

"That's for later in one's career, when one can get away with nearly anything." She thought, but did not say, that there was no guarantee there would be a "later" in her career.

He nodded, mouth quirked at the corner.

And then he swiftly pushed over to her the sheet of foolscap he'd been writing on.

She bent her head. Written in a hand that was neat but dashing and singular, she found several columns of words, in English and Italian, sorted into categories, like so:

stage
costume
wig
shoes
actor
actress
coat

stockings
balcony
conductor
long
hot
cold
soft
hard
fat
velvet
satin
loud
quiet

io
tu
lui
lei
esso
essa
noi
voi
loro
essi
esse

And so forth.

She looked up at him wonderingly.

"I've made a list of words related to the opera and theater, for a start. Both in English and Italian. In this column"—he gestured—"are adjectives. In this column is a list of verbs, in this one, pronouns, and this one, prepositions. I thought we'd use our time by learning categories of words—clothing, food, conveyances, emotions, colors, buildings. You can study them in your spare time and practice what you learn by writing . . . let's say, ten to twenty sentences or more each night, conjugated. I'll test you each day in a different way."

It was a startlingly efficient lesson plan, concocted while he'd simultaneously held a conversation with her. She could only imagine what the inside of his brain looked like. His entire life was probably sorted into neat little columns.

And it was thrilling. She loved knowing that she would soon impose some sense on anything in her world, let alone the swirl of Italian with which she was often surrounded.

"Conjugate," she repeated. "I like satin slippers. He likes satin slippers. She *liked* satin slippers. They like satin slippers. Like that?"

"Like that. Do you like satin slippers?"

"I *do* like satin slippers." She referred to her list. "*Mi . . . piacciono . . . le scarpe di raso!*"

She looked up at him, delighted.

"Very good. Your accent is already creditable. Does this sound like a reasonable approach to our lessons?"

"Oh my, yes, of a certainty." She looked down at the foolscap, gazing at all those new words that would soon be hers, forever. Feeling, for the first time in weeks, something akin to joy. Perhaps the rest of her life had come to a halt, but these words represented both structure and a sort of progress.

Even if she never sang another aria again, by God, she would know how to speak Italian.

She looked up.

To find an expression she could not quite interpret vanishing from the duke's face.

Her heart skipped. She had the oddest impression, though she could not say why, that she'd missed seeing something beautiful and rare. Like . . . a condor in flight.

"Thank you, Your Grace," she said quietly. Somewhat shyly.

"*Prego*, Miss Wylde," he said crisply.

There was a little silence, filled with the two of them studying each other.

"We've a few minutes more." Behind them the pendulum on the clock was swinging its way toward four. "You mentioned earlier that there were a few things you'd like to learn how to say?"

He tapped the quill idly against the table.

"Oh, yes. For a start, I should like to learn how to say, 'Signor, please remove your hand from my bottom at once.'"

The quill froze.

His face slowly went cold.

Then, terrifyingly . . . bored. As if she'd fulfilled every preconceived notion he might harbor about her.

"If this is how you intend to go on, Miss Wylde, I'm afraid we might as well stop right now. If your objective is to disconcert me, it simply can't be done."

God help her, her face was scorching now. "I do

not mean to make you uncomfortable, Your Grace. I fear I am entirely serious. It's a hazard of my business. As I mentioned before, it's mostly men. If I dodge or give their hands a little smack, they think I'm flirting. If I tell them no, they think I'm flirting. If I laugh, they think I'm flirting. If I say no, no, *stop*, they think I'm flirting. And if in the end I seem angry, I'm deemed difficult, and they are disinclined to give me a job. I already know how to say it in English. I should like to say it firmly, in Italian, in a way they cannot mistake for anything other than a refusal."

He remained motionless and silent. But his expression cleared to something thoughtful.

Then inscrutable.

But all the while, he fixed her with the unblinking gaze that made her feel as though he were rifling through her conscience.

"I have a temper, too," she added, somewhat more mildly. "But having one and indulging one are two different things. And I'm afraid until I'm a diva like Angelica Catalani, who makes a thousand pounds per season, my life is entirely strategy. I should like to make it more bearable meanwhile."

There was a little pause while he took this in.

"So you would like to know how to say, 'Kindly do not touch my arse,' in Italian." He said this entirely reasonably.

"Yes, please."

"*Ti prego di non toccarmi il culo,*" he said sternly.

"*Ti prego di non toccarmi il culo,*" she repeated just as sternly.

"Very good," he said crisply. He wrote it down and then pushed the foolscap to her.

"*Grazie*, Your Grace."

"*Prego*, Miss Wylde."

SHE PAUSED IN the hallway as she met Dot, bringing in the duke's tea.

"I have a good word for you, Dot," she whispered. "It's 'serendipitous.' Ser-en-dip-i-tous. It means 'lucky.'"

"Ser-en-dip-i-tous," Dot breathed. "Thank you, Miss Wylde. It's ser-en-dip-i-tous to meet you in the hall."

They stifled giggles and parted.

Chapter Seven

❧❧❧

THE DUKE graciously and sincerely apologized to everyone for his unkindness to Mariana in the sitting room that night. Everyone generously forgave him.

"I expect writing a book would make anyone go a little mad," Delacorte said sympathetically, later, in the smoking room.

The duke fixed him with a level stare.

Bolt and Hardy just smiled.

The duke half wished he could get Delacorte to write his own memoirs, which the duke would then submit to his publisher as *The Untold Story of the Duke of Valkirk*.

"We've all been . . . churlish . . . a time or two," Lucien said slyly.

One and all beamed approvingly upon the new accord between the duke and Miss Wylde, which so far consisted mostly of the duke doing what he normally did in the sitting room, and Miss Wylde doing what she normally did in the sitting room, and the two of them not talking much to each other at all, really, but not in a rude way.

"MISS MARIANA WYLDE is a spirited girl and very talented, and I do feel she has been hard done by," Madame LeCroix told the *London Times*. "I found her to be responsible and kind, and if a girl has plenty of work, why, she won't have time to get into mischief, will she? I think the gossip is exaggerated and that young men are always underfoot when you're a pretty opera singer. A little champagne never killed anyone. I hope we'll have many chances to hear her beautiful voice for years to come. She is not to blame for anything. She's certainly not a harlot. That nonsense must be forgotten."

Suffice it to say, it was not quite everything they'd dreamed of when it came to reputation repair. And Mariana wasn't precisely thrilled at seeing the "h" word printed in the newspaper yet again.

And reading gossip was one thing, some of which was made up out of whole cloth and designed to titillate and inflame.

This was undeniably the *truth*, and it still was just a trifle wince inspiring.

What did that say about her?

Though she was actually rather touched that she'd made an impression on the great diva at all. She would send a little message of thanks over.

"I'm concerned that 'spirited' is code for 'likes gaming hells,'" she said to Mrs. Hardy and Mrs. Durand and Lord Bolt and Captain Hardy, who had gathered around in the reception room to read it.

"Nonsense," said Lord Bolt, who suspected the same thing.

They would just have to wait to see if her name finally disappeared from the gossip page. Lord Kilhone's and Lord Revell's families would have liked to see the end of the matter, of a certainty. They'd scraped the blame off on her the way one might scrape their boots and diverted everyone with the exciting word "harlot." Perhaps their work was done.

She sighed and closed the newspaper, only to be confronted by another article on the front page.

Valkirk Blesses Charity with Generous Donation

Well. It seemed the duke had donated two hundred pounds to the Society for the Protection of the Sussex Poor.

She goggled. Imagine having *two hundred pounds* to just give away.

"His contributions will feed the hungry and keep the desperate in their homes," said a certain Mrs. Sneath in the article. "We are singularly blessed in our patron, one of England's greatest heroes, whom we can never hope to fully repay."

Oh, for heaven's sake.

Nevertheless, it was a rather lovely thing to do with money, considering the kinds of debaucheries that could be purchased for two hundred pounds. Gambling, mistresses, high flyers, champagne, all of which she knew about because—how had

Madame LeCroix put it?—fast young men were always underfoot when one was a pretty opera singer.

But the plans for the Night of the Nightingale continued apace. Delilah and Angelique approached it doggedly, and with a determined optimism.

Mr. Delacorte, whose work selling remedies to apothecaries took him into London's nooks and crannies both bright and dark, happened to know the owner of a stationer, who, after a bit of haggling, agreed to part with a large quantity of silver paper in exchange for a discount on some of the rice papers the Triton Group was importing. They would use this to fashion into roses for their garlands and urns—some of which would be gently colored with watercolors to hues of red and pink—and to fold into little puffy stars that they would then affix with a small quantity of silver spangles and hang from fishing line from the ceiling. The spangles could always be pried off and reused should the day arrive when they wanted spangled gowns or shawls instead of ceiling stars. No one felt that day would arrive soon.

"The effect will be haunting. Haunting!" Mrs. Pariseau declared.

Although they still hadn't decided how they would make the ceiling appear like a night sky, as they certainly didn't intend to paint it black, and they weren't quite sure how they were going to hang all those stars, Mariana was admittedly quite pleased with it.

Then Mrs. Hardy presented an idea that enchanted all of them speechless.

"Commemorative handkerchiefs," she said on a hush. "Can you picture it? Embroidered with the initials of The Grand Palace on the Thames. Because there won't be a dry eye in the place when Miss Wylde sings!"

It was a deucedly clever and profoundly impractical notion. Plain linen handkerchiefs cost about four shillings each, and they fervently hoped to sell one hundred tickets, which made the cost outlandish.

"Perhaps providence will step in," Angelique suggested gently.

They would need it. They were going to need to rely on providence to find one hundred chairs for the ballroom, too. They hadn't the faintest idea where to begin for that.

As for the tickets, Lord Bolt had arranged for a popular jeweler in Bond Street to sell them, which would make it more convenient for gentlemen to purchase. They were printed in elegant script on a palm-sized card: four shillings for a seat, or two shillings if one preferred to stand, or, in the case of the drunk man who liked to lean against the building near The Grand Palace on the Thames, lean. The name of the jeweler was to be printed on the handbill along with the address of The Grand Palace on the Thames, and the handbills would then be distributed about London and posted primarily in places where opera enthusiasts might be found, near Haymarket and Covent Garden and Piccadilly. This ought to make it easy for people with money and a love for opera to learn about it and buy tickets, if the scandal didn't stop them.

Mariana's name would be tall enough on the handbills to see from at least ten feet away, if one didn't need spectacles. Or opera glasses.

She began to feel hopeful. At least things were progressing a little.

And she'd studied her Italian, of course, as though her life depended on it.

She might be a "spirited girl," but damned if she would let the Duke of Valkirk think she was anything like a fool.

"*BUONASERA*, MISS WYLDE."

"*Buonasera*, Your Grace."

Next to his arm was what seemed to be the same stack of foolscap—his book—she'd seen yesterday. Alongside it was a veritable mound of what looked like correspondence, some opened, some still sealed with various wax blobs, and next to that pile was what looked like a miniature tower of crisp, snowy, engraved invitations and calling cards. She'd never received or sent either of those things.

She peered and noted that the top sheet of his book began with the words "Chapter 4." It appeared to be comprised of about five sentences, all of which had been violently scratched out, alongside which were a little drawing of a sailing ship and another of a tiny horse. She was gratified to see that this one had a fluffier tail.

Beneath this he'd drawn three gentle upward arcs. Perhaps he'd been testing a new ink?

"It was kind of you to donate two hundred pounds to the Society for the Protection of the Sussex Poor, Your Grace," she said.

"I suppose it was," he said, politely. "It was kind of Madame LeCroix to reminisce about her relationship to you." He paused. "And yours to champagne."

She regarded him coolly.

Kind, but also a bit of a bastard. How she wished someone would reminisce thusly to the newspaper about the Duke of Valkirk.

"I suppose it was," she said, carefully.

A smile flickered over his lips. "Shall we review what you've learned since yesterday, to ascertain her assessment of your . . . how did Madame LeCroix describe it? Sense of responsibility?"

"I'm ready when you are," she said.

He pulled the foolscap he'd given to her yesterday toward him, and swiftly, crisply, tested her on the words by first reading the English and demanding the Italian. Then reading Italian in a different order and demanding the English versions.

She didn't miss a one.

"Well done, Miss Wylde."

The faint surprise he'd inflected that with set her teeth on edge. But she could not deny that hearing these words from the most irritatingly exacting man in the world was gratifying.

"*Grazie*, Your Grace."

"Do you think you can handle more vocabulary

words this time? I'll send you away with a much longer list and an assignment of, oh, say, fifteen to twenty sentences. How did Madame LeCroix put it? If a girl has plenty of work, she won't have time to get into mischief."

Normally she enjoyed a good piss-taking but was disinclined to let him know. She found herself instead coolly staring again, as if in so doing she had a hope of putting him in his place. The silence unfortunately allowed her to note, once more, that the contours of his face were fascinating. So distinctive and implacably fierce in repose. Those heavy brows. The mouth that bordered on sensual above that hard chin.

"Well done on memorizing the article, Your Grace. May I commend you on your parroting skills."

A swift little smile flashed again. "Before we discuss which categories of words you ought to take away for your next lesson, was there an Italian phrase you've overheard that you'd like translated, or would you like to know how to say a specific phrase in Italian?"

"Ah, yes. I'd like to know what this means, Your Grace. It sounds like this: '*voglio scoparti.*'"

His eyes flew wide.

His entire body went as rigid as the mast of a ship.

Then his face went slowly—and what seemed like irrevocably—hard.

Oh God. Terrifying!

"Miss Wylde," he said icily. "I cannot tell if you are . . . is this *flirting*? . . . in some—well, I can only call it *astounding*—way, or if you're trying to disconcert me. Both are inadvisable, and arguably, impossible."

"Oh, no. Oh, dear. I'm not! You should see your face . . . your expression . . . oh, it's a bad one, isn't it?"

She brought her hands to her face, then deliberately forced them down and folded them tightly together in her lap and regarded him anxiously.

His expression hovered somewhere between scalding indignation, exasperation, and rank astonishment.

Still, her need to know what it meant far outweighed the mortification. He was never going to like her; she would need to get used to not caring. And now she really needed to know what that phrase meant.

He sighed heavily. "Since virtue demands I cannot say the English version aloud . . ."

He dunked his quill, scrawled something on the foolscap, and pushed it across to her.

She read it and she could feel herself going pink.

Her voice seemed to have been entirely burned away. She would never speak again from mortification.

She could not *believe* she had actually said this aloud to a duke.

She could not *believe* a duke had scrawled it on a piece of foolscap and passed it to her.

A silence ensued, during which she could feel his eyes boring into her lowered head.

She finally mustered the nerve to lift her face again.

To find his expression ever-so-slightly less cen-
soriousness, but no less exasperated. The cold
outrage had shifted to something more curious.
Though it was hardly sympathetic.

"Miss Wylde . . . do men actually *speak* to you
that way?"

She cleared her throat. "Not all of them. I should
say most of the Italian performers I meet are perfect gentlemen. But I'm afraid more than a few
have. I've heard it several times. A stagehand,
once. Another time, a man in the chorus. A tenor
with whom I once sang. They slip it in."

His eyebrows shot up to his hairline.

"Into conversation!" she added hurriedly, aghast.
"I've heard it more than once, and something about
the inflection has always made me suspicious. They
slip it in between other phrases, doubtless to . . .
amuse themselves at my expense."

His eyebrows remained in scowl position, and
he assessed her with what she was beginning
to think of as the subaltern glare. It would have
withered a weaker person, and she supposed he'd
cultivated it for that purpose.

Though gradually, before her eyes, she watched
his expression become more thoughtful.

"Where is your father?"

She stared at him. It was the last question she'd
been expecting.

"My father died when I was fourteen years old."

"Your . . . husband?"

"I haven't a husband."

And then she took his point. Men were the *so-*

lution to women's problems as often as they were women's problems.

He tapped his quill thoughtfully, pressed his lips together. She supposed he thought women were bound to learn filthy words if they hadn't men in their lives to protect them.

"Astute of you to notice what those . . . men . . . were doing with that phrase."

Her temper stirred. "Are you aware that when you see fit to appreciate a quality of mine, you inflect it with surprise? It's not as flattering as you might think, Your Grace."

His eyes widened in fleeting outrage.

A tense tick or two of silence ensued. And then his expression eased.

He gave a short nod. "Point taken, Miss Wylde."

"Thank you," she said graciously. Relieved.

After another moment of studying her, he gestured to the filthy little phrase he'd written. *"Non parlarmi in quel modo,"* he said slowly and flatly. Almost menacingly.

She thought about it. "Don't speak to me that way," she hazarded.

There was a little pause. "Yes."

She was almost amused, and rather touched that he'd clearly taken pains not to sound surprised. Her confidence began to recover, along with a little of her cheer.

"It's certainly convincing the way you say it, Your Grace. My hackles fair stood up."

"I was a general. Everything I said was meant to be convincing. Hackle-raising was my forte."

"I shouldn't like to be a general," she mused. She gestured to the sheet of foolscap with her chin. "Men being how they are."

"The loss is the military's, Miss Wylde," he said dryly. "I think that will be a useful phrase for you to know should you encounter that expression in conversation again. Would you like to repeat it to me?"

She took a breath, and squared her shoulders, and lowered her voice an octave. *"Non parlarmi in quel modo."*

It was a creditably menacing imitation of him, repeated with phonetic flawlessness.

Amazement and something like pure hilarity momentarily flared in his face.

"Well," he said finally. "You certainly gave me second thoughts about speaking to you disrespectfully."

"I think you're humoring me, which seems unlike you."

He snorted. "Why don't you write that phrase now, Miss Wylde, so you won't forget it."

She dipped her quill and in her careful, neat hand began to copy what he'd written. And then she paused. "Should I be more polite about it when I use it? Perhaps add a 'please'?"

"Do *you* think you ought to be polite about it, Miss Wylde?"

"If I thought I could get away with it, I would tell them in no uncertain terms where they could put their rude suggestion. And the day I'm able to do that freely will be the day they won't dare to say it. So I suppose the issue is moot."

He cast his eyes up to the ceiling in thought. "In that case, *Ti chiedo di parlarmi con rispetto*. I ask that you speak to me with respect."

He retrieved the foolscap from her, wrote the phrase swiftly, then pushed it back to her.

"I believe *'rispetto'*—respect—will be a useful word for you to know and use. And a useful thing to demand in such circumstances . . . assuming, of course, *'rispetto' is* what you want when someone says those words to you."

She went rigid.

A surge of temper sent heat rushing into her cheeks. She knew, and he knew, what had been written about her in the newspapers. He had a fixed notion of who she was, and the injustice of it scalded.

She clamped her teeth together as she wrote. She could sense his eyes on her, and the fierce tick of his mind. He was as consequential as a bloody planet, sitting there.

She finished and looked up, to find him watching her.

"I'd like to make something clear, Miss Wylde. I—and the other gentlemen in residence here at The Grand Palace on the Thames, and *gentlemen* in general—do not ever and would not ever speak about or to women that way, either in the smoking room or in any other social context."

Which was lovely to hear, of course. Perhaps he

meant it to be reassuring. But the underlying im-plication was that the contexts in which she moved were at fault. That if these words were being said in her presence, then the men in question were surely not gentlemen.

And then what did that make her? *Spirited*, she supposed.

She already knew what *he* thought that made her.

"It's very gratifying to hear that you don't seem to have any difficulty respecting women, Your Grace," she said pleasantly. "Or perhaps your re-spect is reserved to a type of woman?"

There was a pause.

"Women are people, Miss Wylde. All people deserve and are accorded respect until they prove they do not deserve it. It's a simple rule, really." He issued these words with a sort of patient, madden-ing certainty. As though they ought to have been self-evident but he was unsurprised she didn't know it.

"How might someone lose your respect?"

His mouth curved slightly.

He knew precisely what she was asking. Be-cause the splinter, as it were, had not yet been pulled entirely out of their association. Something remained unsaid.

Her heart began to jab at her breastbone. She re-alized she was afraid of the answer. But suddenly she could not endure another day without it.

"If one has ever needed to tell a soldier's mother that he was killed in battle, Miss Wylde, they would perhaps lose all respect for frivolous, careless people who engage in thoughtless, reckless activities that endanger their lives and the lives of others."

The words were elegantly drawled at first, but they gradually grew more taut until the last few fair glittered with ice.

His composure did not so much as shift a hair. But she heard it. It was a sort of futile fury at fate itself, at deaths not even he could have prevented, even with all of his brilliant rules and strategies. It was pain as much as it was anger. She could feel it echoing in the pit of her stomach.

It only surprised her in that she would not have guessed at it. She sat with this realization a moment.

And there they had it.

She breathed in. Breathed out. Mustering her nerve.

"I would like to ask a question, Your Grace."

"Very well," he said easily.

"What is your understanding of the . . . events . . . that led to my being here at The Grand Palace on the Thames?"

"That your two jealous lovers fought over you while you were present, a duel challenge was issued, the duel was fought on the spot, and a promising young man was nearly killed."

He delivered this with brutal, unvarnished calm.

She was still, but her cheeks were hot. "'Lovers.' Plural. That word certainly tripped off your tongue, Your Grace." She said it somewhat bitterly.

"May I refer you to an earlier conversation

wherein I shared with you that it's nigh on impossible to shock or offend me."

"*Irritate* you, on the other hand . . ."

She reviewed his expression and decided it was wiser not to finish that sentence.

"I should like to say that I don't owe you an explanation of what truly transpired that night. Would you agree?"

"I cannot disagree."

"But I swear to you that neither one of those men was my lover."

He tapped his quill slowly. Tap. Tap. Tap. Apart from a single arched brow, his expression did not change. He waited.

". . . at . . . the time," she expounded, a little more quietly.

Two cynical dents appeared at the corners of his mouth. This, clearly, did not come as a shock to him.

It was both unbearable to have to explain this to him, and unavoidable.

She took another fortifying breath. "Two years ago, Lord Revell pursued me rather determinedly. I liked him. And I'll admit I was flattered because . . . well, have you seen the man?" She flicked her eyes up at him, a bravura attempt to be minxy, instantly quelled by the pure flint in the duke's eyes.

"And . . . and one must . . . well, when I hadn't a book full of *warnings* to refer to, one must learn things the hard way, yes? In the absence of books on how to behave or the advice of moralizing dukes, that is."

It was a bit like jousting with a fortress. She was going to come away with, at best, a snapped lance and a scrap or two of pride. As a duke, she supposed there were dozens of ways he could crush her, if the notion took him. But she was certain of one thing: he might be a bastard, but she knew in her gut he would be a fair one, if she could get him to listen to the truth.

"Learning things the hard way is a tried and true method for getting them to stick, yes," he agreed with exaggerated patience.

"And so. My mother had gone to live in Scotland with a cousin until such time I could make enough money to keep both of us comfortably alive. I was . . . lonely. Lord Revell made . . . I shall use the word 'overtures,' given that this is a story that involves the opera. And we became involved."

"I am familiar with how such associations come about, Miss Wylde. But thank you for the history."

He was a sardonic bastard. She might have enjoyed it more if he wasn't wielding it against her.

"I cannot fairly claim that it was an unpleasant or unwelcome association. Or that I was an unwilling participant. But I soon realized the whole notion did not sit right with me, and . . . it did not solve my loneliness."

Her face felt warm with the revelation.

She bravely looked into his eyes.

He blinked.

And his expression—well, she didn't suppose it ever softened—had gone decidedly more thoughtful.

She took it as encouragement to go on.

"Six months into our . . ." She cleared her throat. She could not bring herself to say "friendship," as it was far too coy. She would have to use the more embarrassing and accurate ". . . affair, I explained as kindly as I could that I no longer wanted to go on as we were. We parted as friends, I thought. Or at least civilly. As much as any man enjoys being told he is . . . ah . . . no longer wanted in that way. I never had reason to believe his heart was either broken or even involved. And he certainly is spoiled for choice, when it comes to women. So at the time of the . . ."

"Duel?" the duke supplied evenly.

She nodded. ". . . he had not been my lover for more than a year."

The word "lover," like "duel" and "affair," would forever be a part of her history. How had she been caught up in such a thing? It seemed she could not have escaped the momentum of it, no matter how she'd tried. She might as well get used to saying it bravely and frankly. It could not be undone.

"All of this I swear upon everything I have ever held or will ever hold dear. I do not have many things to hold dear, but they are my mother, my father's memory, my pink ribbon, and my fur-lined pelisse. I would die for them."

She'd tried a joke. Because she couldn't help herself.

He took this in. His expression was difficult to interpret. Like a metronome, the quill between his fingers measured the methodical tick of his mind.

But his eyes never left her face.

"Then I shall be compelled to believe you, won't I?" he said finally. Quietly. Almost gently.

She subtly released the breath she hadn't realized she'd been holding.

"So . . . the night of the duel . . . well, it all began backstage, in our dressing rooms, after my first performance in the lead role. So many encores . . . my room was filled with roses. Roses, Your Grace. Actual flowers from a *hothouse*! I could not believe such loveliness was for me. It smelled like heaven. All the young bloods like to crowd backstage after a show . . . perhaps you know this?"

"So I have heard," he said ironically.

"Lord Kilhone was one of them. He praised my performance and made so bold as to tell me I was beautiful. And . . . well, when someone tells you you're beautiful, it's only polite to graciously receive such a compliment, and perhaps return it somewhat in kind?"

"I cannot say, as I've never been accused of such a thing," he said dryly.

"Well, then everyone's been remiss, Your Grace."

His slow smile was so unexpectedly, wickedly sensual, it shocked the breath from her.

She began to suspect, with a certain thrill and uneasiness that accompanies walking the ledge of a tall building, that he was, in fact, capable of devastating charm. He just hadn't seen fit to expend any of it on her thus far.

It occurred to her that this was likely a mercy.

She did not think this was a man who did anything by halves.

"Do you *see* the difference?" she said. "*That* was flirting, Your Grace. And now we've both learned something today."

"It's a mystery why duels spontaneously happen around you, Miss Wylde."

"*I* think so, too," she said earnestly. "But mind you, it was just the one. Sometimes flirting seems the polite thing to do. Isn't it rude not to say or do a thing about it when men flirt? That is, they *will* flirt, won't they?"

"Do I really strike you as the sort?"

"Oh, I suspect you're capable of anything, if you really put your back into it, Your Grace."

She wanted another one of those smiles the way she'd wanted another sip of champagne that fateful night. And what did that say about her? Both were potent. Neither was wise.

He gave her another one. Fleeting and patient.

She was reminded he was a castle. All but impossible to breach with her meager weapons.

And as far as he was concerned, she was still on trial.

"Lord Revell heard this exchange, and he was outraged that Lord Kilhone would dare to compliment me in his presence, which is frankly ridiculous, as he had no claim on me at all, though they were both . . . ah, foxed."

"You don't say," the duke said cynically.

And even as she said the words, the story seemed unspeakably frivolous and sordid even in her own ears; how must it sound to him? But oddly she felt stronger as she unburdened herself, which spoke to how heavy it had weighed upon her.

"*I* wasn't," she hastened to add, primly. This was true, but mainly because they had run out of champagne. "They used me as an excuse to go outside with pistols and shoot at each other," she said bitterly. "While their friends looked on. While their friends looked on! The papers were wrong. I *didn't* watch. I couldn't bear it. But neither of them gave a da . . . fig about . . . me." She took a breath to steady her voice; she heard the rise in pitch, the stifled anguish in it. "It was about two spoiled men and their pride and reckless tempers that they felt free to indulge like children throwing tantrums. Something I would never dream of doing, and never, *ever* get away with doing."

His eyes were cool and remote, as if he was watching the entire sordid scene inside his mind, the way he might an enemy army amassing on a faraway hillside.

"If they cared at all for me, wouldn't they have minded or noticed that I was terribly frightened?"

Damnation. She kept her chin up, but her voice broke on the last word, anyway.

"You were frightened?" he said sharply, after a moment.

She nodded wearily.

His face was pensive now. Lips pressed together.

She took a breath, and dared to ask the question she'd yearned to ask all along.

"So that is the story, and I swear it on my life.

I am sorry it happened, but I cannot see how I caused it. But what I'd like to know is this, Your Grace. You ought to know. Is it honorable, what they did?"

She asked it as if she were indeed on the dock and he were the magistrate.

Her heart was pounding.

There was a beat of silence.

"No," he said.

It should not have felt like absolution. She was not Catholic. This was not confession. He was not St. Peter at the Gates. But he was the national arbiter of honor, and it was the best she was going to do, and it was enough.

She exhaled.

"And I don't feel as though *my* honor was harmed—im . . ."

"Impugned."

"Even so, one can be angry and not lose one's head. Is that not so?"

"Yes. Being angry without losing my head is, in fact, my specialty."

"I thought glaring was."

A vanishingly swift smile here. "The glaring is usually a result of that."

There was a pause.

"And so, Your Grace, that is my story. Knowing it, you may continue to hold me in contempt if you so choose, but I should be obliged if you would disguise it better."

His eyes flared in fleeting astonishment. His jaw

tensed against a reflexive jolt of temper, or perhaps arrogance.

But she'd been right. He was a fair man.

But what settled in was a certain wry speculation. For the space of a few seconds, he assessed her.

"I hold you in the utmost respect, Miss Wylde," he said quietly.

She gave him a little smile.

He continued to study her, a tiny furrow forming between his eyes.

"Gentilmente non sparatevi l'un l'altro," he said suddenly, firmly.

She gave a start.

"Kindly do not shoot each other," he translated.

"Sono spaventata," he continued. His voice softened. "I am frightened."

He wrote them down for her to take away.

SHE DEPARTED IN possession of a sheet of foolscap that said, "I want to fuck you" in Italian and English, below which were written the word "impugn" and two new sets of Italian nouns (buildings and food) and some more verbs. All in all, representative of a satisfying day's work, if a confusing document for anyone who might happen to come across it out of context.

Chapter Eight

❧

MARIANA TAPPED the feathered end of her quill against her lips, mulling the last sentence she wanted to write in order to complete the assignment the duke had given her. The clock downstairs had bonged the quarter hour. She was due in the Annex in about fifteen minutes.

Now that they'd peeled away the last of their previous mutual resentment, she'd felt oddly a bit exposed and off balance during the last three days' worth of lessons with the Duke of Valkirk. As if she'd been dressed for and braced against a stiff wind all her life and it had abruptly stopped blowing.

Because her experience of the world of men had thus far included three types: the men who wanted to employ her to sing; the men who wanted to shag her; and the men who needed her to sing and also wanted to shag her.

The duke was an entirely new type. He was a gentleman in every sense of the word, not in the Lord Kilhone or Lord Revell sense of the word. He was *very* brisk, frequently impatient, but always respectful and polite, and unless she counted the occasional devastatingly sensual smile that implied he knew *precisely* what she was up to, he did not take up the flirtation baton that she could not resist, every now and then, extending.

Every one of those smiles were like a swift peek through a crack into the earth at something molten.

Every one of them knocked the breath out of her, unsettled her in a very primal way, and all but guaranteed she would try for another one, whether or not that made sense or was wise. (It didn't and it wasn't.)

His barely restrained impatience implied he knew she could do well, he expected her to do well, and he wouldn't tolerate if she *didn't* do well. She set out to impress him.

And his brisk yet fervent "well done's" were frankly as satisfying as the thunderous applause of a stuffed-to-the-brim theater when she sang Giancarlo Giannini's aria from *The Glass Rose*.

This morning over breakfast, Mr. Delacorte, bless his heart, offered to take a message explaining her whereabouts to Giancarlo at the theater since he was meeting a friend at a pub across from it, and to fetch their handbills advertising the Night of the Nightingale from the printer.

"Tall, dark wavy hair, lots of blinding teeth," she told him. "Signor Giancarlo Giannini. They should be in rehearsals. But please don't give it to anyone else."

The lurking possibility that someone might shout, "There's the 'arlot! Get 'er!" and lunge at her with a pitchfork or a knife kept her very close to The Grand Palace on the Thames, which ironically was located in what was considered one of the more dangerous parts of London. She was uncertain whether she ought to gauge the emotional temperature of a city by the one small murderous mob that had appeared beneath her window. She'd worn an enormous wig for one of her Opera House performances, but only a tiara and rose-colored silk dress for the afternoon performance. It was conceivable she'd be recognized.

Somehow she'd failed to consider that singing to a crowd of thousands at the Opera House would ever be a *dis*advantage.

No more gossip items had appeared in the newspaper at least. Perhaps Madame LeCroix had confused everyone about her character, and they hadn't the faintest idea what to say now.

So she was safe for now here at The Grand Palace on the Thames.

And because Valkirk was a gentleman, for the first time she was offered a space in which to be entirely herself. But in some ways she missed the relative buffer of their previous mutual resentment.

Because this space began to fill with an awareness that felt anything but safe.

She supposed that was all her own doing. He sank into her imagination the way the sun from the window warmed her skin. She memorized the interesting cragginess of his face. She estimated that his shoulders were about twice the width of her own. And when she thought about it, the entirety of her skin seemed to hum with restlessness, imagining how it might feel . . . to be covered with the entirety of him.

She did not know how any of this could be helped, and she supposed that was her own weakness. It had been documented in the newspaper that she was not, er, made of stone.

He certainly never fixed his eyes on her cleavage, for instance, and it was right *there*.

And yet she was truly glad he didn't.

But there occurred every afternoon a moment more potent than a cleavage gaze, and it lasted all of a few seconds.

When she arrived in the doorway of the room and first laid eyes on him, there was always a distinct stillness to him. As if his breath was held. It was rather like the stillness of an arrow after it was shot into the red heart of a target.

Each time, she could have sworn that those embers in his eyes flared hotly. But vanished swiftly.

And this took her breath away every time.

She was now ten minutes away from this moment. She'd one more sentence to write to complete her assignment.

She scrawled, "The duke has brown eyes," reached for the sander, and then happened to glance down. She froze.

Shocked to discover that what she'd actually written was:

The duke has beautiful eyes.

Her heart jolted. How on *earth* . . . ? It had sprung from somewhere within her that apparently was outside the jurisdiction of her senses.

She stared at it. Her heart began to jab painfully at her as she mischievously entertained leaving the sentence just like that. Imagining him discovering it at the end of all those other sentences.

What if she did?

What then?

She swiftly realized her nerve did not extend to that. He was, indeed, a gentleman, and she was grateful. It seemed intrusive and unfair to spring such a thing upon him.

And dangerous and absurd to reveal such a vulnerability in herself.

She scratched out "beautiful" and replaced it emphatically with the infinitely safer "brown."

And went off for her lesson.

Heaven forfend she should be late.

* * *

On 5 April 1799 we rode into Seringapatam and by nightfall took the village of—

VALKIRK GLARED AT the partial sentence he'd written. It was so inert he punished it by fiercely and with prejudice scratching it out as though he were murdering a pirate.

He pushed it aside with a gusty sigh.

He used to know how to write, did he not? Perhaps he did not quite make prose *sing*, but surely he was capable of crafting a narrative with verve.

He'd written a book before, and it seemed the whole world had read it; it suddenly felt as though he'd done that almost accidentally. His life had occurred in distinct chapters—birth, school, marriage, son, war, general, duke. He remembered all of them clearly. How difficult could it be? What *was* the overarching message of his life?

At the moment it felt like: never promise anything to a publisher.

Poor, poor long-suffering Mr. Alcock, of Alcock & Sons Publishers, who sent him polite letters inquiring about his progress that were clearly seething and frantic between the lines. He was counting on this book to contribute to the ensuing year's profits.

James yanked the sheet back for a moment to draw an "O" in a grid of noughts-and-crosses he'd been playing against himself in the margins of it. Then paused to slowly draw again a small subtle curve that his pen seemed to suddenly take great, delicious pleasure in making. It was a bit like what the back-and-forth swing of a pendulum might describe, if a quill had been attached.

A stack of correspondence sent over by his Man of Affairs throbbed accusingly in his peripheral vision—letters from people all over the country, requests for donations or recommendations or endorsements or introduction, friendly letters from old acquaintances. His Man of Affairs sorted through all of it first, so he knew the ones remaining deserved his attention.

In it, right on top, most accusingly of all, was a

letter from his son. Last year, the duke had given
Arthur, among other wedding gifts, a farm in Sussex, with the stipulation he ask for the duke's bless-
ing before he ever thought of selling it. Because it
was where the duke had been raised. His father
had lost it to debt, and James had repurchased it
the moment he was able. It seemed critical, somehow, to keep it in the family. An emblem of his
triumph over the terrible loss of it. Evidence of his
vow to himself and to his family and to generations
to come: never again would they lose or suffer.

The farm was stocked with Leicester Long-
wool sheep; it could make a tidy profit, if properly
worked. He'd thought work of some sort might
help shape Arthur's character into something a
little . . . craggier. He both liked and loved his son,
but as heir to the wealthy first Duke of Valkirk,
Arthur would never have to work a day in his life,
and in truth, never had. And this, oddly, was why
the duke had very little in common with him.

He suspected Arthur wanted to sell the farm.

James didn't want to.

He stopped drawing curves when he noticed it
was two minutes until three o'clock.

In about one minute, one of his new favorite
moments of the day would occur.

At one minute until three, she always paused for
a second or two in the doorway. He didn't know
why, but he suspected Miss Wylde was gathering
nerve to enter. This oddly and quite unaccountably moved him. The light always slanted across

the room at that time, and gave her rose gold hair a bit of a halo. If he looked up just at that moment, it was like catching a glimpse of a shy forest creature.

She was *not* a shy person.

Her confidence was a unique hybrid between earned, innate, and cocksure, not a blend unfamiliar to any military officer who had ever dealt with an infantryman. Brazening her way through things she didn't know had clearly long been a habit, but each day, a little more of a certain native grace and steely self-possession shone through, probably because he would neither let her get away with anything nor make her feel like a fool, which she patently—sometimes unnervingly—was not.

And her approach to the desk was always diverting to witness. She carried herself as if she were strolling out onto a stage, and she was as made of curves as a violin. The neckline of the green muslin dress she wore straddled a line between demure and daring, which described the necklines of all of the dresses he'd seen her wear so far. Each one exposed a pearly expanse of skin from her throat to her bosom and a tiny but intriguing shadow between her breasts. All of this was no doubt by design, and while it somewhat amused him, he could not truthfully say it went unappreciated.

"*Buonasera*, Your Grace."

"*Buonasera*, Miss Wylde."

She learned with gratifying speed, and was

now in possession of a decent-sized vocabulary
of nouns in various categories (buildings, occupa-
tions, clothing, food, animals, moods), verbs, and
adjectives.

The sentences she brought with her each day
were a disarming revelation into the workings of
her mind. The denizens of The Grand Palace on
the Thames featured frequently. As did two people
inexplicably called "Primrose" and "Phillip," because, as she'd explained, "I liked the names."

"Let's have a look at your sentences, shall we?"
he said, and pulled the foolscap she placed on the
desk over to read it.

"'*Gordon diverte a mangiare grandi ratti,*'" he read.
"'Gordon has fun eating large rats.'"

Gordon was the cat who lived at The Grand
Palace on the Thames.

"I'm only surmising," she said. "I haven't actually seen him do it."

"Well, it's not something you'd want to sit about
and watch, is it?" he said absently. "Your verb tense
is a bit off here. Do you know what bit is missing?"

She studied it. "Oh! the '*si*' part. *Has* fun." She
leaned forward and with her quill corrected it.

"'*Dot salì le scale e lasciò cadere il tè,*'" he read.
"'Dot walked up the stairs and dropped the tea.'

"Has this happened, or is this rank hearsay?"
he asked her.

"I heard that it happened, but we all know not
to believe all the gossip we hear, Your Grace."

"'*Mr. Malloy guida una carrozza ed è triste.* Mr.
Malloy drives a carriage and is sad.'

"I can't think why driving a carriage would make Mr. Malloy sad," he said.

"It's a hack," she explained. "I couldn't pay him the full fare when I arrived at The Grand Palace on the Thames, and now the guilt is excruciating. I truly hope one day to find him and pay him."

He looked up at her swiftly. She appeared entirely serious.

"*'Primrose indossava un ampio vestito verde e mangiava pasticceria, torta, pane, uva, e carne.* Primrose wore a large green dress and ate pastry, cake, bread, grapes, and meat.' Primrose certainly has a healthy appetite," he said.

"I think it's because she might be"—she lowered her voice to a whisper—"with *child*. But lest you feel too scandalized, Your Grace, read the next sentence."

He did.

"*Primrose and Phillip si sono sposati.* Primrose and Phillip were married."

"I see. Felicitations to them. A thrilling conclusion to the story that began with yesterday's 'Primrose wore a pink dress' and 'Phillip is a baker.' The last must be why Primrose has plenty to eat."

She laughed.

He realized he'd lately taken to saying things to get her to laugh, the way he might reflexively open a window to allow in fresh air.

There were little gold flecks in her green eyes, and when she laughed, they lit up. More of these faint gold flecks were scattered across her nose. It was as if her maker had finished her off by flinging a handful of fairy dust at her, and then, whimsically, pressed a little dimple into her chin with a forefinger before calling it a day.

"I almost married her off to a cobbler," she said. "My father wanted me to marry a cobbler. I might have done, if he'd lived."

He coughed a shocked laugh. "I *cannot* imagine that."

Her silence and stillness were so sudden that he looked up from the foolscap sharply, surprised.

To his astonishment, she looked stricken.

"Why not?" she said finally. Her voice was quiet, thin, and wary, as if she knew he was a doctor bound to deliver bad news.

It seldom happened that he was surprised unto speechlessness.

But he was.

"It would have been a perfectly nice life, Your Grace," she said indignantly into his silence. "I'd have a family. Maybe we'd have some rooms over a shop, with a little parlor a bit like the one here at The Grand Palace on the Thames, and a pianoforte if we'd been able to get one at a bargain, and we'd stand about it singing some nights . . . I would know how my days would look. I'd have . . . people to care for."

It almost sounded like an enviable life. Truthfully, a lot like the one they'd managed to create here at The Grand Palace on the Thames.

Moreover, one would never be urged to write their damned memoirs if one lived that life.

"It sounds like a fine life," he said finally, somewhat gently. "It's a far cry from the King's Theater and . . ."

She tipped her head. "Lovers and duels?"

"Exactly," he said, rather ruthlessly.

There was a pause. "I had no extraordinary ambition at first. I sang for pleasure. But after my father died, I sang for money in the hopes that my mother and I could keep our rooms over the shop. I was able to get better and better singing roles, but I never did earn enough money to keep it. My mother was compelled to go to Scotland to live with a cousin, who had more room for her. It's safer and more comfortable for her there than in my tiny room on Haywood Street. I send money to her when I can."

She wasn't complaining about any of it. But through her words ran a current of almost bewildered wistfulness, as though the life she'd imagined was something she could see receding inexorably into the distance. Borne away by the damned caprices of fate, like a boat that had slipped its moorings while she stood on the shore.

I would know how my days would look.

He'd never even thought about that. A military life meant he'd known, for the most part, how all of his days would look, often to the minute. Not precisely what *occurred* during a campaign, of course, but he knew that there would be one. It had been a fact of his methodical, rung-by-rung climb to the rank of general. And then, as a commander, he'd been able to determine how his day and the days of thousands of others looked now.

How difficult would it be to find and keep one's bearings in life when the road wasn't at all defined? When life came at you as though you were a moving target?

When one was falling, the reflex was to flail out for any steadying handhold, he supposed. He conceded to himself that what she had managed to accomplish—from the cobbler's shop to Covent Garden and the King's Theater—was actually rather astonishing. When viewed in this light, it was rather a miracle that she'd been made visible at all by the gossip columns.

He sat with this realization quietly. He considered what to say.

"I spoke hastily, Miss Wylde. A habit of barking orders, and I apologize. I instinctively could not picture it, because . . . I think extraordinary circumstances are, for better or worse, the lot of extraordinary people. Not everyone is equal to the caprices of fate. Most would lose their heads, literally or figuratively, when confronted with some of the challenges you've faced. It just seems to me that you are destined for a more remarkable life."

As he said it, he was bemused to realize he did, indeed, believe this.

Before his eyes, gradually, slowly, a glow gorgeously suffused her. As though his words had reached every corner of her. It was as elemental as a sunrise.

He had somehow forgotten the simple, piercing joy of making someone happy.

He hadn't thought her anyone's notion of a siren,

with the pale gold dust on her cheeks and the dark gold tips of her lashes and the rose gold hair that seemed to want to burst from its pins.

For that fleeting instant, he couldn't imagine preferring to look at anything or anyone else in the world. Those idiots who'd shot at each other had gotten one thing right: she was unequivocally beautiful.

Her bodice lifted and slowly fell as she seemed to take a steadying breath.

"'Caprices' . . . ?" she ventured quietly.

He'd been staring.

More accurately: staring and frowning.

"Whims," he said shortly. "'Vicissitudes' is another word you might like. It means very nearly the same thing."

He wrote the words down for her.

There was a little silence.

"So you've not yet wed at all, Miss Wylde, unlike Primrose and Phillip?"

It hadn't occurred to him to ask this yet. It was possible her husband had died.

Or abandoned her.

Men being what they were.

For a moment he thought she wouldn't answer; she was under no obligation to do it. Uncertainty flickered across her face. Then she quirked the corner of her mouth. "Opera singers don't precisely fit into anyone's notion of a good or proper wife. And then, once you get that first scandalous duel under your belt, well . . ."

She shrugged one shoulder.

She wasn't wrong. She now occupied a singular place in their very stratified society. People liked their labels; they wed to climb rungs, to cement a place in the world. Marriage was a strategic initiative, not a whim.

But Miss Wylde, he suspected, still possessed more than a drop or two of romanticism.

It was difficult to fully kill, romanticism was. Worse than a weed.

War killed it neatly, though.

So, for that matter, did marriage.

"I should think there are some compensations in the theater. I imagine it is all drama and passionate declarations and so forth all day long."

"Oh, *those*," she said so offhandedly he bit back a smile. "That's not love, is it? Possessiveness. Posturing. A whim of mood. It's all, 'Oh, your hair looks wonderful by candlelight, now I'm in love.' Of course, should the day come when I rise to the top of my profession . . . I shall have anyone I choose." She paused. "Or no one at all, if I choose."

This bit sounded like bravado. The thing she told herself to dull any lingering wistfulness.

But then, she'd had the presence of mind to cast off a lover who wasn't right for her.

"No doubt," he said shortly.

He dropped his eyes to the foolscap. "Have we looked at all of your sentences?"

"Yes," she said hurriedly, just as he said, "I see there's one left."

She reached for the foolscap to pull it back.

But he'd already silently read:

Il duca ha gli occhi marroni.

"The duke has brown eyes," he said.

The unadorned nature of the sentence was striking amidst all her others.

In the English version she'd written, a longer word had been hatched out; "brown" was its replacement. The word she'd originally chosen also appeared to start with a "b." He was also certain he could detect an insufficiently scratched-out "l" at the end of it.

"I was wondering if I'd make an appearance in your sentences. Why have you not dressed me, perhaps, in a green coat and yellow trousers?"

Startlingly, she did not reply. She seemed to have gone mute.

He looked up. "What did it used to say?"

She appeared to give it some thought.

"Seventeen," she replied.

"It used to say, 'The duke has seventeen eyes.'"

She inspected his face. "Yes."

He smiled slightly. "What did it used to say?" he repeated pleasantly and evenly, as if he hadn't asked the question the first time at all.

She met his eyes, but she was distinctly, curiously uncomfortable. Her cheeks had gone a hot pink.

"Refuse," she said.

His eyebrows began to dip as he prepared a frown. Immediately, he schooled his features to careful stillness and regarded her in silence.

He was fairly certain he knew what the original word was.

He hadn't the faintest idea what to do about it.

He knew a twinge of irritation, mainly because he'd been taken by surprise, which had happened perhaps twice before in the last decade.

All at once, with a disconcerting epiphany, it occurred to him that she was not so much hesitating in the doorway of the anteroom before she entered . . . as taking that moment to look at him.

Precisely the way he took that moment to look at her.

He was utterly still.

And then, in order to look at anything else at the moment, he glanced at the clock and noted three minutes were remaining.

It was, surprisingly, a second or two before he could think clearly.

But then he had it.

He wrote something on the foolscap.

"Tu non mi ami. È solo il lume di candela," he said evenly.

She looked up at him curiously.

"You do not love me. It is merely the candle-light."

She gave a laugh.

He pushed the sheet of foolscap over to her so she could see what he'd written. She dipped her quill and bent her head, and diligently began to copy the words, so that she would make them her own.

He picked up his own quill, to return to the work of writing to his solicitor.

He noticed a strand of hair clung to Miss Wylde's cheek, and the sunlight through the rain-washed windows picked out little rainbows in it. He obviously had no choice but to look at that instead.

AS SHE LEFT, Mariana passed Dot in the hall bearing a tea tray laden with scones on a plate, a pot of tea, and a cup for the duke.

"Vicissitudes, Dot," she whispered. "Viss-iss-i-tudes. It means whims."

"Viss-iss-i-tudes," Dot repeated slowly. "So fun to say! Like a snake. Sssssssss. I have a word for you, too. I learned it in the kitchen this morning. It's 'beleaguered.' 'Beelee,' then 'grrr' like a dog growling, then a 'd.'"

"Bel*ea*guered," Mariana repeated. "I like it! It's a very strong word. What does it mean?"

"It means bothered or annoyed. I overheard Mrs. Durand say that Lord Bolt told her that the duke is *beleaguered* by all the invitations he receives to dine with lords who want to marry their daughters off to him. She says he's bound to marry one of them."

Mariana was silent, frozen in place, for a long moment. Shocked by the fact that this, briefly, had taken the breath out of her.

"Well, that would beleaguer anyone," she said, finally.

THE DUKE MADE short work of the tea and delicious scones Dot brought in (the food here was divine), made use of the snowy napkin provided, then pulled his stack of work back toward him and dipped his quill.

He went still and frowned. Staring at the curve he'd drawn yet again.

Another epiphany struck.

He tentatively, almost angrily drew atop it two shorter, rounded peaks.

He now was looking at Miss Wylde's lips.

He laid his quill gingerly down, as if the feather had grown talons. Might then spring to life and attack him.

He'd been spending the last two bloody days tracing the swooping curve of her bottom lip.

The duke has beautiful eyes.

That's what she'd written.

He hadn't sensed this approaching.

The legend of General Blackmore had it that he could hear the movements of an enemy army from a hundred miles away, like some sort of primordial forest creature sniffing the wind for wolves. It was an exaggeration. He had vision: he could cast his eye over a circumstance—limited munitions, cruel geography, depleted troops—and then apply inspiration and cunning to eke out a triumph. He had, time and again.

Perhaps he hadn't sensed this thing with Miss Wylde because it wasn't an advancing army, and battle was all he knew.

But if he'd been a deer at a watering hole, the wolf would have gotten him.

With brutal and funny astuteness, she'd suggested that a duke chess piece would only be able to move in a straight line. But it *was* always the swiftest, most powerful way to move. Life *ought* to be conducted within defined contours. And honor dictated that he could take note of the charms of this opera singer and not feel compelled to veer outside those lines.

Because that's where a woman like Mariana existed: quite beyond the bounds of his world.

But he understood now that her earlier implication that he was cold had landed painfully raw because of his suspicion that it was a quality of character he could do nothing about. As if "cold" was merely his personal climate, like Siberia.

He began to suspect that it was a condition he'd merely been needlessly suffering.

And that the cold was not a climate, but a season.

Somewhat darkly amused, he dipped his quill, and drew a long, careful, vertical, curving line. Then next to it, an inch or so away, a matching one. As deliberately as though he were drawing a battle map of enemy territory. The shape of her beautiful body, the way he saw it as she approached each day.

Chapter Nine

༺၆၅ၐၐ༻

$\mathcal{D}$OT SURPRISED everyone that evening with a show of initiative: earlier that day, when she'd been out to buy the newspaper, she'd purchased for three pennies of the household money twenty silk handkerchiefs from "a nice gentleman on the street! It must have been providence, like you said, Mrs. Durand!"

She beamed at them proudly and brandished them in the sitting room at the top of the stairs.

Delilah and Angelique eyed them warily.

It was, of course, entirely possible that a man had been taken by Dot's big blue eyes and general air of don't-mind-me-I'm-up-in-the-clouds and offered her a bargain out of the goodness of his heart. But given that a good plain linen handkerchief usually cost four shillings at least, and that pickpockets usually did a brisk business reselling stolen handkerchiefs after they'd picked out the owner's embroidered initials, the conclusion was that she'd brought contraband goods into the house. Providence, in this case, was likely a pickpocket.

Captain Hardy had spent the first half of his life running smugglers to ground. Delilah was glad her husband wasn't around to witness this. And now they would have to explain the matter to Dot without crushing her initiative.

Poor Dot, who had begun her life as the worst lady's maid in the world to a duchess, albeit an evil one, was now buying stolen goods near the docks.

The handkerchiefs pulsed wickedly and temptingly before their eyes. It was no good. They simply remained enchanted with their idea of giving them away.

"I'm so torn," Delilah whispered to Angelique that night. "What does it mean that I'm both horrified and amused that we might be giving our guests back their own handkerchiefs?"

Angelique was quiet.

"We shouldn't like them to go to waste," she said carefully.

Delilah bit back a smile. "Moral decline is a slow but slippery slope, Angelique."

"At least we'll have each other for company on our slide down."

Delilah stifled a laugh. "We can hardly sell them *back*, or find their rightful owners. Perhaps we'll accidentally *return* them to their rightful owners."

"Perhaps it was providence that a stack of stolen handkerchiefs appeared today."

"Just like the appearance of Miss Wylde."

They laughed with just the *tiniest* bit of muffled hysteria. They knew their ambitions for their program slightly overflowed their abilities to get it all done in a month.

"I wonder what the duke would say. Is it honorable to take something just because we want it?"

And they were both quiet. They'd both done exactly that at least once. The fact that they had both acquired husbands who had shown up at The Grand Palace on the Thames at different times was proof of that. However, it had hardly come easily to either of them.

Certainly not as easily as these handkerchiefs.

"We'll give them a good laundering first, shall we?" Delilah said finally. "And . . . perhaps we won't tell Captain Hardy. No need for him to, ah, suffer over it, too."

MR. DELACORTE HAD promised Mariana that he'd safely delivered her message right into the neatly manicured hand of Mr. Giannini. "Pleasant bloke!" he'd said, cheerfully.

Bless his heart, he was willing to believe most people were pleasant. Which, she knew, had more to do with Delacorte than with other people.

"He can be," she agreed with a sigh. But Giancarlo hadn't appeared at The Grand Palace on the Thames with her money yet.

Mariana had begun to feel nostalgic for the milling, dirty streets around Haymarket, and the theater itself. The sky-blue boxes, the flowing red curtains, all those eyes beaming down upon her, all those ladies in brilliant silks and satins studding the curving boxes and balconies of the theater like jewels in a crown. The crowds jostling each other on the benches. Wax from the thousands of candles overhead dripping down on poor and wealthy alike. Feeling the song move through her body as she released it into the theater, feeling the audience stir as it filled the ears and hearts and bodies of those listening.

And yes, the handkerchiefs, those white flashes she saw in the crowd, rising to dab eyes.

She knew she possessed a rare talent; she was unsure whether she considered it a calling, or whether she would even have missed it if life had progressed in the way she'd once hoped for. But she'd come to realize that the only place she truly felt powerful and safe was in the midst of song. She rather wished she could retreat into one and live there for a bit now. To be the one with all the power.

Rather than the one who was beset by a shocking, faint agony at the notion that the duke might soon choose a wife from that stack of invitations.

She sat at her little writing desk, unable to think clearly enough to study her words or write her sentences. Held fast by something that felt nearly like panic, or perhaps urgency, like a fine needle driven right down through the center of her.

Surely he was lonely. He'd been widowed for five years.

And she knew that despite his respect for her, and despite their accord, and despite his, daresay, present kindness that had nothing of condescension in it, there was in fact an ocean-sized gulf between their stations in life. That signet ring he wore might as well be a crown.

But in other fundamental ways, they were very alike.

Which was why the agony was offset by a glimmer of something that left her breathless. As though they comprised a miser's hoard, she sifted through her impressions: the way his eyes kindled when she appeared in his doorway each day. The way he looked at her during silences, taking note of her features the way she noted his. The way, yesterday, he had been utterly nonplussed by her sentence. He must have guessed what she'd written.

And therein lay the glimmer.

It seemed, in this moment, that her life depended on following it to whatever the conclusion might be.

VALKIRK FOUND THAT Miss Wylde was unusually subdued the next day, following their usual exchange of "*Buonasera*'s."

So was he.

He'd kept his head down as she'd approached.

He understood now that she moved like a woman who understood the kind of pleasure her body was capable of giving and receiving. She brought sensuality into the room with her every day like a perfume. It lingered long after she left.

This was why he'd appreciated her entrances so thoroughly.

He promptly assigned her the task of translating five English sentences into Italian while he addressed an urgent inquiry about repairs to the roof of a property he owned in Northumberland. The room was quiet, apart from the scratching of quills on foolscap.

He pointedly did not draw curves of any kind on his.

Mainly because the curves remained in his mind and right in front of him.

She finished first. He could feel her eyes on him. He could also almost feel her formulating a question, which both amused him and made him a little wary.

"You seem to have many invitations, Your Grace. You must be quite popular."

"Indeed," he said shortly. He continued writing.

"What a torment it must be for the mamas of the *ton* to have a widowed duke of reasonable age just roaming free. Is it honorable to inflict such suffering upon them?"

"I am indeed 'spoiled for choice,'" he said, grimly amused by the entirety of her sentence. He gave the last three words a sardonic lilt. *Spoiled for choice.* He wished he didn't remember so clearly that this was how she'd described the handsome Lord Revell.

"*Are* you going to choose one?"

"Refuse," he said at once, distractedly.

He caught the flash of her tiny smile out of the corner of his eye. A bit like a shooting star darting past a window.

A long silence followed.

"No doubt you'll fall in love with just the right one when that time comes."

He tensed. He recognized that little sentence,

with its loaded "l" word, for the stepping stone it was. She was laying a conversational path of sorts that he could walk down.

If he chose.

"Your faith in my judgment upon such short acquaintance is very touching, Miss Wylde. But 'falling in love,' as you put it, is hardly necessary for a successful marriage."

He could sense in the silence that followed a number of things she was tempted to say.

He wondered which ones she was discarding.

"It is so generous of you to share your expertise on the subject of love. Perhaps you ought to write a book on it as well."

"If I feel that life has gotten dull for want of suffering, I shall certainly do that."

He could sense her smiling.

He finally signed his name with a flourish and reached for the sander.

"Do you miss your wife?"

He went still.

Then he pulled his arm slowly away from the sander and straightened. A quick flame of anger flickered, a certain reflexive imperious resentment at being so deftly cornered.

He *was* a bloody castle.

And she, like a wildflower, had been seeking out the chinks between the stones from the beginning.

To what end?

But of course he knew.

He ought to stop it now.

Her gaze was steady. But she hadn't his years of expertise with cold inscrutability. He found himself unaccountably moved by the cant of her chin; it betrayed a little uncertainty of her own presumption. She was poised to turn her question into a jest should he decide to deflect it.

Odd to think of her as an innocent, this girl who'd willfully taken a lover. In many ways she was.

He fiercely disliked the realization that, in some ways, at the age of forty-three . . . so was he.

Not only that, but possibly also a little awkward.

He was buffeted between two things: what he knew were the right things to do and say, and where he, the ruthless strategist, could lead this conversation if he so chose. Which was to the room adjacent, where a bed was.

He found himself turning slightly away, toward the window. The water seemed a safer view than her green eyes. He told himself that she'd asked a question, and he owed her an answer.

This was, after all, their bargain.

His breathing seemed too audible suddenly.

Two breaths were all he allowed himself before he answered.

"At the time of my wife's death," he said, carefully, the words maneuvering around the forces of reason that attempted to stop them, "we had not lived together for nearly eight years. She was the daughter of a viscount. She preferred the city, near her family. I preferred the country. I was often away on campaign during our marriage. I have reason to believe she was satisfied with the arrangement. And I . . ." He gave a small, humorless smile. "I confess that I was, too."

It was unlike him to cushion bald truths. But this one, he knew, would ring brutally in the quiet room:

He didn't miss his wife.

He wasn't going to say that out loud.

He didn't want to say it because he couldn't anticipate how Miss Wylde's expression would change, because of a certainty it would. He didn't think he would ever forget the muffled anguish in her voice when she'd spoken of the duel, as though she hadn't mattered at all to them. It had been yet another offhand, crushing erasure of a woman by a man.

Mariana had taken a lover and enjoyed him and left him. And still she hadn't mattered much to him at all.

It did not solve my loneliness, she'd said.

It seemed impossible to believe in this quiet room with the light pouring in that the woman sitting across from him had wound up in the middle of chaos, scandal, and bloodshed, in part because, once upon a time, she'd attempted to solve it.

He was now on guard.

Because his admission had introduced into the room the phantoms of lovers he'd had in those eight years. Not many. Never for more than a night. Nevertheless, he'd hardly been celibate. She knew this must be true, of course.

He'd revealed this deliberately.

And, of course, it was this she had sought to uncover.

He was mordantly amused to realize that he wasn't much accustomed to considering himself an object of desire outside of his title and money. It had never mattered.

Loneliness was so much a part of him now that at times it seemed to be the inalienable force, like gravity, that held him to the earth. The invisible plinth that held him up and apart from everyone else. It was simply the fact of who he was. It came along with the supposed greatness.

He undeniably missed the *fact* of his wife. They had not been compatible; Eliza had neither loved nor understood him, not after the first flush of infatuation so many years ago, but they had not been enemies. He didn't know whether she'd ever taken a lover, but he would not have begrudged her that comfort. He knew only gratitude that if she had, she'd clearly been discreet. But he missed the fact of a life with all of the parts he thought it should have: a duchess, a family, a title, a fortune, property, a legacy. He'd had all of them, once. But they'd been like a collection in a cabinet. He supposed, long ago in his callow youth, he'd thought they'd be more like a garden. Like lush rolling green fields, growing, surrounding, sustaining him.

"I miss the life we once had in the early days, before the war, when my son was small. And I know my son misses her greatly."

He turned to look at her again.

She was regarding him with a warmth so new

to his experience that it altered his breathing. He could not look away. He ought to. He didn't think he deserved it.

"And that's why their miniatures are on your table. So they can look across at each other, and not be alone," she said.

He stared at her in surprise.

"Yes," he said finally. Quietly.

They heard the rattle of the tea tray as Dot made her careful journey down the hall.

THE NEWS WASN'T entirely good.

Then again, she chose to think it wasn't entirely bad, either.

"We've sold five tickets."

Mariana appreciated the way Lord Bolt delivered this news without editorial. Though five out of a hundred available tickets—she didn't need any formal training in "maths," as the duke had put it, to know this wasn't ideal for an event scheduled for less than a month away.

It seemed there was a bit of tension at White's between gentlemen who had grown quite fond of the reformed Lord Bolt and truly *wanted* to attend a fine musical evening and didn't want to offend him; and those who were well acquainted with Lord Kilhone, Lord Revell, and their fathers, and didn't want to offend *them;* and those who were jealous of Lord Revell because he'd once been the lover of a pretty opera singer. Then there were those who could not be dissuaded from the notion that she was a harlot and would never pay to see her even if she sang like a nightingale.

The sum of this conflict apparently was five tickets.

Lord Bolt shared all of this in detail with Angelique and Delilah and Captain Hardy. Miss Wylde was given a kinder, sparer version of the truth.

She was no fool. She could certainly surmise what was going on.

Sergeant Massey, a personal friend of Captain Hardy's who lived in Dover, would be in town with his wife, Emily, through the end of the month, and he'd purchased two of the tickets.

Still, she wasn't displeased that three possible strangers had purchased tickets to see her. Perhaps it was only the beginning. It was insupportable to think of it in any other way.

She looked into Mrs. Hardy's and Mrs. Durand's faces. They did not seem at all bowed.

There was one more thing she needed to ask, though she suspected she knew the answer to this, too.

"Did you speak to the string quartet I told you about? I think they may agree to play for forty minutes in exchange for standing them a round or three at The Wolf And. *After* the show," she added hurriedly.

The Wolf And was the little ancient pub adjacent to The Grand Palace on the Thames. Much like The Grand Palace on the Thames sign featured a ghostly extra word, The Wolf And's sign was missing a word, and no one could remember what it used to be.

She'd performed with these particular musicians before she'd sung at patent theaters. They knew her repertoire well.

Delilah cleared her throat. She and Mrs. Durand were clearly struggling to formulate a feelings-sparing response.

"They've been told not to play with me, is that it?"

Her gut went cold. It was so thorough, the ostracizing. She'd been one man's lover briefly, and the effects of that had spread like a stain, until suddenly these poor musicians had been told to *avoid* her. What did that mean for her career in general? Was there naught left of it? What would she do then?

"Delilah and I know all the songs you intend to sing save one, and both of us will learn the aria from *The Glass Rose*. We shall take it in turns. We aren't professionals, but we won't embarrass you," Angelique said firmly.

It was so kind to say, given that it seemed more than likely she would embarrass them.

THE MOMENT SHE'D arrived today, Valkirk had assigned Miss Wylde the task of transcribing the lyrics from an aria from *The Glass Rose*—one of her favorites, she said—from Italian into English.

She was doing a credible job of it. Many of the words in this particular song—"delicate," "fragile," "transparent"—were similar to the English versions, and were precisely the sort of words one would expect from an opera called *The Glass Rose*.

Every now and then she looked up, silently, for guidance. But she was determined to do as much as possible by herself, and of this he approved. It was how lessons stuck.

He'd removed all the invitations from the anteroom and tucked them instead in his bedroom. For some reason he refused to examine closely, he did not want her to see them.

Perhaps more accurately—and more troublingly— he didn't want her to have to look at them.

He'd be dining with the Earl of Balfe and his family a week hence. Who, unsurprisingly, had a daughter of marriageable age.

He watched Mariana perform her careful, slow, even, graceful writing, head bent studiously.

"You can ask me about a word before you frown yourself into a headache."

She paused. "Was I frowning?"

"As if you could intimidate the word into yielding its meaning."

She smiled. "Then I'm learning more than Italian from you. *Per sempre?*"

"Forever."

"Thank you. As it turns out, it's a beautiful aria about the fragility of love," she told him, as she wrote that word.

"Shocking. Such original lyrics, too," he said.

She quirked the corner of her mouth.

"Why 'jetty,' Miss Wylde?"

She went still.

Then she gently laid down her quill, straightened her posture, and stared at him. "You remembered." She sounded both pleased and not about it.

"It isn't the sort of metaphor one easily forgets."

Fascinatingly, she seemed reluctant to share the story.

And then she sighed. "Very well. I shall tell you." She seemed to be deciding where to begin.

"Do you remember when I said that I had gone twice to the seashore with my family?"

"I do."

Delight flickered in her expression. She was pleased. "Well, this was the second—and last—time we went to the seashore. My father and mother and me. And it was quite a blustery day. The wind tried to tear off our bonnets, and it whipped our coats out behind us, but the day was clear and beautiful. And we were all in such jolly moods. The three of us walked along the beach until we reached a jetty that reached a long way out into the ocean from the shore. And then Papa decided to be silly—he could be impulsive and silly—and ran out onto it, all the way to the end. He smiled and waved at me on the beach. I could see his teeth."

Her lips twitched wryly at the memory.

"And I smiled and waved back at him. And then . . ." she took a breath ". . . a huge wave appeared from what seemed to be nowhere and crashed over the jetty. He disappeared. And we haven't seen him since."

He was struck dumb.

Of *all* the stories he might have anticipated.

He'd seen more than his share of impossible and terrible death, so he was surprised by a jolt of devastation, as though that wave had come for him. He was immediately haunted by the image of her smiling father disappearing before a young girl's eyes.

Words momentarily eluded him.

He already knew, from the warmth in her voice, what her father had meant to her. And what the loss of him had done to their family. They'd all been blown off course.

"I'm terribly sorry, Miss Wylde. The sea is capricious even for seasoned sailors."

She plucked up the quill again, and drew the feathered end of it through her fingers, over and over. She nodded.

"The strange thing was . . . at first it was almost like those Punch and Judy shows. You can't believe it's real. It doesn't seem real. There was a second or two where I felt nothing at all, and then for a moment I thought it was almost funny—surely Papa is playing a joke. Surely he'll pop up again at the end of the dock. I suppose that's the thing that helps ease you into the shock and . . ." she cleared her throat ". . . loss of it."

He considered what to say to her. He was conscious of a peculiar jolt of anger. As though it had been his duty to be there, and prevent that from happening. He could not undo it.

"I think it's a common enough reaction," he said gently. "Some years ago, when I was still a lieutenant colonel, I had in my platoon a soldier by the name of Josiah Gunderson. That boy had no talent for being a soldier. But he was game and had a good heart and a ready wit, and he reminded me of my son, whom I saw very rarely. I tended to choose battlegrounds with upward slopes so I could hide more of my troops on the reverse of them—we could surprise our enemy. I knew I could win a battle that way even when we were far outnumbered. I gave the orders for my troops to flatten themselves against the ground. But Gunderson heard a sound, and lifted his damned head," he said grimly. "And . . ."

Too late he realized he probably shouldn't have gone straight to gore in order to sympathize.

"*Ha perso la testa?*" She whispered it.

"Yes. He lost his head. One minute there. The next gone."

She stared at him, pale and absolutely silent.

"Oh God. I have gone and frightened and shocked you," he said finally.

"No, Your Grace."

"Oh, yes, I have. My apologies, Miss Wylde. Like a heathen, I've forgotten how to speak to women about things beyond the usual social niceties."

"And Aristotle and St. Thomas Aquinas."

"And them."

"Your Grace," she said firmly. "Perhaps it isn't ladylike to say so, but I'm neither unduly delicate nor unduly horrified, and, well, arguably, not a lady." She flashed him an ironic little smile. "Because war *is* horrifying, isn't it? Terrible death is a feature of war. One would hardly be shocked to hear the sky is blue or that there is a cloud in it, because those are the features of the sky. I'm a little shocked because it's shocking. Even to you. I don't suppose shock will ever kill me if it hasn't yet."

It was quite an astounding thing to hear, or for a woman to say. But it was increasingly clear how Miss Wylde had survived fatherless in London from the age of fourteen: a filament of steel in her spine.

"I'm just terribly sorry you witnessed such a thing," she added. He could hear the sincerity and the ache in her voice. "And lost someone you cared about. And sometimes feeling . . . terribly sorry for someone . . . makes it very hard to speak, doesn't it?"

The disarming, astute loveliness of this stopped his words yet again.

"I do not want you to spend a moment of your time feeling sorry for me," he said quietly. "I'm a bloody general and a duke, and here I am, alive, tutoring a notorious soprano in Italian as a punishment for being rude in the parlor. I only hope you shall not be scarred by my awkward attempt at commiseration."

"Nonsense. I am *comforted*," she assured him, perhaps a little too vehemently.

He snorted.

She smiled at him.

He took a moment just to do nothing more than enjoy that smile.

He leaned back in his chair. Drummed his fingers once.

"If it helps at all . . . given that I've been *so* helpful thus far . . . life is cheap and fragile, but ultimately it's all we've got, isn't it, when we have nothing else? And that makes it such an outrageously precious thing that we'll do anything to preserve it. It's quite the paradox. It's a wonder we're entrusted with it at all, given how easy it is to lose. And fate can make ridiculous rag dolls of us at any time, even the wisest of us. Even kings and dukes. But when you realize no one is exempt from the caprices of fate, well, that's the greatest gift of all, I think. A good humbling early on is marvelous for building character."

It was a rare pleasure to speak this way to anyone, let alone a woman, and to know that she listened because she was actually interested.

"That was a little better," she said.

He smiled slowly.

At once her face went still and rapt, as if that smile had surrounded her and held her fast.

They were quiet.

He grew more serious. "The last thing on earth your father saw was your smile, Miss Wylde. And as I'm sure you've surmised by now, there are far, far worse ways a man can go."

He literally saw her breath hitch.

Once again his words made her luminous. He watched it, restless with the kind of hunger one watched any lovely thing—a sunrise, a sunset— destined to vanish quickly.

He did have a sense of the potency of his own

presence and his own gaze. He was not surprised when she ducked her head.

He also did not think she'd remain overwhelmed for more than a second.

"Do you suppose someone on a ship somewhere found him?" she asked, quietly.

In all likelihood, her poor father had fed hungry eels, or a shark. Perhaps the eels had been made into a pie sold by a monger out on the street. He could no longer be sentimental about bodies themselves; it was so clear in death that they'd just been vessels of transport through life, like a ship.

She must have read his expression. "Don't answer that," she said hurriedly. "I'm not delusional. But sometimes I lie awake at night and I imagine him, oh, in China, cobbling shoes so he can make enough money to finally sail home. Or perhaps he's in Egypt, and making sandals, and he has a lot of friends because he always did."

"It's very difficult not to know for certain what became of him," he said gently.

He tapped his quill. There was something he, for some reason, very much wanted her to know.

"Losing men never became rote, for me, Miss Wylde. Every one of them, I think, is scored somewhere on my soul. Assuming I still possess one." He tipped the corner of his mouth.

It was yet another thing he'd never said aloud to anyone.

Her face suffused with that ache again, which she quickly disguised.

"Just as some women are made to hold an audience captive with their voices, some men are built to withstand war. The more you endure, the more you can endure. Until one can easily bear weights—troubles, responsibilities, grievances, deaths, triumphs—that look to someone on the outside inconceivable. It happens over time. I was the one able to do it." He paused. And said, quietly, "So I did it."

He had not ended that sentence with, *until all you're doing is enduring*.

But with a sudden violent clarity, Mariana knew that it was true.

His calling had been consuming. And it was such that now it isolated him. He was unique among men—all men—in the world, and had seen and done things most other men would never see.

That was the source of his gravity. That presence one felt when one was in the room with him.

Who had ever borne weight for him? It stole her breath to think he'd done it alone.

Somehow she knew it hadn't been his wife. She was certain he'd married the right person, of course. What a funny word that was, when one thought about it. "Right." It ought not have shades of meaning. It ought to be like day or night.

Perhaps that was why his memoirs were going badly. Perhaps he just couldn't see beyond the horizon now. Perhaps with less weight on his shoulders, he felt unmoored. His hand, heavy with that signet ring that represented all he now was, lay flat on the table.

"Your Grace . . ."

He looked up at her.

She took a breath. "I should like to say . . . I am very sorry that I hurt your feelings when earlier I implied . . . that you were cold."

He went still.

Clearly absolutely stunned.

And then, before she realized she was doing it, she reached across the table and slowly, gently laid her hand on top of his.

It was, on the surface, an instinctive transferring of comfort to another human.

His eyes flared at once in surprise. Then, she felt an unmistakable heat at the base of her spine as surely as a torch had been swiftly touched there.

And from there it spread everywhere, everywhere in her body.

Oh, he was too much for her. She'd already known that.

But the deeper truth was that she could not go another moment not knowing if she could feel that force that hummed inside him. The thing that shortened her breath when she walked into a room that contained him. That made her brace herself as if she was about to go off the jetty.

They both stared at her hand over his. His skin was hot.

If she shifted her hand a very little, she could feel his pulse.

Her courage did not extend that far.

And then she withdrew her hand, and folded both hands together as if sheathing weapons.

She fancied her hand still buzzed.

She kept her head ducked.

Neither one of them spoke for a long moment.

She looked up to find him motionless, his expression carefully unreadable, eyes fixed on her, and the clock hand twitching forward to four o'clock.

They heard the rattle of the tea tray borne by Dot coming down the hall.

"I don't think I want to learn the Italian word for 'jetty,'" she said, finally. "Hopefully I'll never again find it terribly useful."

Chapter Ten

❧❧❧

𝒯HE SITTING room that night was filled with chatter and the homey, domestic snick of scissors and the rustle of industry. All feminine hands were needed to fashion stars and roses and to embroider the initials TGPOTT into twenty surprisingly fine white handkerchiefs. No consensus had yet been reached about how to make the ceiling of the ballroom midnight blue.

Captain Hardy, who knew how much handkerchiefs cost, had eyed them askance on his way into the smoking room.

So far he hadn't asked any questions.

The duke was out. Perhaps dining with a family who were blessed with a pretty daughter or two. Mariana could hardly stop it. Why wouldn't he enjoy their company?

But she'd excused herself from the sitting room earlier than usual that evening, to be alone with the enormity of the things she felt that she had no business feeling.

She settled gingerly in at the little desk in her room and stared at the foolscap, her old friend, and thought:

Dear Mama,

I hope this finds you well.

Help me. Oh, help me please. I need help.
I am worried.

I think you would be pleased to know that
the duke called me extraordinary. I was so
proud. He would know, wouldn't you think?
Because he is.

But how can I be? He has already
endured so much. He can be a bit of a
bastard, but he is practically a bloody
national saint. He is expected to be good, and
he is. He is a very fine man. I am grateful
to know him.

Oh, but Mama. When I am with him . . .

The way I feel about him is neither small,
nor wise, nor bearable.

I so wanted a very different life. A life
like the one we had. At the moment, I've no
business wanting anything at all, unless it's a
paying job.

I suppose some would call me a fallen
woman. But I still feel just like myself—just
Mariana. No different inside. So I am
worried that what I did with Lord Revell
was not so much a mistake as simply my
nature. And then, what does that say about
me? Am I what the newspapers say I am?

Is that why I want to tempt the duke?
Is that why he is tempted? Would I be his
downfall?

But what are bodies for, if not for this?

THE NEXT AFTERNOON, Dot tapped on her bedroom door just as Mariana was drawing heavy lines through a sentence she'd written that she didn't dare allow anyone to see.

She'd just heard the clock downstairs chime out two o'clock.

"Miss Wylde, a gentleman has arrived who wishes to speak to you. He talks very quickly and has very white teeth. And his name sounds like 'eeneenee.'"

Mariana shot to her feet. "Oh! Mr. Giannini is here?"

"He's *very* handsome, Miss Wylde," she whispered. She fanned herself. "Cor! Italian! Like Queen Charlotte's lover!"

"He's a charming rogue, Dot," she said firmly. "Don't lose your heart. Thank you for telling me. If you would bring in tea? Would that be all right? And will you kindly tell him I'll be down presently."

Dot darted back down the stairs.

Mariana rubbed a bit of shine from her nose, pulled a few tendrils of hair down to trace her jaw, bit her lips, and rubbed her cheeks. It wasn't Giancarlo in particular she was attempting to impress. But she knew he would tell the world how he found her.

She gracefully made her way down the stairs. She took the descent at a regal, leisurely pace, as if she were mistress of the manor.

Thusly, Giancarlo was able to admire her as she passed beneath the crystal chandelier.

He looked the same, of course: lean and elegant, all flashing dark eyes, teeth like pianoforte keys, a cravat tied with Gordian knot intricacy, and a perfect swoop of Byronic dark hair.

He covered his heart with his hat as she approached, and bowed.

"Mariana, *tesoro mio, luce dei miei occhi*—I have found you."

"Giancarlo! So you have!"

"I ask at every inn in every town. Where is she, the most beautiful girl in England? You must tell me."

She'd almost forgotten how absurd he was, and how amusing, in his way.

"Only in England?"

He smiled. "In all the world. I would have said it properly, but my charm, she has some rust since I do not see you every day I have no need to use it. NO one else is worthy."

She snorted. He flirted liked he breathed, and she had no doubt he did indeed suffer if he had no current target.

It wasn't *unpleasant* to see him. Or to bask in extravagant compliments.

"And then I ask at this inn and my prayers are answered," he concluded. Ignoring that Mr. Delacorte had sent him.

"Are you about to answer mine?"

"I am here on business, *cara*. I bring you gifts." He reached into his coat and, with a smile that began slowly and grew wide, retrieved something that rustled promisingly.

He held it out to her.

She tried not to be too eager about snatching it. She realized at once the stack was a good deal thinner than she'd anticipated.

"Seven pounds! That's . . . only a third of what you owe me! Did you think you'd blind me with a smile and I'd forget how to count?"

"Mariana, believe me when I say I wish I could pay you all now, but I have only been paid for part of what I am owed, and it is . . . it steals my sleep. I am truly sorry. I cannot yet pay you all of it."

She believed him.

Mostly.

"And we *will* make it all—it will rain down like leaves in autumn, the money—if *you* were singing. But La Fleurina . . . she is not you. While she once was the queen of all sopranos, she no longer has the range, and certainly not yours, *mi amore*. And my beautiful opera, it needs it. And she is"—he lowered his voice and whispered, as if confessing a shameful secret—"getting *old*."

"Well, so are all of us. So is the audience for opera, for the most part. Surely they can't see a line or two in her face from where they sit."

She could feel herself aging as she sat there, no closer to diva-hood than before, or to that one thousand pounds a season Elizabeth Billington once made. No closer to ever being employed again.

He put his fists up to his eyes and mimed looking through them. "With the . . . how you say . . . *costosa* . . ."

"Expensive glasses."

". . . *sì*, the expensive and beautiful opera glasses."

He mimed a rich audience inspecting the singers on the stage. "They can see if I miss a whisker beneath my chin." He scraped his hand beneath his chin illustratively. "They will see her lines in her face, and the powder she covers over them with, as she sings of being an innocent virgin, and they will not be kind in the papers. And they will mock. She does not deserve it, but neither do we."

"It's a beautiful score, Giancarlo, but I'm hardly an improvement at the moment, am I? They will throw fruit and worse things and hiss at me. They might not go at all if I'm in it. They will not hear a word of your beautiful opera or all the controversy—'trouble,' that word means, that is—"

"I think they are all now deciding to, how do you say . . . pretending you never were?"

He said this appalling thing so blithely.

"*Shunning* me?" she said weakly.

Her heart flipped.

This boded ill for any more ticket sales for the Night of the Nightingale. Or any other work of hers, for that matter. It went a long way toward explaining the quiet, though.

"So I have heard. They do not want to kill you or maim you, just ignore you!" he said brightly. "But soon they will forget it happened, and then I can hire you once more. You are my muse, my angel."

"Forget it happened? Are you *new* to London, Giancarlo?" She was a little frantic.

"Someone will shoot someone else soon enough, and they will forget," he said confidently. "For now, Mr. Tanniger will not allow me to hire you. He agrees that you are best for the role, but he thinks it will be very bad for business."

Mr. Tanniger, a wealthy businessman, was financing the production.

She was speechless.

"Do not look so sad, Mariana. You have still your glorious talent, and I . . . have another gift!" he said wheedlingly.

From his pocket he retrieved what appeared to be a very plump letter.

"It was sent to you at the theater, and I retrieved it. It's from Signor Roselli in Paris."

Signor Roselli was the director of a smaller opera company there—she'd met him. A kind and respected man. Her heart picked up a beat. Paris!

"Thank you, Giancarlo."

"*Prego.* Oh, Mariana," he sighed. "I have missed you. You turn winter into spring. It is always so *dull* now. No one is like you."

It was funny. Now that she was learning Italian, she suspected that his compliments were so dramatic because he was making use of the English words he knew in the best way he knew how. He'd likely learned them the way she was learning Italian. Hot cold good bad beautiful sun moon.

"Surely you exaggerate, Giancarlo," she said, dropping her lashes, partly because she was just a bit parched for flattery and this reliably encouraged more, and partly because Giancarlo was as gifted at creating drama as Helga was at crafting an apple tart. He could be counted on to do it the moment serenity threatened.

He startled her by stepping closer to her. "No, Mariana, *cara*. It is true," he said, suddenly, startlingly ardent. "Scandal agrees with you. You glow like the moon and have roses in your cheeks . . . and your . . . lips . . . your eyes are like spring . . . your . . ."

He lowered his eyes to her bosom and dragged them up again a little too slowly. His lips tipped in a crooked, confiding little smile, and he stepped closer still and lowered his voice. "Do you recall, how the night was"—he cast a hand up as though tossing confetti—"so many, many stars, and we kiss?"

She hesitated. "I might," she said carefully. She was not in the mood to reminisce. They'd had ratafia. He had purred things in Italian she could not understand, but they'd sounded like a lullaby, and then he had seized her impulsively in his arms. He'd unsurprisingly smelled marvelous, and her vanity and sense of competition made sure the kiss that he'd gone in for and that she could not escape had been one he wouldn't soon forget.

But that was all she would give.

She'd gone heavily limp in his arms immediately after, which made him break his hold on her, and he'd laughed, and so had she, and escaped.

He had not pressed her for more then.

But he did tend to put his hands on her far more than she preferred, especially if he'd had a little wine.

And right now—and probably never again—she did not want to touch or be touched by him.

She felt a sweep of crushing exhaustion. She didn't want to play this game at all, ever again.

She wished she were in a quiet sun-washed room, watching those russet and amber lights stirring in the eyes of the duke. In a world that seemed unsafe, it suddenly seemed the safest thing, the only place she wanted to be. Although it was hardly safe, either.

"We are alone and the light is so beautiful, as are you, *cara*, please . . . *dammi un bacio.*"

Ah, hell's teeth. Thanks to her Italian lessons, she knew what that meant, so at least she was somewhat prepared for what was about to happen.

"Oh, I don't think so, Giancarlo. Not now. Not here." Not *ever*, but since he could employ her, since he wrote music she would die to sing, she could not produce the sterner commands she'd learned.

"Oh, come now . . . we are alone. Just think how it could be . . . *Voglio baciare il tuo seno . . . Voglio le tue mani su tutto il corpo . . . Dammi un bacio.*"

"Giancarlo!" she said firmly. "*Ti chiedo di parlarmi con rispetto.* I must ask that you not speak to me that way. Not even in jest."

She didn't think he *was* jesting, but she thought she'd give him an opportunity to back away gracefully.

"We need not speak at all if we are kissing," he explained, logically. Teasing.

"Giancarlo. I don't *want* to kiss you. Please stop." Her voice escalated in pitch.

He didn't seem to notice that she wasn't laughing. He laughed and snaked an arm around her.

She pushed it away. She pivoted, but he was too fast, and he got the other one around her, too. She pushed at that.

And he half waltzed, half backed her toward the mantel, where she would not be able to turn around. All the while grinning as if this were merely a game of charades.

He transferred one of his hands to her hip. She twisted again, but he'd managed to plant the other hand on her hip.

And then another voice seemed to come everywhere and nowhere at once, like God, or perhaps Satan. It was low, calm, and so menacing all the fine hairs at her nape prickled erect:

"Se non le togli subito la mano dal culo, la rimuoverò con una spada."

Giancarlo's hand flew from her body as if it had been lopped off, and he staggered backward and whirled around.

Mariana adroitly stepped away from his reach and spun.

To find the Duke of Valkirk standing in the doorway. Pure, cold fury in his eyes.

A long silence ensued, during which invisible flames of wrath seemed to lick at Giancarlo's ankles. Giancarlo was motionless. Unless one counted the sudden rapid rise and fall of his chest.

"Would you like me to remove him, Miss Wylde?" the duke said politely. His voice was all taut, and nearly dripped icicles. He didn't move his gaze from Giancarlo.

"From . . . this earthly plane?" Mariana nearly stammered.

It was just . . . he looked capable.

His lips performed the slightest of taut curves. "From the premises." He turned to Giancarlo, and added, shortly, "For a start."

Giancarlo had gone as white as the marble-fronted fireplace. Other than this, and a certain tautness of his own features, his composure remained admirable. He raised his palms in self-deprecating surrender. "There is no need to speak of me as if I am not here. Or to . . . cut off my hand with a sword." He lowered his hand and circled his wrist with the other hand. "I shall take my leave. Miss Wylde, I apologize if I offend"—he looked the duke full in the face, his own speculative, awed, and resentful—"or trespass. If you will please allow me to pass, I will go."

He bowed quite beautifully—first to Mariana and then to the duke—because he was a graceful man, and second only to his instinct to flirt was his instinct for self-preservation.

Mariana held her breath while the duke's eyes followed his swift progress from the building. No doubt he was counting Giancarlo's pores, memorizing his eyelashes as he passed.

Mariana was surprised not to see two smoking holes in the back of Giancarlo's head.

The slam of the heavy door echoed in the foyer.

Mariana put a hand to her heart as if to steady it. Her face was still hot.

He remained in the darker foyer. She remained in the light of the reception room. In silence, she and the Duke of Valkirk regarded each other.

No man had ever before come to her defense.

"*Grazie,*" she said. A little ironically. Almost shyly.

"*Prego,*" he said shortly.

James found he could not quite produce a smile for her yet.

His fingers were still curled; they buzzed as though they'd been deprived of the feel of that man's throat. Emotion entirely out of proportion to the situation simmered in his veins.

"Anger" was the safest word to call it.

She was so pale that the little gold spots on her face stood in stark relief, but two hot, pink, embarrassed spots sat on her cheeks.

"But he's a *brilliant* composer," she said finally, ironically, as though they'd been exchanged in a long, silent litany of Giancarlo's grave flaws.

He managed a short, humorless laugh.

She cleared her throat.

"I'm terribly sorry you were forced to witness that, let alone intervene." Her hands went to her cheeks. "I'm just so embar—"

"No. Please don't apologize. There is no need. I am only glad that I was here and could be of some assistance."

There were questions he wanted to ask. Of her, but mostly of himself, when he was alone. Because he could not catch hold of the ragged ends of his outsized rage to trace it back to its source.

She cleared her throat. "Signor Giannini is a

composer, and our relationship is professional. He brought about a third of the money he owes me. He's dissatisfied with the current casting choices for his opera, and since he cannot hire *me* at the moment, for obvious reasons"—she grimaced wryly here and she flashed a quick little smile—"and he claims he missed me. One can hardly blame him for that, yes?" Her voice faltered. "Though he tends to express such sentiments . . . with his hands."

Her words began in a brittle, cheerful rush. They ended nearly inaudibly.

Mariana, he wanted to say softly.

She looked so alone, standing in the middle of the room. He realized he'd never fully understood her actual aloneness so acutely until now. The absolute singularity of her position.

"I hope," the duke said carefully, "I have not introduced a complication into your milieu by interrupting your . . . shall we call it a conversation?"

She quirked the corner of her mouth. "Oh, what's one more complication? It seems I've an infinite capacity for them. Rather like Mr. Delacorte has for gravy."

James smiled a little, only because she seemed to need it.

"Will you be all right now, Miss Wylde?" he said finally, a little stiffly.

"Oh, of course," she said quickly. A flush rose swiftly again. "I'll just sit here a moment and drink my tea. Please do carry on with your day, Your Grace. Thank you."

"It was no trouble at all."

He turned at once to leave. And as he moved across the foyer, he did not slow his pace. But he could not keep his head from turning, just slightly, to look back.

She was still. The light that always seemed to animate her, so that she perpetually glowed like a little lantern, seemed dimmed. She looked weary, stunned, and ashamed.

He was shocked by how this cleaved him.

He turned away abruptly, as if to protect her from his gaze.

ONCE BACK IN the anteroom, James lowered himself slowly and stiffly into the chair, as if he were gingerly carrying something volatile.

He did not recognize his mood.

He did not recognize himself.

He took up his quill and aimed his gaze out the window, but he didn't see the river, the milky-blue sky, the man urinating against the building, the black cat making a slinky left turn into the alley.

A knot like a spiked, mailed fist sat between his ribs. His mood eluded naming, and its persistence remained all out of proportion to the circumstances, which had been common enough: he'd come upon a man behaving like a cad, and he'd put a stop to it. Young men, especially charming, good-looking young men, had seized upon such opportunities since the world began, and it was the job of honorable men to stop it when they could.

That was it. Something about that word.

Common.

He closed his eyes as he again saw Giancarlo's hands at Mariana's waist, her elbow, her hip again as she twisted and dodged and backed away. If a duke had not issued a threat to his life in the doorway, the man would no doubt have kept at it until she'd had no choice but to knee him in the baubles. Or capitulate. It had been a diversion to that man. It was clear he'd done it lightly.

The *wrongness* of this. It had felt like watching someone use the grail for a spittoon. Or an emerald for a shuttlecock. "Sacrilege" seemed like hyperbole, considering, but James couldn't think of a better one.

All he knew was that she was not common.

The more accurate—and troubling—word was "rare."

He knew, in a way that made his breathing go peculiarly shallow, that she was rare.

The flustered, shamed spots of pink in her cheeks, her chin resolutely hiked as she visibly gathered the tinselly shreds of her usual composure about her—he understood viscerally now something he suspected she did not yet fully realize, and he saw it because he was a man. There would be no ultimate winning against the Giancarlos of the world. Flirtation and charm and firmly issued Italian or English requests to behave might forestall them. But she could not ever fully stop them.

And it would surely wear her out in the end.

Unless and until she acquired the armor of a diva.

That mailed fist between his ribs clenched more tightly.

He drew in a long, long breath to prove he could, and released it. He had frightened her, which he regretted, and awed her, which he did not. Her gratitude felt like a warmth against his skin, felt like a medal pinned to his chest.

And then, as he'd stood there unable to speak, a slow-dawning radiance supplanted uncertainty as her eyes searched his. She'd found something there.

He wondered what she'd seen.

SHE DRANK HER lukewarm tea, and sat in the reception room. She wanted to be alone for a while in a room where, for the first time in her life, a man had come to her defense.

And looked at her the way the Duke of Valkirk had just looked at her before he'd left the room.

She was chagrined she hadn't finished her assignment, but she fetched the foolscap from her room anyway, before she took herself off to her Italian lesson. There was no sense in wasting it.

She paused for a moment in the doorway, as usual.

"Good day, again, Miss Wylde."

"Good day again, Your Grace, Duke of Valkirk."

He flicked a wry glance up at her. A sheet of foolscap lay before him, and a glance—she saw a salutation, what appeared to be a column of numbers—made her think he was writing a letter to his Man of Affairs.

The pages of his manuscript were stacked and

pushed to the far side of the table, as if he couldn't bear to look at them.

She settled herself into her chair.

"How is your work on your life's story proceeding?" she asked. Rather wickedly.

"Apace," he said shortly. He flicked his eyes up to her again, went still, and a faint furrow appeared between his brows. He was distracted.

"'Apace.' What a usefully vague word that is. I suspect it means 'not at all.'"

This ought to have won her a reasonably good-humored scowl at least. But he seemed lost in thought. Between his fingers the quill pen was poised, the feather trembling, as though impatient to return to the work of writing.

Then he leaned back and regarded her, his brows knit.

"I think I ought to learn the word for 'sword,' Your Grace. Because I suspect that was the difference in your success and mine, when it came to Giancarlo."

He snorted. *"Spada."*

"I wondered if—"

"Miss Wylde," he said so abruptly she froze.

He didn't speak immediately. He seemed to be choosing his words carefully.

"I should like you to know," he began, as though he was picking his way through unknown terrain, "that I am not in the habit of threatening anyone with sword violence as a first line of defense, especially an unarmed man. I will assess a situation and, if it seems necessary, step in and at once break a man in half like a bundle of twigs. I will do that without announcing my intention or issuing threats. I don't believe in wasting words or actions."

She went breathless.

"A bundle of twigs?" she repeated softly.

"Yes. That is to say . . ." He took a breath. "I regret the means by which I accomplished my ends today. I do not regret the ends."

She sat quietly a moment.

"Perhaps it is just you were out of practice in threatening composers. One often overshoots the mark when attempting something new."

"Nevertheless."

She wanted a smile from him, but given his mood, it seemed clear she wasn't going to get a complete one, just one of those little taut affairs.

"Perhaps you were simply overcome with emotion at witnessing a friend in distress, Your Grace."

There was a little silence.

"Ah, yes. 'Overcome with emotion.' That sounds like me."

She smiled at him slowly. He was regarding her with a little furrow between his brows. He didn't take up the word "friend."

She was as absurdly glad as if she'd gotten away with an epithet in the drawing room.

Finally he returned his attention to his foolscap and said nothing more, which she took to be her cue to write her sentences.

After tapping her quill to her chin, she thought of a sentence, and began to scratch it out.

Then she paused.

"It might reassure you to know, Your Grace, that Giancarlo has only a basic command of English, and it was likely a charity to him that you were direct in a way that could not be misconstrued. I suppose it's an impulse of his age. It seems a reflex with men to have a go if they think they can get away with it. That is, why haven't you tried to kiss me?"

Those last words emerged like a bullet she hadn't known was in the chamber.

She'd shocked herself breathless. She felt as though they'd entered the room like a cymbal crash.

The duke didn't seem to hear them.

His head remained fixed on his foolscap; his quill continued scratching in leaps and darts, making those consonants like the masts on ships and the swoops below like their decks. "Because if I were to kiss you, Miss Wylde . . ." He jabbed a period at the end of a sentence and looked up at her. "It would ruin you for all other men."

There ensued an instant of absolute silence and stillness.

Such that when the gold sliver of the second hand on the clock shifted, it echoed like a gunshot.

She sat, airless, as the words all but detonated in her, sending a shocking onslaught of heat through her, tensing her muscles, waking something raw and new and so needful that her eyes burned, and she could not say whether it was longing or fury.

She knew, with a certain despair, that he only spoke truth.

He did not lift a brow. He didn't duck his head to fix her with a smolder. Such embellishments were wholly unnecessary. After all, everyone understood what went on inside volcanos. It was why one did not recklessly tiptoe about their rims.

Now was the time for a light, insouciant laugh, or a joke.

She parted her lips to do it.

There emerged a sound like the wheeze of a gently squeezed concertina.

He gestured to her foolscap. "Shall I have a look?" he said mildly.

He seemed to have complete command of his voice. His expression hadn't changed.

But she had no doubt that he'd read her as clearly as he read Italian or the map of a battlefield.

Mutely, her palms damp, she pushed it over to him.

She didn't take her eyes from him when he lowered his head. She studied the severe lines of him: the narrow part in his hair, the vast horizontal shelf of his shoulders. The gold-brown hands with the copper hair at his wrists. She realized only then that while she was learning Italian, she'd also been learning him with an unseemly hunger.

She'd written only one sentence.

But his head stayed lowered a second or two longer than this warranted.

She wondered—it occurred to her—that perhaps his own composure wasn't entirely shatterproof. That perhaps he had shocked himself.

And at this notion, her heartbeat became nearly painful in its slamming.

He read aloud finally.

"'I use my sword to cut the roast of beef.'"

He slowly raised his head. His eyes had gathered that light she had come to so appreciate, to count on, when he looked at her. His expression was difficult to interpret. He, too, was schooling his features. She was certain of it.

However, she suspected part of this was because he was tempted to laugh.

"I thought they ought to be put to some use during peacetime," she said, subdued. "Swords."

He nodded once, gravely. "Swords might indeed languish in peacetime if there were no women to defend from composers."

Damn.

He was *funny*.

And if she was being truthful with herself, she'd thought he was funny from the very first.

His wit was as subtly dangerous as the rest of him. It sneaked up on you like a sunrise and took you over until you were lit all through with a sort of quiet and total delight.

She couldn't speak. They regarded each other across the table. Her eyes still burned strangely with some suppressed emotion. As did her heart. Like joy or fury, only too bound in thorns and brambles to get a good look at it.

And that's precisely how it would stay: bound. It could strain all it wanted at those bonds.

She had more sense than that.

He pushed the foolscap back to her.

"Write it using all of the pronouns and verb tenses," he suggested. Then he dipped his quill, and he resumed writing, and in seconds it was as though she was forgotten.

Chapter Eleven

⁓⦿⁓

TWILIGHT WAS his cue to change into a fresh shirt.
He would not be dining with the boardinghouse
citizens tonight; instead, he would be dining with
the Earl of Langley and his family, and he saw
no reason to beg off. The Earl of Langley, who, of
course, had a pretty daughter.

He slowly wound his cravat while he studied
his reflection in the mirror. He was no Byron. He
was no Giancarlo Giannini, for that matter. But he
saw nothing to lament, unless it was the passage of
time. He looked the way a man ought to when he'd
lived a life like his. He'd seen himself reflected in
the eyes of women and men; he was satisfied with
what they reflected back to him.

But he'd never seen any woman look at him the
way Mariana had this afternoon.

He finally understood the single word that described how he'd felt when he'd seen Giancarlo's
hands on her:

Mine.

James had been willing to do violence for her,
because he wanted her.

It was perhaps precisely that primal.

Why have you never kissed me?

Simmering beneath their civility, beneath his control, beneath the tightening weave of intimacy, this feral *want* had been biding its time.

This notion played hell with his equilibrium. *He* was the one who commanded. He had imposed his masterful control and order on the chaos of war. And his entire being had been shaped around protecting, as best he could, people—and an entire country— from terrible dangers and bad decisions. He'd made excruciatingly difficult choices and shouldered impossible responsibilities without complaint because he was needed. Because he could.

And because his pride would not release him from a contract with himself.

He might be known throughout the land; he knew he was admired, if not revered.

He didn't suppose he was loved.

He drew the silk folds of his cravat slowly through his fist. Imagining, as he did, sliding his hand along her lovely throat to cup her breast, and thumb her nipple erect beneath the muslin as her eyes went dark and hazy.

Lust was a bolt through him. His vision all but blurred with it.

He breathed through it like pain.

How the *ton* would laugh at him if they knew the run of his thoughts: Valkirk brought low by the Harlot of Haywood Street. Because he was just one more man who wanted Mariana. One more man on the precipice of making a fool of himself over a woman other men had made fools of themselves over.

He'd spent a lifetime ensuring he'd never be spoken of in the same breath as "other men." And he wouldn't tolerate being thought of as a fool.

And it was quite the irony that his desire to take her was precisely as ferocious as his desire to protect her from men like himself. And from nasty little bits of gossip like that. So she could go on being herself, safely. So she could have what she wanted from the world. So she could rise.

Because other men would not *see* her. They would only partake of her. And this notion, for some reason, he found unbearable.

He could not deny that his pride was satisfied that she wanted him, too. Not because he was a duke. But because she, like he, just couldn't help it. It was simply how things were between them.

What is the honorable thing? What is my duty here? Those had always been his lodestars. Once he located them, it was easy enough to navigate his way through any thorny circumstance.

He jammed on his hat, reached for his walking stick and his overcoat.

Took one final look at himself.

It had always been up to him to protect everyone, including himself. He'd do that here, too.

If he burned, he could, and ought to, marry one of those young titled women.

It would be the right thing to do.

And he always did the right thing.

THE DUKE WAS out all evening at the behest of one of those engraved invitations he was forever receiving, so he'd missed Mr. Delacorte's triumphant announcement in the star-and-rose-making factory the sitting room had become.

"The Cain and Abel Theater burned last night!"

Captain Hardy winced. "That place was bound to, eventually. Den of vice," he informed a room of wide-eyed listening ladies.

"But not *all* of it burned." Delacorte was full of suppressed excitement. "Guess what remains?"

"Chairs?" Lord Bolt got it on the first try.

"Hundreds of 'em, so I'm told. I've never been inside." Delacorte's taste in amusements didn't run to any vices outside of a truly rank cigar or interesting liquor. "Do you know what they might be like?"

"Haven't any idea," Lucien said at once. Rather smoothly.

Captain Hardy flicked a sidelong glance at him.

"I suspect a number of interesting things have happened in those chairs, however," Captain Hardy suggested carefully. It had to be said.

Thusly were the ladies presented with a second philosophical dilemma. Or was it moral? Or amoral?

"They're free of charge. We'll go pick out the best ones, slap on some whitewash, cover 'em with paper roses," Delacorte suggested.

"More providence," Delilah murmured to Angelique. "Den of iniquity chairs to go with our contraband handkerchiefs."

Neither of them mentioned the previous history of The Grand Palace on the Thames, but there was a reason the word "rogues" was still faintly visible on the sign outside, and why every now and then a young man would show up with an ancient, yellowing printed price list and request The Vicar's Wheelbarrow. He would be sent away, red-faced.

The Grand Palace on the Thames was such a fine and *respectable* establishment now.

The current presence of notorious opera singers notwithstanding.

"Shall we have a look at the chairs?" Captain Hardy turned to them.

"Yes, please," Delilah and Angelique said at once.

Mariana listened as she alternately folded a paper rose and studied her Italian vocabulary, excruciatingly conscious that all of this fuss was so she could earn her room and board and launch their new ballroom. She could only hope they hadn't wagered on the wrong horse, because she was accruing so many benefits she wasn't certain she deserved, including Helga's cooking, chess lessons, Italian lessons, and the expression she'd seen on the duke's face this afternoon in the reception room, after Giancarlo had unceremoniously departed.

She had reviewed this in her mind, over and over. Taking it out as though it were a new treasure, a bit like the pink ribbon given to her for her tenth birthday, for the pleasure and terror of it. For the way, each time, a stab of exhilaration stopped her breath. For the rest of the day, the weather inside her was like that moment during their trip to the seashore when she'd smelled salt on the breeze well before the vast, endless ocean came into view. In comparison to this feeling, the whole of her previous eventful life might as well have been a small locked box. A trip inside a carriage.

She thought she might die if she did not ever kiss him. Although how this death would occur she couldn't quite envision. She could imagine the item of gossip: "Diva sets fire to The Grand Palace on the Thames with her burning loins. Nothing remained but the chairs."

She did not know where it would lead if he did.

She already knew, however, that if she went down that road, there would be no return.

THE FOLLOWING MORNING, Mariana awoke to find that anticipation seemed to have shaved away a fine layer between her and the rest of the world. Between the moment she opened her eyes and three o'clock, every sound, every color, landed exquisitely and painfully on her senses; anticipation flavored the very air she pulled in.

She knew the duke would not pretend nothing had changed. He didn't say frivolous things; he was not a flirt. Like the duke chess piece she'd imagined, she knew he would only make forward moves. She knew she could not use that expression she'd seen on him yesterday as a crystal ball to predict her future.

She tried very hard not to want anything at all, and instead focused on the things she knew would happen. She completed the work he'd asked her to do. She had a good look at the dress she'd decided she would wear for the Night of the Nightingale, reviewing the nacre-colored satin for stains or tears. The hem needed some delicate sponging. She would wear her hair down, she'd decided. Like a nymph the audience had stumbled upon out in the dark woods.

She did, however, imagine the letter she might write to her mother, if she dared.

Dear Mama,
   I hope this finds you well.
   I think my life will change today.

* * *

AT FIVE MINUTES until three, she was moving down the hall to the anteroom, feeling much the way she did before she walked out onstage, emerging from the dark into the light.

She paused in the doorway.

She was surprised to find him standing behind the table, rather than sitting. All six feet infinity of him.

"*Buonasera*, Your Grace."

"*Buonasera*," he said politely. "Miss Wylde, upon reflection, I've decided that my time here at The Grand Palace on the Thames would be better served by working to complete my memoirs. I should think any debt to you incurred by my previous thoughtlessness has been satisfied, so I am drawing our Italian lessons to a conclusion. I wish you good luck. Good day."

A few numbed seconds elapsed during which it felt as though her spirit had been neatly bisected from her body. As if with a *spada*.

She could not move, or breathe or speak.

She stared across at him from the doorway. He seemed to pulse, somehow, before her vision.

He was watching her, expression inscrutable. Posture erect.

Or, if she was not mistaken, braced.

He did not seem to be breathing, either.

You coward.

He was hardly, of course, a coward.

But she supposed some things were more terrifying even than staring down the French.

She opened her mouth to say something clever or cutting. Or perhaps gracious. A "thank you for your time, Your Grace, I understand." Something that would impress him, and that he would not ever forget.

And then the pain set in with a shocking totality.

She said, "I hate you."

It was appalling. Her voice was low and sincere and faintly surprised. It trembled, which she regretted. She would have liked to have sounded emotionless.

The violence of her own emotion embarrassed her. But she decided she didn't mind. She instead felt a peculiar, dark exhilaration. She so seldom said precisely what she felt, and this was her purest truth in the moment.

She watched those words enter him like a dart. The tensing of his features, the tightening of knuckles on the quill he held. The shadow of pain about his eyes.

But he said nothing.

She supposed he was not the sort of man a woman like her could ever hope to really hurt.

She turned and departed with dignity, closing the always-open door quietly behind her.

JAMES STARED AT the smooth, blank white door long after she'd departed. It suddenly bore a disorienting resemblance to the lid of a coffin.

The knob winked like a blade.

And his ears rang as though she'd slammed it.

So he closed his eyes. All of his senses, in fact, suddenly felt raw and amplified, as if he'd sampled the wrong thing from Mr. Delacorte's case and had awakened naked alongside a sleeping tiger.

He rubbed his forehead. He pulled his hand away and stared at it. It was trembling, as if he'd just done murder.

It's how he knew he'd done the right thing for both of them regardless of how he, and she, felt now. He had learned it was always best to make a cut brutal and swift. There was no mercy in it otherwise.

He'd lately come to know that his very spirit was always contracted like a muscle to bear all of the things expected of him. He'd understood this the instant her radiant face had lifted to his in the parlor the day of the Italian composer. Because for that brief moment, for the first time in his life, his feet had simply not felt the ground.

Firmly rooted to earth again, accustomed territory where he would always have the lay of the land, he sat down and picked up his quill pen.

He dropped his forehead in his hand.

He couldn't make the pen move. All he saw on that foolscap was the image of Mariana's white, stunned face.

And it was this—the need, the attempt to think of anything else—that resulted in a few words. He wrote haltingly at first.

Then ever more concertedly.

And before the hour was out, he'd filled an entire, very surprising page, word after word emerging as if something had broken open inside him.

And thusly, at last, he began to tell the story of a life.

But not, his publisher would be chagrined to learn, the one he'd already lived.

In her room, she wept.

Only a little, and as quietly as she could. Palms pressed hard against eyes and mouth. Hot tears leaking through her fingers. Ribs aching from the blows of her stifled sobs. But she could bear this. Couldn't she? It was just emotion; for heaven's sake, if emotion was capable of killing her, it would have done it by now. And fury and embarrassment were practically part of every day in the typical opera career, weren't they? Onstage and off. She ought to be able to manage that much without coming apart.

But grief was so much harder.

Grief was . . . hope's ghost.

The grief was how she knew hope had taken up residence in her like a sneaky lodger. She did not dare give this hope a name or assign it an objective. She only knew definitively that it had been there, because now she was leaden and hollow with the disbelief that accompanies a death.

Hope. That was the gleaming thing she'd sensed on the horizon. It had borne her aloft. Like a cloud. It had sneaked in, despite her ramparts.

She felt like a fool. And worse than that: uncertain. She was suddenly forced to recast everything she thought she knew about herself in this discovery. Because a lot of new questions were begged. How much of what she considered her courage was merely bravado? How much of it was really . . . just her *lying* to herself?

She could not afford to feel uncertain. She could not afford to miss a trick. Any emotional condition other than pragmatism was sheer luxury at this point in her life.

He was a bloody duke! What had she been *thinking*? He could say and do very nearly anything he liked to anyone at any time, of course. And he was better at denying himself unwise things, and perhaps that was all to the best.

Surely he was right.

Because wasn't the bastard always right?

It was just . . .

She was going to miss him.

And he, she knew, was going to miss her.

She sighed and pulled her palms away from her face. She took another few good, long breaths.

She found a handkerchief and dampened it in her basin, where the water was still cool, and gently dabbed at her eyes.

She inspected her reflection. It wasn't unpleasing. She tried a smile; it wasn't unpersuasive. She did not look ravaged by disappointment. But there was still a tension about her eyes, at the corners of her mouth. That wouldn't be going anywhere until—and if—she found a paying job.

This reminded her that she was luckier than most. Because she knew what to do with emotions. She could turn them into glory.

And one day again, hopefully, into more money.

FINALLY SHE MADE her way downstairs and followed the smells and laughter down one more flight of stairs to the kitchen. She found it as usual, filled with the warmth and laughter of kind and clever women. It was a balm, it truly was. A balm she was borrowing, like a balm from Delacorte's case, a temporary remedy, but a remedy nonetheless. She did not truly belong here.

She hovered on the threshold for just one moment.

"Miss Wylde! We have decided on lemon seed cakes for the Night of the Nightingale, and punch," Delilah told her happily.

"Oh, divine!" she told them, sincerely. "How lucky our guests will be." She was beginning to feel as though it was a bit of a pantomime, this pretending there would actually be guests. But life had surprised her before.

"Did you come to help?" Helga was teasing. One did not press the guests into folding dough for apple tarts.

"Well, I did come about work, but it's of another sort. I know I usually use it earlier in the day, but would you mind terribly if I availed myself of the ballroom this evening before dinner? Privately, if you don't mind. To rehearse a bit. I know I normally do it earlier, but the urge suddenly took me."

"Oh, we should love for you to sing in the ballroom anytime you like, Miss Wylde." Mrs. Durand gave her the key from the ones jingling merrily at her waist.

Mariana had in mind the aria from *The Glass Rose.* Sung at full voice. It was full of all those—how had the duke dryly put it?—very original words. Perhaps they *were* mundane. Nevertheless, they could cut like a sword, and they would, when she sang it.

HE'D LIFTED HIS head from the world of his writing to find that Dot had apparently come in with the tea and a scone, and he hadn't so much as noted it. The tea was, naturally, cold. The sky outside his window was twilight-mauve, and the river had gone pewter.

It rather felt gray inside of him, too.

He lifted his body from the chair to go out for the evening. Dully he performed a shave, splashed in the washbasin with some soap for a few of his other parts, dragged on a fresh shirt, and tied a fresh cravat.

He'd been gravely injured in battle once. Took a musket ball, bled until they'd thought he would die. He was surprised to note that he felt a bit like that now.

It was how he knew Mariana had already become more a part of him than he'd realized. It was not something he would recover from overnight.

He buttoned his coat, reached for his hat, inhaled a deep breath in order to sigh it out again, and made for the stairs.

The sound reached him before he'd fully descended.

His breath caught. He stopped abruptly.

She was singing.

And oh, the sound. Full-throated, glorious waves of it reached him through the walls as though he was hearing it from a distance as far away as heaven.

And he moved toward it. Slowly. Breath shallow, heart beating slow and absurdly hard.

He stopped again.

The door of the ballroom was ajar.

Entering to witness her seemed like something he had irrevocably forfeited the right to do.

But it seemed he could neither stop nor deny himself, because stealthily, quietly, as though he was stealing this moment, he moved into the room and pressed himself against the wall.

Mariana was onstage, head tipped back, eyes closed. Her arms, crossed over her chest, unfurled outward as the note she held grew in breadth and depth until he could feel it everywhere in his body.

He was motionless. Held fast by awe.

That such a small person should possess such *power*.

It wasn't just the volume, which seemed otherworldly. He was helpless against the tide of its outrageous beauty, against the sorrow and yearning.

He couldn't recall the last waking moment he'd felt truly helpless. He couldn't remember the last time he wasn't at least somewhat conscious of the full weight of who he was.

But all of it was borne up, and then away, on her voice.

He'd hurt her, and this glory was what she'd done with her pain.

Suffice it to say he felt things. Things for which he had no vocabulary, possibly because they could not be captured in mere words. Why one of them should be pride—pride like a sun in his chest—he didn't know.

She hurled skyward a final glistening note, and held it aloft, elongating until its edges frayed with a sort of weary, bitter triumph. Then, like a handful of leaves tossed, down in half steps the notes drifted into a forever-altered silence.

Battlefields had that kind of silence, he thought, even when the smoke had cleared and the bodies buried. One always sensed something of consequence had happened there.

Perhaps one would call this room a beautyfield, instead.

And when that last note receded like floodwaters, hidden things were suddenly revealed to him: old wounds and terrible griefs and guilts. Dormant ecstasies and needs.

And painful, unpalatable truths.

Perhaps he'd done the right thing when he'd sent her away.

But it was also the fearful thing.

He'd done it because he was afraid. As afraid as a green lad.

And *therein* lay his crime. He could not see what lay on the other side of this.

Her shoulders moved swiftly as she caught her breath. She dropped her chin to her chest, briefly, then lifted her head.

And then she went still.

And she suddenly looked toward him.

Her features were indistinct in the twilight, but she seemed to glow more than the light warranted. Perhaps she simply had a diva's instinct for finding whatever light there was, and standing in it. Perhaps there was a light in him that illuminated her.

IN THE BLACKS and grays of his evening clothes, he might have blended seamlessly into the shadows, apart from his posture. It had the profound stillness of the transfixed.

Her traitorous heart leaped higher than her highest C.

There was really no mistaking who it was. She fancied she'd still know he was standing there if her eyes were closed.

He showed no sign of moving.

But then she realized she was already moving toward him, as if the floor between them were a river bearing her along, inexorably, in one direction. No *one* should possess such power. She wanted no one to have that kind of power over her again, not to hurt her, not to save her.

But she yearned to hear his voice again speaking only to her, alone in a room.

The heels of slippers gently ticking on the wood floor was the only sound.

He waited.

She'd meant to pause before him, and to formulate, and say, something clever, cutting.

But then she saw the raw need in his expression.

She paused only to get her bearings, then walked right into his already reaching arms as if he were a lifeboat.

They all but collided.

One of his hands fanned to cradle her head as it tipped back and his face came down.

It was a mutual siege. At once swift and hard and ruthlessly, searchingly erotic, frank and drugging. A kiss they broke only to drag in hot, swift, rough breaths so the next and deeper kiss could begin. Her arms went around his waist; his muscles, taut as iron, contracted when she touched him, and he pulled her closer still. He was everywhere in her senses. Velvety and hot against her tongue, his cock hard at her groin, his fingers delicate at her nape, his other hand sliding stealthily down to the curve of her arse to squeeze, to stroke in a coarse claiming. Bolt after bolt of lust shivered through her, and she could hear her own breath coming in short sobs. She hadn't known that desire had a taste. It burned like whiskey in her throat.

But she had known he would be like this.

He ended the kiss abruptly, with a soft oath.

He didn't release her. She clung to him, and he held her close. His hand was soft on her back now.

For a second or two, she held on to him. Her eyes remained closed. His breath gusted against her temple. His chest rose and fell hard against hers. His lips were against her brow. He brushed the gentlest of kisses there. Her hand remained over the hard thud of his heart.

She'd felt his words forming; they'd rumbled in his chest before he murmured them.

"Forgive me."

She supposed he meant for everything.

For the liberty taken, because he wasn't a man who simply took things, even though he was a duke, and even though he could.

For hurting her with his words. But they both knew why he'd done it. He flailed for any weapon to hand when pulled by forces he could not command. She understood it. She didn't like it, either. She would fight dirty, too, to save herself. And that's what he'd been trying to do.

For ruining every other man for her, precisely as he'd said he would. He was indeed a man of his word.

For leaving her with an impossible choice.

Although she supposed he had one, too.

He loosed his arms, and they eased away from each other.

Stepped back and assessed.

His face was now a veritable chessboard of shadows.

But she felt rather than saw his watchful wonder, the near fury, the desire that, even from that distance, made her shiver.

All for her.

She felt powerful and frightened. Dizzy from kisses and from an elation she ought to thoroughly stamp out before it killed her. Surely, no matter what, devastation would be the end result.

But oh. The bliss between this moment and then.

She couldn't find her voice to answer him. But she did forgive him, and he likely knew. Because she would have given him anything in that moment, except she could not give him what he likely wanted most, which was to not want her.

Well, that was mutual.

Then the war hero gracefully bowed to the harlot as if she were a queen.

Once upright, his mouth tipped at the corner in another wry salute.

He turned and departed, patting his hat back into place.

Just as he disappeared out the door, his hand rose. And wonderingly, he touched his fingers to his lips.

LADY BEATRICE GALWORTHY had clearly been told that her eyes were beautiful. And they were—sable

colored and doe-limpid, her lashes so luxuriant
they bent against her cheekbones when she was
seen in profile. Which wasn't often, as she had
clearly been instructed to aim them unrelentingly
at the Duke of Valkirk. The hope was no doubt to
mesmerize him into falling in love.

And this took courage, he thought, blackly
amused. She was half his age and clearly frightened of him. But her mute awe at his presence
was offset by a self-congratulatory gleam in those
doe-eyes. Very few of the other young ladies of
the *ton* would be able to say they had watched the
duke take another helping of peas in sauce. He
suspected she knew about everything he owned
and its value, to the penny. Her mama would have
made certain.

All in all she was very pretty, a veritable rep-
lica of her mother, who watched over the dinner
like a sparrow hawk in green satin. He liked her
father; he'd been a good soldier and was an intelligent man. Of course he was going to try to get his
daughter a triumphant match.

Valkirk was so bored he did not feel as though
he fully occupied his body.

The fault of this lay in the few hours earlier
when he had fully occupied his body for the first
time in what seemed like years.

Her hot mouth open to his.

That catch in her throat at the pleasure.

The curve of her arse.

As he maintained polite conversation with the
Galworthy family, his senses continued to riot.

Every cell of him was ravenous and amazed. *So this is who and how I truly am*, he understood with surprise and a certain resignation. He hadn't known, because he had never before met a hunger that matched his own. He had, in fact, never been this hungry for *any* other woman. He had the oddest sensation he was meeting his true self for perhaps the first time, and Mariana had somehow affected this introduction.

And yet. Slim silver candlesticks that had likely been in the Galworthy family for centuries marched down the middle of the table, and he approved of this. He'd spent a lifetime amassing a fortune and building a legacy, and he imagined his descendants dining at tables just like this one, in front of silver owned for a hundred years. He saw his own face now distorted in the smooth, bulging side of a silver tureen, as though he was already inextricably a part of this way of life.

He thought about declarations of love caused by candlelight.

He wondered how Mariana would look naked, by firelight. Which caused him to surreptitiously dig his nails into his palm.

Marrying again meant life with a girl like the dark-eyed one sitting in front of him. She would lie alongside him at night and accept his attentions dutifully. He'd leave her a rich widow, no doubt, he thought mordantly. Free to happily traipse about England and Italy like Mrs. Pariseau, having done her duty by her husband.

He thought of a little girl witnessing her father

disappear off a pier and how she had scrambled, valiantly, to find her footing ever since, and his breath went strangely short. It suddenly seemed imperative to be where she was. As if he could forestall anything like that happening to her ever again.

He didn't know how he felt. Only that he did. He was suddenly all feeling, and the identifiable emotions that rose to the surface were restlessness and irritability.

He should leave it lie. One passionate clinch with a diva in a ballroom. Followed by an apology to her for the indiscretion. A line firmly drawn. Propriety restored.

Easily enough done. Who knew more about discipline than he did?

He was suddenly glad Lady Beatrice had a decent man for a father, and that she would never need to learn another language just to protect herself from the eager, casual hands of men, because no young woman ought to endure that. She should be allowed her innocence.

And he was glad that he was a duke who could say things like:

"I'm afraid I must offer my gratitude along with my heartfelt apologies. I am unable to linger after dinner. Duty calls."

And shortly thereafter he was gone.

"WE DID NOT expect you to return so early this evening. Did you enjoy your dinner with the Earl of Galworthy?" Delacorte asked when Valkirk appeared in the entrance of the sitting room. He had known, courtesy of conversation in the smoking room the night before, where the duke intended to go.

"He has a pretty daughter, doesn't he?" Mrs. Pariseau wondered, slyly.

"Everybody does," the duke said grimly.

Mariana hadn't known where he was going, but she'd suspected. She had not expected him to say. What mattered now was that he was back much, much sooner than anyone had anticipated.

"How go your Italian studies, Miss Wylde?" Mrs. Pariseau wanted to know cheerfully.

Mariana froze.

And the pause seemed inordinate. For perhaps the first time in her life, she had no idea how to reply.

The duke did. "Miss Wylde is an excellent pupil. I should be pleased if she should wish to continue for the duration of her stay here."

She took a long and surreptitious breath, and an unseemly yet delicious heat pooled between her legs.

"I should like to continue. *Grazie*, Your Grace," Mariana told him, gravely.

Mrs. Pariseau said happily, "How delightful! Soon we'll *all* be chattering away in Italian."

"*Imagine* all the things in the world that can be learnt when you know words," Dot said, with a happy sigh. "Chess, Italian, who is shooting who."

"Whom," Mrs. Durand corrected her absently.

Chapter Twelve

⚜

THEY DIDN'T speak of the kiss at all the following day between three o'clock and four o'clock.

Out loud, at least.

She arrived at the usual time to find him seated at the desk, attending to what appeared to be a stack of correspondence, also as usual.

"*Buonasera*, Your Grace."

"*Buonasera*, Miss Wylde."

"At least the day is clement."

"It is indeed, calm," he agreed.

This, absurdly, was more or less how the hour proceeded.

They exchanged these polite sentences as though they were passing back and forth something that could scald them if it spilled.

They were absorbed in separate thoughts that were wholly about each other. The air was dense and buzzy with portent. It was as if yesterday they'd stumbled upon an underground cavern, in the depths of which they'd detected a seductive glitter.

Which could either be a treasure, or the eyes of a dangerous man- and woman-eating beast.

Or could be the whites of the judging eyes of the *ton*, who might strip the duke of his reputation like so many termites stripped wood should they ever learn he was consorting with her. Or run Mariana out of town on a rail.

It wasn't comfortable. But it was thrilling.

There were any number of times in her life when she had asked, "Why me?"

But she knew the answer to that was, "Why not you?" Fate had such an insouciant shrug it must be French.

He would be an animal in bed, she thought. It was what she wanted. She suspected this said less about their natures than the alchemy of the two of them together.

She was furious—it seemed grotesquely unfair, yet another in a series of events that seemed grotesquely unfair—that her lust was adulterated by emotions she had no business entertaining. Ones that all but guaranteed pain.

And there he sat, a man of absolute composure. She thought of how many people had relied on him for safety. How in large part the reason everyone in England still spoke mainly English instead of French was because the man sitting in front of her somehow had risen to the occasion.

She imagined her arms wrapped around his waist.

She imagined screaming into a pillow while she came with him inside her.

"Is there anything new you'd like to learn in Italian today?"

Do not bother flirting with me, as I have been kissed by the Duke of Valkirk, and he has ruined me for all other men. That would be a useful sentence.

"Oh! I forgot to tell you that I received a letter—a rather plump one—written entirely in Italian. It's from an opera director called Signor Roselli in Paris." She did not add, *where word that I am a pariah has not yet reached the populace*, but it rather went without saying. "Mr. Giancarlo Giannini brought it to me when he, er, visited the other day."

The name "Giancarlo" narrowed the duke's eyes.

"I am able to read many of the words thanks to you—and I think he may be offering me a job, and I think he's sent along a libretto. But his handwriting is quite shockingly bad." She paused. "And he failed to include any illuminating illustrations in the margins."

His mouth curved, but he didn't lift his head, and his quill didn't pause. "Did you happen to bring the letter with you today?"

She watched, transfixed, as the hand that had so lately squeezed her arse in order to press her up against his cock made what looked like a question mark, based on the swoop and dart of the quill.

She took a surreptitious breath.

"I fear it slipped my mind. I left it in my room."

"I see." There was a little silence as he continued writing. Scritch scritch scritch. "If you should find that some of the language contained in the letter eludes you, Miss Wylde . . ." He paused and looked up. Then leaned back in his chair.

"I should be happy to assist with the translation when I return later this evening. I've a meeting with my Man of Affairs after dinner, but I will be back in my rooms just before ten o'clock."

Her heart lurched.

She stared at him.

She *was* a good pupil. She understood at once what this was.

And he was an extraordinary tactician. He'd seized upon an opportunity, and he'd made a decision. And he'd played a card.

The man who did everything right intended to break a rule for her.

Which meant, of course, it was now her turn to play one.

"Thank you." Her voice was arid. "Your offer is kind."

He gave a short nod and resumed writing.

If he was invested in a particular outcome, not a twitch betrayed it.

"Shall we review what you've learned today?" he asked politely. He put aside his work.

HIS MAN OF Affairs had foisted upon him more requests for donations, sponsorships, quotes, and speeches, and he'd carried it all back with him to The Grand Palace on the Thames, joining the group of ladies in the sitting room, sitting apart at his usual little table. The other gentlemen were out for the evening on a matter of business for the Triton Group. Mr. Delacorte had, it seemed, gone to a donkey race.

A sudden palpably anguished, tense silence made him look up abruptly.

"It's the ballroom ceiling, Your Grace," Mrs. Pariseau explained, gravely, noticing his gaze.

Everyone involved in the planning, and even those who were not, were deeply, passionately committed to a midnight-blue sky twinkling with stars for the Night of the Nightingale, but no one could agree on the best way to achieve it. Tammy, velvet, tulle, and silk were variously rejected as too expensive, too outlandishly expensive, or pure madness. And the notion of affixing the number of stars necessary to enchant all the guests was daunting, and neither Delilah nor Angelique was eager to put holes in a ceiling they'd only recently fully repaired.

"Fishing nets."

Everyone in the room swiveled to stare at the duke. It was the first thing he'd said all evening.

"Dye fishing nets indigo or black. Attach the stars using fishing line to the holes on the net and then hoist the nets up. The stars will be easier to adjust in height that way if you wish. No need to attach anything to the ceiling. Use the chandelier as a center point to help support the nets but don't light it, of course. Any hooks you install on either end of the room will be practical and support the weight of bunting or anything else you might use to decorate the room in the future."

They listened to this crisp recitation with wide eyes.

And their expressions transformed as though he'd just won the war again.

"We'll layer the nets," Delilah said at once. "To get a denser sort of blue."

"And I suspect we can get them, and the dye, free or cheaply or for trade of some kind, given the Triton Group's dealings with shipping and the like," Angelique added.

"I thought so," he said pleasantly.

"Thank you, Your Grace," Delilah said fervently.

He nodded.

It was the least he could do for spending the last half hour imagining the Night of the Nightingale's star naked beneath him, her fingers digging into his shoulders as he thrust.

It seemed every breath he took was hot, as if the room was a blacksmith's forge instead of a parlor full of pleasantly bickering people. Every muscle in his body, his every cell, was as alert with anticipation as the night before a battle.

He was balanced on the knife-edge of propriety.

He never equivocated. He either did things or he didn't do things, as his moral compass dictated. He never wasted time on sexual reveries. He knew how to get satisfaction when he needed it.

For the first time in his life, he was conscious of rationalization. Of searching out a reason he could live with for what he wanted to do. Because the only compelling reason to break the rules here at The Grand Palace on the Thames with a notorious soprano was that he wanted to, and it was a weak man's reason.

Even as the stack of mail upstairs congratulated him, in part, for being the inspiration that kept the young men of the *ton* out of the clutches of women like her, he knew it was less about wanting to fuck someone than it was about looking down into Mariana's face and watching how her eyes changed when the pleasure he gave her became too much to bear.

He—they—had set this thing in motion. He knew full well that every avalanche began with a few pebbles. But that didn't seem to be a compelling reason to stop it, either.

Mariana, imagine how it will be. You know how it will be with us.

Come to me.

He could see her now in profile.

She turned slightly. Met his eyes.

She turned away, with obvious difficulty.

Mariana, don't come to me. I'm not the sort of man who has sex with notorious opera singers just because he can.

I'm not the type of man who takes advantage of a young woman's sensuality and fascination for me to get her into bed.

I do not ever want to hurt you.

But if you come to me . . .

She might not come.

And if she didn't, he would not seduce. He would not coerce. He would not beg. He would, and could, pretend as though nothing had ever happened between them, and he would protect her decision, and her, from his desire as if it was his sacred duty.

But he would take note of every minute between now and ten o'clock as if they were punishing lashes.

SHE'D DRESSED IN her green silk, the one that made her eyes "bewitching," or so Lord Revell had said, before she'd broken with him. Before all of this.

And then she'd put on her fur-lined pelisse that Revell had given her, as a gift. *Not* a payment.

She sat on the edge of her bed for a long time, in the dark. She took long, deep breaths. And with each one, instead of feeling steadier, she felt weaker. She hadn't the duke's chessboard, whip-crack mind. She couldn't reason through this.

She glanced over at that unwritten letter on the desk, and imagined writing:

> *Dear Mama,*
> *I hope this finds you well.*
> *I want him.*

That's all she could think. Three mundane words when taken separately. Rather drab to look at, when written. But: *lo voglio.* She knew just how she'd sing them. She would tear the hearts out of her listeners with a howl of equal parts anguish and ecstasy, a cry for help.

Her breath seemed uncommonly loud in the dark of her room.

No one could save her but herself.

As it turned out, she wasn't up to the job.

Ten minutes later she stood in front of the door
with a lit candle in her hand. For a time, she did
nothing but experience the bass drum thud of her
heart. It seemed to vibrate her entire body and
send her blood whooshing like waves in her ears.
Surely it would wake the house.

She passed rows of doused sconces (and all the
maids were in bed), and the floor upon which Mr.
Delacorte snored (all the guests were sleeping). She
crept down the stairs, skipping the creaky ones
(surely it was the first thing any person who was
not a saint sussed out upon moving into a house).
Then through the passage, which was chilly at
night and dark. The great, sturdy door with the
peep window was barred and locked for the evening. The shutters were latched and the heavy
curtains drawn against the night chill. The chandelier scattered only one or two amber twinkles
on the marble floor, as the fires in the parlor were
allowed to die and the crystals only shone by virtue
of its light.

If anyone should come along, there was no way
this could be construed as an innocent visit. She,
and her trunk, would be thrown bodily out of the
building.

The door swung open so abruptly, she gasped
like the heroine in *The Ghost in the Attic*.

The duke filled the doorway.

He was in shirtsleeves, cravat-less, rolled up,
bootless, and the firelight cast the V of visible
skin at his throat in copper. Dark hair curled up
from it.

Her head went light.

"Miss Wylde." He managed not to inflect the words with anything other than conviction: she was indeed Miss Wylde.

She did not reply, because she couldn't. She could not move her eyes from his bare throat. She thought if she touched her tongue to the bones at the base of his throat, his skin would taste like toasted bread coated in honey.

Her skin was everywhere warm suddenly, like the pelt of an animal. It remembered how it had felt to be crushed up against his body, and every inch of her wanted that again.

"My apologies for startling you." This was how he interpreted her speechless stare. "I saw the toes of your slippers flash in the crack beneath the door."

She looked down. "Oh. I suppose they are shiny by candlelight." She was mildly pleased by this.

She looked up again to find a slow smile spreading across his lips. As if no one had ever said anything more charming or absurd in a doorway of a boardinghouse.

Which made her realize: he'd likely known precisely how long she'd been standing here.

Her cheeks went hot. She hadn't realized it was possible to simultaneously feel like a virgin and a whore.

And then it occurred to her: he might have been waiting by the door, too.

Nothing about him betrayed impatience. But his silence was unlike him. Perhaps he was mesmerized by her in candlelight.

But his silence made her wonder if he had rifled through a rash of reservations between this afternoon and this moment.

She cleared her throat. "I . . . I brought the letter I told you about." She brandished it. If she clutched it for one second longer, the ink would transfer to her damp palms. "I've come to believe the other pages are a libretto or lyrics."

"Ah. Very good," he said. There was a pause. "Shall we read it together?"

He slowly turned like a drawbridge lifting, and the room behind him was revealed in flickering gold firelight and dense velvety shadow. The lamp next to the dark contours of a roomy bed put out a hazy nimbus of light. The light picked glints off a decanter of brandy, a snifter, a vase next to the bed.

Tomorrow. During the daylight. That's when they should read the letter. That's what she should have said.

She looked up at him, mutely.

He gently, chivalrously took her candle from her.

He closed the door behind them and slid the bolt once she was inside.

"I WAS SITTING on the settee and reading and having a brandy. May I offer you a . . . or would you rather . . ."

He didn't know the protocol for whatever this was, either, clearly.

"Brandy would be lovely." Did ladies drink brandy? Did it matter? She was hardly a lady at this point. It needed to be something. Sherry seemed far too tea-with-the-ladies for the occasion.

She stood just inside the room, rule breaker that she was.

The room smelled of him. Manly, expensive, perhaps a little sweaty. Excellent soap and the *best* tobacco and a little of the citrus, woody scent that had haunted her since she'd kissed him. He didn't baptize himself in scent the way Giancarlo did.

And then there was actual leather, which could be ascribed to the Hessians standing next to the hearth as erect as if he was still in them. They were considerably shinier than the toes of her satin slippers.

She was a cobbler's daughter. She knew Hessians like that cost the earth, relatively speaking.

It was ridiculous, but suddenly, the beautiful boots, and the great distance between where they stood at the hearth and where she stood at the doorway, underscored their stations in life. This room was vast, and she could only *imagine* what his actual home looked like.

She took in a breath, feeling absurdly shy.

The settee was long and tall-backed and looked shiny and plump. Perhaps the finest piece of furniture she'd met in person, and this belonged to a room in a boardinghouse.

"If you'd like to have a seat there, we'll have a look at the letter together."

She took his suggestion, and discovered the fine settee was nicely sprung. She could not resist giving a gratuitous bounce.

He sat down beside her, almost gingerly, close but a decorous distance away. So close to touching, but not yet touching.

She wondered if he was nervous.

"What have you been able to read?"

She flattened the letter in her lap and pointed to a scrawled paragraph. "I think he is inviting me to Paris to work? A role in a new opera? But I do not know what this part means. *Aragosta*? His handwriting is a bit unusual."

He read the letter carefully. "Excellent. Yes, you *are* being invited to work, and I believe your role will be . . . you will be a . . ."

He turned to look at her, his expression carefully blank. "A lobster."

She stared at him, dumbstruck.

"A . . . l-lobster?"

"Yes," he said gently, as if breaking the news of a death in the family. His eyes, however, glinted. "I believe you're being asked to play a singing lobster."

She was speechless.

"Operas don't have to make sense, Miss Wylde," he reminded her, his tone entirely sober, his eyes pure, dancing wickedness.

Dazedly, she slowly raised one arm, bent at the elbow.

Then the other.

He watched her face, taut, then trembling with some suppressed emotion.

Slowly, experimentally, she turned her hands to face each other, like claws.

And then clacked them.

They both gave shouts of laughter. And then they doubled over with it.

"Oh, oh, no. Oh, dear," she sighed happily, and wiped her eyes. "Oh, my goodness."

"Hold." He held up a hand importantly, catching his breath. He coughed. "Now let's think a moment. It could be very poignant. Think about how lobsters wind up in cages . . . there could be an injustice done . . . perhaps it will be like Lobster Newgate!"

That set them both off again.

He referred back to the letter. "Before you get too excited about your role . . . wait one moment . . . let's be sure." He cleared his throat and scanned the page. "It's possible I was mistaken. It's possible he means for you to be a mermaid. He mentions a *sirena*, and I believe that's a mermaid . . ."

She dropped her jaw. Then made an indignant sound.

"But . . . that's . . . are you sure?"

He referred to the letter again and squinted, as if he could bring the man's scrawl into better focus. "Yes, I believe it does. The lobsters are . . ." he frowned ". . . merely . . . stage dressing? I believe? Or they might be minions. Ye Gods, was this man drunk when he wrote this? His handwriting is abysmal. It might be a chorus of lobster minions. *Please* let there be lobster minions," he muttered.

She studied his profile as he read. He still had tears in the corners of his eyes from laughing. She stared at the glint of them. She stopped breathing from the sheer, untenable happiness.

"A mermaid is much better," she said, distractedly.

He turned to her in all seriousness. "Is it?"

"Well, I could have a very pretty tail for a costume. Just imagine! Perhaps done in net and paste jewels. And a magnificent wig," she said dreamily.

As he studied her, his face settled into that bemused wonderment.

"Even so, Mariana, no matter what . . . you'd be the most riveting lobster to ever grace the stage."

"That's the nicest thing anyone has ever said to me."

He gave a soft laugh.

They sat in the kind of silence Mariana had never known. It was perfect.

"You are gifted," he said.

"I know."

He smiled at that again, and damned if he didn't look pleased with the answer.

"But that's precisely it, isn't it?" she said. "It's a gift. I hadn't much to do with it. I'm a . . . vessel for that voice. I got lucky."

"No. You're wrong," he said firmly but ruefully. "One person might look at a little cloudy rock and say, 'What a nice rock.' It's the dedication, the determination, the instinct, the . . . *spirit* . . . that ultimately tumbles that rock into a glittering diamond."

She knew he was right. He delivered it as if it were gospel. What must it be like to be so certain of things? What would it be like to be able to rely upon him as a rudder through life? He was so often right.

"If that is in fact true," she said carefully but firmly, "you may have to contend with the notion that you are in fact a hero deserving of statues and accolades. Not just a man with the conveniently right temperament for an impossible job. Because the same concept applies."

He was still. Then his head went back a little, thoughtfully, and then came down in a nod.

And then he smiled at her, and that's how they sat for a moment or two, enmeshed in a bemused glow of mutual appreciation.

He stirred abruptly and handed the letter back to her. "Why don't you read this paragraph aloud. I think you'll be able to translate all of the words in it. The one at the bottom of the page. I'll help if you need it."

"Very well. I shall give it a try." She cleared her throat. "'We . . . should like to' . . . . this word that looks like . . . prove?"

"*Prova*. Prove. Rehearsal. Rehearse?"

"'. . . three weeks . . . *cominciando*'? Beginning?"

"Yes. Very good. Beginning."

"'We should like to commence rehearsals in' . . . oh my . . . that's nearly three weeks away. I've only a very little time to get there! And here are the words 'Signor Antonio Grieco'—oh, I do like his work! He's a fine composer. And look at this. The money is good! Am I reading this correctly?"

"Oh, yes. That's what he's offering to pay you."

They had begun by sitting a few inches apart. Somehow, as if they'd slowly been melting, their thighs were now touching, and their shoulders were touching, and suddenly James could no longer think.

A few strands of hair lay against her throat. They glowed like filaments in the firelight. They might as well have been actual gold.

Tension spooled. Tighter and tighter.

Her words grew quieter, faltered, trailed off, stopped.

Her eyelids had shivered closed. And now the little tendril of hair behind her ear fluttered with her breathing. He could see the pulse beating in her throat.

And then finally, delicately, gently he swept those red-gold strands away, his own hand shaking a little from all that he held in check.

He felt like an animal. He wanted to mount. To ravish. Devour.

He warned her of this. Into her ear he confided, each word soft with amazement, scorching with intent: "I want you."

She turned up to him a heavy-lidded, fully surrendered, lust-drunk gaze, pupils black as the hearts of pansies.

Her eyelids dropped. Her lashes shivered, casting shadows on her cheeks. Her lips were parted; her breaths were uneven. He watched, mesmerized, the lift and fall of her breasts, her nipples already ruched and hard against her bodice. He took her earlobe between his teeth, lightly, as he unlaced her dress with a pickpocket's vanishing touch. Then dipped his tongue into her ear, softly tracing its contours, chasing his tongue with his breath, until her head fell back on a helpless "oh." Then he dragged his lips to the silky hollow where her pulse thudded and opened his mouth to place a hot kiss there. He could feel the little skip in her breath as he dragged her bodice down, down.

And she turned to him, nude to the waist, her arms reaching to wrap around his head. Her head fell back to meet his lowering lips, and her moan hummed against his lips as his hands filled with her breasts.

The sweetness of holding this particular woman's body against his. The sheer bloody luck of it. It seemed this unsatisfied craving for her, just for her, had lurked in him a lifetime.

The warm, silky weight of her breasts nearly did him in. He stroked; his fingers teased her until her breath was sawing. She reached for his trouser buttons; they gave beneath her fingers. She found the jut of his cock beneath the folds of his shirt and wrapped her hands around it as their mouths met in slow, carnal kisses. She dragged her fists over him again, and then again, then paused to trace the dome of it with a delicate finger, teasing. He hissed in a breath; his head dipped to touch her forehead, then fell back again as he struggled to accommodate the ramping pleasure.

He urged her back against the settee. His miles of shirt were in the way, and her skirts threatened to impede, but they were, to their everlasting relief, somewhat naked, positioned groin to groin, lips clinging to lips, hands searching for bare skin to savor, to conquer, to arouse.

He dragged his hand down her softly fuzzed thigh and slipped it between where the skin was tender as a petal, his fingertips cherishing the feel of that as they skated down, down, until they dipped into the satiny, hot slickness hidden by damp curls. His eyes never left her face as he teased at first, stroked and withdrew, circled lightly, watching her eyes go hazy, her lids slit, her neck arch back. The lust was a madness, a pressure in his head, pulsing in his veins. Their eyes locked, both in thrall to the pleasure she took and he gave; her sighs evolved tattered edges, then became moans, then oaths hoarsely whispered against his lips.

"Oh, James . . . oh God . . . please, James . . ."

She came apart with a silent scream, her body whipped upward; she pulsed around his fingers.

He hovered above her, the muscles of his arms all trembling from coursing need. She wrapped her legs around him, locked them about his back, to pull him close, as he thrust himself into her.

The glory of that tight fit, of moving in her for the first time. The triumph of watching her eyes go dark yet again when the pleasure banked. The wonder and amazement and ferocious want evolving in her expression as she felt another release building. He teased both of them at first, or tried; he kept his rhythm deliberate, leisurely; oh, but it cost him. Need had its claws in him. Her hands dug into his shoulders, until she slid them down to his bare hips and gripped him, arching to urge him on, to take him deeply. "James . . . let go. Please . . . oh God . . . I *need* . . . I need . . ."

It was the permission he sought. Their bodies colliding and arcing as he drove into her, driving them both to the brink and over it into that shattering bliss that blacked his vision.

He went still. He buried a roar against her throat. He pulled from her just in time. She clung to him while their bodies quaked, the bliss still rippling through them.

It was a moment before his sense re-met his body.

He lowered himself carefully beside her. Turned so that her body was half-draped over his, and held her. So she could use his chest as a pillow.

There was nothing quite like the texture of quiet with a woman's soft, sated weight against his body. He drew a finger along her quivering lashes. Her mouth curved in a little smile.

Her cheek rose and fell with his breathing. His heart thumped against her skin.

This was like the moment after waking, before all of the things of the world sifted in.

They lay still and listened to the clock softly bonging twelve times.

She stirred, and he sat up.

She gave a soft laugh. "Your hair," she said. "It's every which way."

He went to smooth it with his hands.

"Don't," she said. "Not yet. I like knowing how it got that way."

They smiled at each other. With a certain awe-filled caution.

There seemed no need to review what had happened: *Sex! Gosh! There's nothing like it, eh?*

But he had never before experienced sex—or himself—or a woman—as an uncontrollable and irresistible force. It had owned him.

There was really no smooth or direct route back to dignity after a sexual frenzy. He found a handkerchief and handed it over. She cleaned her thigh. She pulled up the sleeves of her dress and he, without asking, did up her laces while she held up her rummaged hair. She did the best she could with it.

He suspected he was going to have an affair.

With, to boot, perhaps the most notorious woman in London.

Although he was certain that they would both spend the rest of the night reviewing the wisdom of everything that had just transpired. Wisdom was never present when a man and a woman were naked together in a dark room. The light of day might reveal some stark truths to both of them.

He only hoped she did not and would not regret this. He found he did not dare ask if she did. And this—the not daring, because there had never been a thing he hadn't dared—was new, too.

"Thank you for the Italian lesson," she whispered.

He gave a soft laugh.

Her cheeks were still flushed. Her hair was still a bit anarchic, albeit re-pinned. Her lips were rosy and a trifle swollen.

And then gently, almost tentatively, she laid her hand against his cheek. They looked into each other's eyes, solemnly, in a sort of wary tenderness.

He turned his head to lay a hot, lingering kiss in her palm.

He closed his eyes and breathed her in.

And then he threaded his fingers through hers and stood, and pulled her to her feet, and released her hand.

He found her candle, and handed it to her.

And by tacit agreement, she slipped silently out of the door.

As SHE MADE her way through the darkened house, she balanced the candle in one hand lest a stray draft douse it. She carefully closed her other hand into a fist.

As if the kiss he'd put into her palm was another tiny flame she needed to delicately tend and keep until she reached her room.

She slept with her fist against her cheek.

Chapter Thirteen

⨳⨳⨳

MARIANA AWAKENED feeling as though her little room was filled with sunlight.

Given that this was London and her room was on the non-duke side of The Grand Palace on the Thames, the one without the water view, this seemed unlikely.

She realized it was just her very being.

She basked in the sensation, drowsing while the maids came in and made her fire and brought the tea, then slipped out again.

The real world and its concerns would leach through.

She lay still, and thought:

> *Dear Mama,*
>   *He called me extraordinary.*
>   *But I don't think I am. How can I be?*
> *I did not resist.*
>   *I thought about it. I truly did. You raised me to be a good and cautious girl, and as the years go by, the reasons for that seem all too clear. I only know that I wanted him—* <u>*him*</u>*—more than I wanted to be good. What*

does that make me? We tend to label things, don't we?

But what we did was extraordinary.

And it didn't feel wrong.

* * *

"*Buonasera*, Miss Wylde."

"*Buonasera*, Your Grace."

She settled herself into the chair gingerly. Parts of her were still a little tender. She hadn't slept nearly enough, but she'd had a lot of coffee this morning at breakfast, and the net result was that everything seemed both hazy and more pronounced.

She looked at him, with his smooth, clean-shaven face that had scraped her only hours earlier as she'd kissed him, and thought last night and this moment were like the difference between backstage and onstage.

Suddenly, however, it was difficult to know which was more real: the feverish, firelit naked grappling, or this: the duke in his spotless black coat and cloud-like cravat, looking as coolly brisk and unapproachable as he had the day she'd met him.

Except for his eyes.

As far as his eyes were concerned, she was a feast.

But only briefly. He screened them carefully. A habit of being a general, no doubt, and forever in the public's eye.

"How are you today?" he asked.

A little sore from locking my legs around your naked back so I could take you deeper, thank you for asking.

"Very well," she said, politely. "And you?"

"Never better."

If only he was a blusher. One of them was hot and pink at the moment, and it wasn't him.

He smiled, though, slowly.

She had never fainted, but she was beginning to understand what it was like to swoon in place.

"I thought we would write your letter accepting the job that we can have a messenger take at once to Signor Roselli in Paris."

"It is so very kind of you to offer."

"It's no trouble at all. Would you like to write the letter yourself? I'm certain you're able to by now."

"Yes, please, I would."

"Why don't you do that, and I'll review it when you're done?" he said gently.

They sat in silence.

His pen scratching.

Her pen scratching.

Cozy, if not for the lava-dense atmosphere.

In Italian, she wrote:

Dear Signor Roselli,
  I would be pleased to take the position.
I shall arrive in Paris a week before
rehearsals begin, as you requested. I am
pleased to accept your offer of accommodation.
Thank you for offering me the position and for
the chance to review your lovely libretto.
    Yours sincerely,
    Mariana Wylde

He sealed it with a blob of wax, but not with a press of that enormous signet.

And then, just as if it were an ordinary day, and not the day after a night she would remember for the rest of her life, he tested her on vocabulary words. Because she would be leaving for Paris and would be surrounded by Italians, and she would need them.

When the hour had nearly come to a close, he gestured to the message. "I'll have it sent straightaway."

"Thank you."

There was a pause.

"One more thing, Miss Wylde." He slowly reached into his pocket.

And then gently, with a little clink, he placed something on the table between them.

It was a hairpin.

She stared at it.

She slowly looked up at him.

He was indeed masterfully still. His expression inscrutable. His eyes slightly hooded, and watchful.

But then, out of the corner of her eye, she saw that the quill was ever so slightly trembling in his grip, and this was nearly as thrilling in the moment as his body covering hers.

"If you think you may be missing other hairpins, Miss Wylde . . . I'd be pleased if you'd come have a look for them. I'll be in all night." He paused. "I will abide by whatever you wish to do."

She reached out a hand and dragged the hairpin toward her.

"Thank you, Your Grace."

HE'D LEFT THE decision up to her.

And she ought to stay right where she was, in her little room. She was capable of rational thought. She possessed intelligence and reason. She was not at heart a taker of risks, though some of her choices could certainly be construed as risks.

She *was*, at heart, an enjoyer of pleasure.

Once, and she could say she'd done it for the experience. She could perhaps rationalize it away. How many women could say they'd made love to the Duke of Valkirk?

Twice, and, well. Making love to him twice was about as reckless a thing as a woman could do.

Twice meant she would do it again . . . and again.

Twice moved her further away from a position of singularity and more emphatically toward that word that began with "h."

She decided she would not go.

Ten minutes later . . .

HE MUST HAVE heard her heartbeat from the other side of the door, because it opened again before she'd knocked.

As he had the night before, he took the candle, set it lightly down, and closed the door.

"I brought the letter again. I thought perhaps we could translate the lyrics," she whispered.

He didn't say a word.

His eyes never leaving hers, he gently took the letter from her hands. Laid it aside atop a little table.

His hands rose to cup her face.

Oh God. Oh God.

His mouth touched hers.

She heard her own sigh as if from miles away. Soft as a breath at first, his lips then gently insistent, then her whole, spinning world. He was hot, and tasted of brandy. Her knees gave way, but he was there to softly crush her against him. She curled her fingers into his shirt and clung.

Her head fell back into his cradling hand, and while she was at the mercy of his kiss, his other hand managed to loosen and spread her laces at the back of her neck. Her bodice collapsed into something like a swoon. "Off," he ordered, pushing at the sleeves of it.

He gently tugged, and she helped him, tugging and shimmying until it pooled at her ankles.

She stepped out of it, feeling like Venus disembarking from her half shell.

The *sound* he made when she stood nude before him.

He pulled his shirt off over his head, and while he did that, she reached for his trouser buttons with trembling, greedy fingers, and when they were all undone then he pulled the trousers off and gave them a kick for good measure.

She could not have in her wildest dreams imagined anything as glorious as his naked body.

His hands glided along her throat, the blades of her shoulders, following the nip of her waist to the flare of her hips. He was savoring her, and the pleasure he took in her body, the pleasure he gave, made her outrageously glad to have skin. This was the whole point of it, surely. She could feel his hard cock against her thigh, and shamelessly she ground against him. With a low growl he lifted her up, his arms banded hot across her back.

He lowered her until, to her surprise, she felt the give of the bed against the bare skin of her back.

He knelt between her legs, gently parting her thighs so he could dip his head between. And when his tongue first touched her, then stroked, the sound she made, an animal keening, shocked her. She had not known such pleasure could be had.

His tongue and his fingers colluded in driving her nearly mad. The velvet heat of his tongue against her slick heat, the searching glide and stroke of his fingers, mustered an unendurable need from all corners of her being. It was sinful sorcery, and she was the wickedest, luckiest woman alive. She moved with him, abetting him, begging him shamelessly.

She was going to scream. She threw her forearm over her mouth and did, coming apart with a sob of hallelujah.

He was on his feet to hook her legs over his shoulders, and the mad speed with which he plunged told her that he'd been wild, too.

She lay sprawled and sated on her back beside him, while he lay on his stomach and propped himself up on his elbows. He'd fetched the letter and read to her what appeared to be lyrics.

"'Queen of the Deep, why must you' . . . I believe this word is 'abandon'? 'forsake'? . . . 'me. I am your humble servant.'"

"I think the lobster is singing to the mermaid," he told her.

"Well, that's very sad, don't you think? Is the lobster in danger? Poor thing!" Her voice was drowsily amused.

He smiled at her and read on.

"I think it's jealous of . . . I think this word is 'Neptune'? The lobster is jealous of her lover Neptune. 'My heart is on fire with jealousy,' I think it says."

He lowered the letter.

"This is a bloody *masterpiece*, Mariana."

"It will be, when I sing it," she said, placidly.

He smiled at her.

She'd been watching his face while he read with a little smile. When he turned to her, they gazed at each other silently for a moment.

She reached up and gently, with one forefinger, traced his eyebrow. Then the other. Her smile faded when she moved her finger to his mouth and traced it with a feather-soft touch. He drew her finger into his mouth and sucked gently.

Again and again, the luscious beauty of her stunned him like a club to the head. The tapering line from her full breasts to her round hips was his idea of a masterpiece. If the ceiling of his London townhouse had been painted with her image, he'd never see the floor again.

He dipped his head and closed his mouth over the little raspberry peak of her nipple in a languid, teasing caress of tongue, and teeth, and lips. Her eyelids fluttered closed, to isolate herself with the pleasure, and she absently stroked the back of his head. Her breath was ragged through parted lips.

"Oh . . ." she sighed.

He moved his lips to her other breast, and she shifted her body so that she was beneath him, and his swelling cock pressed against her hip. She combed her fingers up his neck, lightly around the whorls of his ears. It made him wild.

He knew from her shuddering, desperate breaths, the jump of her ribs, when she was ready, and he pinned her gently. She arched her hips up so he could ease into her, and she clung to him, her breath hot in the crook of his neck as he moved in her, slowly, slowly, teasing both of them, prolonging the mad, wicked bliss of being so tightly, hotly sheathed. The friction of his chest against her nipples. The heat of their gazes, locked.

"James . . . *please* . . . I . . ."

Her head whipped back and her body bowed beneath him. He followed her, seconds later, into the heavens, shattered into light and cinders, her name on a hoarse cry.

The clock softly bonged two o'clock.

"We've less than a fortnight before you leave for Paris," he said.

The word "we've" was the first formal acknowl-edgement of their conspiracy. That this flagrant breaking of the rules at The Grand Palace on the Thames and sex after dark was something they were mutually deciding to do, and intended to continue doing until she was gone. They were officially lovers.

"Yes," she said.

But there was no reason to think of anything other than this moment.

He had never before felt so full of things that he could not form into words. And he supposed that was the point of operas and sex, so that you could feel and communicate things you could never say.

She left with the full complement of hairpins she'd had when she'd first arrived.

Chapter Fourteen

୧◌◌◌◌◌ঌ

OF THE hundred tickets optimistically made available for the Night of the Nightingale, ten now had been sold.

"Perhaps people come the day of the show. Perhaps on the day of the show we can send Dot out with a bell to lure people back for a shilling," Delilah said, half joking. But only half.

There was a silence.

"May I?" Dot asked quietly.

She loved the idea of shouting and ringing a bell. She fervently *longed* one day to do it. She hardly dared hope she would be allowed.

"I think not," Delilah said regretfully.

Handkerchiefs, neatly folded and embroidered with TGPOTT, awaited early guests. Bowers of paper flowers bloomed in the sitting room.

The days seemed to pass rather too quickly.

Several of their handbills advertising the event had been slid under the door of The Grand Palace on the Thames. One had been violently hatched through with an "X," on a second someone else had written, "Are you mad?" and on the third someone had drawn a surprisingly accomplished, very detailed penis.

They all mutely stared at it in astonishment.

I think I recognize him, Mariana was tempted to say.

She thought they might laugh. They were not milquetoasts, these ladies.

Then again, they might not. Recognizing penises was probably what harlots did, and her reputation had only recently been mildly rehabilitated by one article.

"It's going to be a triumph," Delilah maintained, firmly.

JAMES COULD NEVER possibly answer, let alone read, all of the letters sent to him.

His Man of Affairs did that for him, sorting out and setting aside the ones he thought he ought to see, or would prefer to personally answer. A fresh stack of these had just been delivered to him at The Grand Palace on the Thames. He reached for the one on top, from a Mrs. Anne Jenkins of Portsmouth.

He broke the seal on the letter. Something that flashed silver like a coin spilled out into his hand.

He exhaled. It was a Waterloo Medal. The heft of it was familiar; every man who'd been at Ligny, Quatre Bras, or Waterloo had been given one. He had one, too. He ran his thumb across the name engraved on the edge: *William Jenkins.*

The letter read:

Dear General Blackmore,

My son Billy passed of an illness recently. He said to me on his deathbed, "Send my Waterloo Medal to General Blackmore, and tell him he's the finest man I ever knew. He's the one who brought me home to you." He was on a rough path, my Billy, before the army. I thought I would lose him to gaming hells and bawdy women and other bad sorts. We scraped all we had to buy a commission, and he said you made a man of him. He never left home without your book in his pocket. He married a good woman and we have two grandchildren.

Billy was my heart. I should have liked more years with him. This is a small thing indeed, but I wanted you to know that you had Billy's gratitude and his mother's. There are no words for how much you have meant to us.

Yours Sincerely,
Anne Jenkins

His breath left him in a short gust.

He dropped his forehead into his hand and thought: Jenkins. Did he remember Jenkins? He thought so, yes: an ensign when he was a lieutenant colonel in India. Blue eyes like wide, terrified circles when they'd first met. Quick learner. Ultimately a very good soldier. He'd been the boy's first commander.

He could not recall when he'd last wept for one man at a time. He wasn't certain he even could now. He'd needed to learn how to accommodate that kind of loss swiftly early on, and besides, the English were not weepers. Grief was part of his soul's geography; it had formed a canyon of sorts, through which it ran, deeply and contained. It did not slow him. He did not hover on its banks and stare into its waters. But it was there, nevertheless. Always driving him on to his victories. It was one of the things that gave him gravity. It made him grateful for every bloody day he still walked the earth.

He knew what it had cost this mother for Billy to be a soldier. And that's what he would write to her. *Thank you for your sacrifice and for your son. His service was exemplary.* And more. Whatever he wrote would never be enough, but it would mean the world to her.

He experienced a swift internal whipsaw between irritation, then guilt over the irritation. The pendulum always steadied itself at duty again. This adulation and gratitude formed the confines of his world. He was a blessed man. He was a trapped man.

He picked up the miniature of his son. Closed his hand around it as if he could protect that twenty-two-year-old from any harm. How bloody lucky he was that he still had his boy.

As he'd told Mariana, he had no awareness of being a hero as he apparently went about being heroic. Would it break this mother's heart all over again to know that her son's hero was something less, or something more, than everyone thought?

Would it dishonor the memory of the son she'd given to the war, would she think him a hypocrite, if she knew that he'd willfully broken rules and violated the hospitality of The Grand Palace on the Thames to have vigorous sex again and again with the kind of woman who'd been to a gaming hell and had inspired a duel? A woman who would generally horrify a mother like her?

What on earth was he doing with Mariana? Was he mad?

Would Jenkins think he'd lived a lie if he'd discovered before he died that his hero had feet of clay?

How many Jenkinses were out there, even now?

He was in many ways perfectly ordinary. Last night he and Mariana had discussed Helga's apple tarts, and he'd found it a very satisfying conversation. It seemed, in fact, that a conversation merely required her participation in order to be enjoyable. In fact, increasingly, moments merely required her presence in order to be enjoyable.

He was capable of being diverted by stories of a cobbler's shop. He liked, but did not require, ceaselessly elevating conversation. He was learned, but he wasn't Aristotle. The blood of his peasant ancestors still ran through his veins. She was dazzlingly clever and funny. But she was also, surprisingly, a source of peace.

He glanced down at his heavy, gleaming signet ring, the first one in his family's history. The one he hoped to pass down for generations to come. The seal that had become synonymous with all that was good and right and brave. What he wanted for his family and for his legacy remained unchanged, and what he needed to do to ensure it remained unchanged, too.

Christ.

If they could only see the way Mariana looked at him at night. That welcoming, fiercely joyous, tender, almost too-open generosity. *Take all you need*, she seemed to say.

He hadn't known. He hadn't known what he'd needed. Or that he'd needed so much.

"WHAT DO YOU call this?" she murmured as she trailed her tongue along the cords of his neck.

"Neck. *Collo.*"

James was flat, naked on the bed, like a great, beautiful beast she'd slain.

She was going to devour him.

The thrilling, massive, hard, dangerous beauty of him. He looked built to conquer. The ditches between the rises of muscle. The dips between his belly and hips, where she could fit her hands and hold him fast when he was inside her. Thighs like furry cannons. Her head was light, too filled with lust and admiration.

"And this?" She traced the outline of the furred chest with a single finger tangling in the dark hair, a thread or two of silver in it.

"Chest," he murmured. *"Il petto."*

She did not know if the gully between those muscles had a name. He was sectioned in quadrants, like armor. She found scars.

She ventured there anyway, with tongue and fingertips, with teeth and breath. She loved feeling the ripple and tension of him as he hissed in a breath of pleasure.

She smoothed her hand across it, laid her cheek there. Applied her lips.

"This?" she murmured.

"Belly. *Pancia*."

She felt his voice rumbling beneath her lips.

"And this." She dipped her tongue.

"*Ombelico*."

"And this?" she whispered. She closed her lips over his cock.

"*Paradiso*," he sighed.

Heaven.

She laughed softly and pulled away. "I am getting *quite* an education."

She closed her mouth over his cock again.

His low groan of pleasure was more inebriating than a pint of bolted liquor. More drugging than anything Mr. Delacorte might sell to an apothecary.

"Mariana . . ." He half laughed. "I beg of you . . . *succhi . . .*"

"*Ti succhio adesso*," she whispered, and did just that.

It was quiet apart from the tiny sounds of the crackle of the fire, and of her lips, her fists, her tongue, her fingers moving over him in the rhythm and friction that she had learned, in a few short nights, drove him near to insanity. He twined his hands in her hair. There was a part of him that battled the pleasure, and she understood. To be so wholly owned by it, to abandon yourself to the mercy of desire, to another person's mercy—it wasn't in his nature to surrender. But the deep and molten seam of passion was in his nature. And the primal hunger was. And the gift he had for giving pleasure was. He understood pleasure the way he understood war.

Or maybe all of this was just the alchemy of the two of them, the duke and so-called harlot, together.

His low groans and soft oaths, his hips lifting from the bed.

"Dear God," he rasped. "Please."

And who was this person she became? She wantonly sought her own pleasure. She wanted to look down into his face consumed with his own lust. Watch the stunned wonder in his face at the sight of her body moving over his. The dark ferocity as he raced toward his release.

She lowered herself onto his cock.

And for a time she controlled it. Until she heard him growl, and he arced his hips upward as his release rocked him. Whipped from her body, she heard her own voice as if from a thousand miles away, frantically calling his name.

They collapsed side by side. He turned and wrapped his arms around her, pulled her against his body, and she burrowed in.

He felt ferociously protective of this small, lush, velvety, feral, gentle, generous person. How dangerous, in some ways, it felt to just hold her.

For four mad nights in a row, she had come to him.

Last night he had closed the door and had at once gently pinned her against it. He hadn't said a word, but she'd read *now* in his face, and she had reached for the buttons on his trousers. He took her against that locked door, his hands scooped beneath her buttocks as he thrust, her legs wrapped around his waist, her breath in his ear, whispering oaths, begging him, urging him on.

The night before, on a blanket laid out in front of the fire, she'd crouched on her knees, round arse up in the air, while his hands glided over her back and between her legs as he moved in her. He'd watched her fingers curl into the blanket to withstand the pleasure, her little muffled moans of amazement at the sheer magnitude of pleasure the two of them could conjure together.

And conversation meandered, lazily and idyllically as a spring, between lovemaking. Profound and utterly mundane. Laughter and lulls. Those moments were the easiest his life had ever been.

Now, behind them the pendulum on the clock swung toward one o'clock in the morning. Gently, softly, he stroked her shoulder, her arm, her hip, her thigh and back again.

"Lovely as velvet," he murmured. *"Velluto."* He would love to dress her in velvet. Shower her in shiny things.

"Velluto," she murmured. He could feel her smile. Feel her body begin to melt into surrender again.

He slipped his fingers softly, softly between her thighs. Drew delicate patterns with his fingertips.

"Like satin," he murmured. *"Raso."* She would glow in satin.

"Raso." Her voice lulled. Her breath was swifter now.

"Wet," he predicted on a whisper into her ear, as his fingers delved to stroke. She was hot and slick again, and he caressed until he heard that sweet sound, that little whimper in her throat.

"Luscious," he whispered, as he moved his other hand to her breast. He did not know the word for "luscious"; he could not think of words at all anymore.

His hands traveled this path, teasing, languorously arousing, until she was rippling against him.

"James . . ." His name on a frantic breath. As though some cyclone threatened to pull her away and only he could save her. It made him wild.

He had never felt more valorous than when he made her come, her body borne upward on a silent scream.

"Yes?" he whispered to her. "Once more?"

"Yes. Again, yes."

He guided his cock into her, and once again they moved together, languidly, entwined, toward that bliss that seemed to have no end.

And as they lay quiet, recovering their breath and their senses, the clock hand made its inexorable journey toward the time she would return to her room.

"Mariana . . ." he said softly.

He drew her long, long rose-gold hair out between his fingers. Soon she would have to bundle and pin it up again. *"Sei bella sotto ogni tipo di luce."*

She waited for him to translate.

"You are beautiful in every kind of light."

VALKIRK HAD DRAWN a small picture of a horse with a fluffy tail and had written three paragraphs that thrilled him and, unfortunately, that had nothing to do with his book he was supposed to be writing, when there was a tap on his door.

He glanced at the clock.

Mariana had just departed. She'd brought with her today ten sentences involving the words "velvet," "suck," "the duke," "naked," and "hairy," among others. Even Primrose and Phillip made love in exciting ways.

As a result, he was semiaroused, and he suspected he would remain in that condition for the rest of the afternoon.

And then would come the night. He lived for nights now.

He got up, regretfully threw the filthy little sentences on the fire, and answered the door to find Dot.

"Your Grace," Dot whispered, and curtsied. "I'm so sorry to disturb your concentration."

"You don't need to whisper, Dot. It's broad daylight, and my writing is not so easily addled by interruption."

How he wished that was true.

"You've a visitor in the parlor down below," she said loudly. "He says his name is Arthur. Your son."

Christ.

"He looks just like you!" she added, quite pleased. "Thinner, perhaps."

"How in the bloody hell did he . . ."

He trailed off at Dot's wide eyes.

"There's no jar here, Your Grace." She was back to whispering. "And I won't tell."

"But I've to set a good example at all times, Dot," he said gravely.

"Oh, right, of course," she said quickly. "I forgot."

"Will you please tell my offspring I'll be down in about five minutes? Thank you."

"I'll bring tea!" she said, and dashed off.

HE COULD NOT deny that, exasperated or not, his heart gave a leap when he saw his tall son standing in the center of the little reception room. It was admittedly good to see him. He was as lanky as James, and better-looking, and probably a nicer person. He had his mother to thank for that.

"Arthur. How did you . . ."

Arthur spun around to greet him, grinning. "I pestered your Man of Affairs to tell me where you were staying. You haven't answered my letter."

"My Man of Affairs is a bit of a tough nut to crack, given that he both worships and is frightened of me. Well done on the pestering, I suppose."

"I learned conquering from the best. What *are* you doing *here*, Father?"

"I've promised my publisher I'd have my book finished by the end of the month. It was a bit difficult with all the hammering going on at the town-house, and too many other distractions."

"Ah! So you've taken a room in this little plain place . . . a bit like . . . like a monk's cell?"

If only he knew how far, far from the truth this really was.

James snorted. "No. Not at all like a cell. Good God, I think perhaps I've allowed you to live too sheltered a life if you think this place is anything like a cell."

"But . . . the furniture doesn't even match, does it?" Arthur looked more puzzled than censorious.

"Of course it does. It all has legs and backs and seats. What more does it need?"

James was being deliberately perverse.

"It's . . ." His son, unbeknownst to either of them, was looking curiously around the little room as every guest who'd seen it had previously done, with its worn but pretty furniture that didn't quite match, and the carved pilasters fashionable last century, and wondering at the source of its charm.

Because it *was* charming and welcoming immediately.

"It is actually rather nice," Arthur said finally, sounding surprised. "For a little building by the docks."

"It's very comfortable and pleasant, it came highly recommended by a friend I hold in high esteem, and it was peaceful up until five minutes ago. I have a feeling you're going to say something to change that," the duke said dryly.

"I'm just . . . well, I came about one thing, originally. But on my way here, I saw this in a shop on Bond Street."

From inside his coat he produced a handbill for the Night of the Nightingale.

James took it.

> *Mariana Wylde. One Night Only.*
> *The Grand Palace on the Thames.*

It was instantly, oddly disorienting.

He'd been so nearly cloistered here that he'd forgotten the name of the woman with whom he'd spent mad, endlessly sensual nights was currently distributed around London. Because she was an entertainer. Not only that, a notorious one.

He remembered very clearly how he had once viewed her.

How his son no doubt viewed her now. *Common.*

For a mad, jarring moment, he wondered: was his affair merely the inevitable result of forced proximity?

Was this, indeed, how men like him became fools for women like her?

One Night Only.

Soon, it would be all they'd have left.

The thought of that tensed his muscles again, and his face went grim. He knew at once that proximity had nothing to do with the inevitability.

"So I wondered . . . why on earth are you living in a boardinghouse haunted by a woman like that?" Arthur sounded a little amused. But mostly deadly serious.

James slowly lifted his head.

"Women . . . like . . . what?" he said softly.

His son's eyes flared widely in surprise. He'd heard that tone often enough to know he needed to tread carefully.

"It's just that I was surprised to discover that"— he lowered his voice—"it was thought she'd fled the country, or drowned herself, due to the scandal, and now suddenly all is well and she's putting on a show?"

"The whole mess involving Kilhone and Revell, you mean."

"Of course."

"To my earlier question. Could you kindly elucidate how she differs from other women of your acquaintance?"

He was simultaneously coldly incensed and genuinely curious about what Arthur would say.

But his son was both clearly reluctant to elucidate and baffled by James's tone.

"You've known me your entire life, Arthur. Tell me, what opinion do you have of my patience?"

"Well, they've *wiles*, don't they?" His son had lowered his voice again. "Women like her. And their morals are . . ."

Something in his father's expression killed the end of his sentence.

"Are you laboring under the misapprehension that the ladies of the *ton*, young or old, do not possess wiles? You're married, for God's sake. How do you suppose you got that way? I hope you're not thinking it was entirely your idea."

"She . . ." He paused and furrowed his brow to think about it. "Do you think . . . my wife was . . . She wouldn't *dream* of . . . having wiles." He trailed off, amidst a dawning comprehension.

Valkirk snorted. "Thank God for women and their wiles, or men would never get anything done."

"Hmm. Well, Miss Wylde had *two* lovers, whom she set against each other, and one shot the other, and he barely survived. I shouldn't like to see that happen to you."

And this was what happened to gossip. And why, even when it vanished from the newspaper, it grew on, misshapen, like a cancer, and spread among society. At the center was something approximating truth, but the farther it traveled, the more contours grew ragged and wrong and increasingly evil.

"Lies," James said coldly.

Which brought his son up short. "It was in the *London Times*," he pointed out cautiously. "Kilhone was shot. Two men were involved."

"Yes. That much was true. They printed lies. It was gossip, and the rest was lies."

Since his father was so seldom wrong, and arguing with him had always proved a fool's errand, his son fell quiet.

But he was clearly still confused.

For God's sake. He'd managed to keep his son out of gaming hells and away from lightskirts who excelled at getting young aristocrats, particularly drunk ones, to part with their money. He was educated and erudite. He was a kind person, and perhaps a trifle too lazy and too innocent.

But what had tested him? Did he *need* to be tested?

He'd wanted him to be innocent of the worst of the world. Who would wish upon his own child the things he'd seen? God willing, there would be no more wars in England in his lifetime. He'd thought doing some actual work might help shape Arthur's character into something sturdier and more distinct. It was why he'd given him the farm—raising sheep and selling quality wool seemed like just the sort of thing a clever man could transform into a useful, profitable enterprise.

And yet here they were.

"Three things, Arthur. Do you really think one small woman can cause an outbreak of duels? Secondly, do you really think I'd be so reckless with my life or anyone else's? And thirdly, do you really think *anyone* is going to *best* me in a duel?"

"It's just . . . at a certain age . . . men take notions to . . ."

He wasn't brave enough to continue that sentence in light of the duke's expression.

"I'm forty-three years old. I may yet live another year."

A tense silence ensued.

And then James understood his son, was, in fact, genuinely worried.

He'd lived with a father whose job could have killed him anytime. He thought of Mariana watching her father blown off a jetty, lost forever, and the pure joy she took in the memory of the mere sight of green fields, and all the boys lost in the war, and— His astonishing good fortune swept over him, and suddenly all frustration with his son gave way to patience. And gratitude.

He took pains to gentle his tone.

"You've naught to worry about. Miss Wylde is a guest in a boardinghouse. I am a guest in this boardinghouse in an entirely different wing. I have no intention of dying anywhere apart from my bed, at an advanced age. I am focusing on completing my memoirs in a place where I thought no one would be able to find me to interrupt me. Clearly this is one of those rare occasions where I am wrong."

His son took this in. "Truthfully, it does sound like something you would do."

"The tea is good, Arthur. Sit. Drink it."

His son sank down onto a settee and obeyed. He poured, sugared, and sipped, then lifted his eyebrows appreciatively.

He had another look around the room again, and the faintly pleased, faintly puzzled look settled in.

The duke sat on the settee opposite him.

"How *are* your memoirs going, Father?"

"Oh, apace."

"What part have you reached?"

"I'm just about to write the chapter about the time my son arrived to warn me about the wiles of women."

His son grinned. "I told a few friends you were writing your memoirs. They're eager to read them. Did you know, every boy I knew at Eton was given a copy of *Honor* as soon as they could read? 'Cor, he's *your* da?' I was so proud. You made the world seem like a safer, nobler place for everyone. I traded stories about you for favors."

The duke took this in. Why, suddenly, this swoop of crushing sadness, and where did it come from?

It was as if something, in this moment, was being irrevocably decided for him.

How could he ever tear down or tarnish the image of himself so cherished by his son?

"I've friends who confided in me that they grew up asking, 'What would Valkirk do?' every time they encountered a particularly sticky wicket."

"For God's sake, Arthur. I'm hardly Moses on the mountain. I wrote *Honor* during the boring parts of war. They could also read Marcus Aurelius, just for starters, if they'd need of some wisdom."

"True. You've not got a patch on Marcus Aurelius."

The duke laughed. Thank God Arthur had a sense of humor.

"Still, it's a comfort to me knowing that when I have children they will grow up with you as such an influence. And that boys who grow up without fathers have someone like you to look to for guidance. So thank you, Father."

James merely gave him a slight wry smile. He had a feeling that all of this flattery was leading to something.

"You look different," Arthur said suddenly.

"Perhaps I'm fatter. The food here is good, and the hospitality is unparalleled."

"Noooo . . . don't think that's it." He fixed his father with a startlingly good approximation of his own patented penetrating look. He had his mother's blue eyes. "On dit says you've been accepting dinner invitations." Now he was fishing.

"Yes," the duke said curtly.

"Galworthy?"

"Yes. Why?"

"The last time I saw him at White's, he mentioned he'd invited you to dinner."

"He did. I accepted. I went."

Arthur studied him, and apparently realized the futility of continued questions along those lines.

He lowered his teacup to its saucer. He took a breath.

"Well, then. As I mentioned earlier, I'm not really here to interrogate you about opera dancers." He said it lightly.

"She's a singer."

Arthur's eyes flared in surprise.

Too late, James realized how sharply he'd spoken. Hearing Mariana reduced to two words, one of them wrong, both of them disdainful, had slid into him like a shiv. Somewhere out of reach of his control.

His son cleared his throat. "Opera singer, then. I've found a potential buyer for the farm," he said quietly.

He waited for his father to say something.

James did not.

"I think you'd like him," he pressed on. "Name of Elkhorn. He was born on a farm in Germany, raised in England. Fought for England, made a good bit of money and inherited some, and he'd like to retire to the country. Knows sheep and cattle. He'll be here four days from Friday. It's Cathryn's birthday that Sunday and I thought . . . I just thought . . . will you come out to talk to him?"

Valkirk sighed.

"We'd be . . . we'd be honored by your visit, just the same. And do you remember that day we went fishing on the Ouse, when I was ten years old?" His son still sounded tentative. Almost wistful.

His son shouldn't need to feel "honored" to get a visit from his father.

Nor feel so cautious about issuing the invitation. Or have so few memories of his father that they both knew precisely which day they'd gone fishing on the Ouse. By rights he would have had dozens of memories of fishing on the Ouse with his father.

And this was it, James realized suddenly, with a bludgeoning guilt. This was his son's challenge in the world; the thing that had tested him and shaped his character, for better or worse. He had a father who was more knowable as a book than as a man. Who belonged more to England than to his family. He had so seldom been present. So often away on campaign. A son who had lost his mother five years ago, and had only him now.

He wanted to say yes.

And yet . . . it meant he'd be away in Sussex on the Night of the Nightingale.

And he imagined Mariana standing in front of the staff of The Grand Palace on the Thames. Perhaps some of the local drunks who spent good portions of their days propped against buildings, who could be lured in by the promise of lemon seed cakes and ratafia to fill seats. He wanted her to be able to look out and see someone who understood that her beauty and greatness was due to far, far more than her voice.

He had four more days with her. Only four more days.

Perhaps his son's appearance was a sign, and a reminder of his duty, and a mercy. The end of their affair demarcated by life's demands, their goodbyes swift. They would go their separate ways.

"You're determined to sell it?" Less a question than an affirmation.

He could not deny he was disappointed.

His son stared into his tea. "I understand the farm is important to you, sir. It's less that I want to sell it, than I would like to build my wife the home of her dreams . . . and I want to design that home myself, and to do it with my own resources. She wants the wing with the dormers and turrets, and I refuse to trouble you for money, sir." He said this firmly. "I know how fortunate I've been and how fortunate my children will be."

"You're interested in architecture?" James said sharply. It was the first he'd heard of it.

"I'm *passionate* about it."

"Well, that's quite a fine thing."

Arthur's face blazed with pride. "Thank you. I've been studying it, to tell you the truth. And . . . I'd hoped you'd give some consideration to my reasons for wanting to sell it. And shouldn't the land and livestock go to someone who has the will and knowledge to make it prosper? And I know . . . I think Cathryn would like to have you. Show you off a bit around town." His son's smile was crooked. A little diffident.

James hesitated.

"Yes. Of course I'll come. I'd be happy to."

Arthur's face went brilliant with pleasure, which he quickly tamped. Probably from force of habit.

Guilt jabbed James in the solar plexus. It was just that easy to make his son happy, and it was a joy to do it. How many of those happy expressions had he missed when he was on campaign? Traveling on business for the crown? When parliament was in session?

"Well, I'll leave you to your work." Arthur stood at once. He was used to leaving his father to his work, too.

James also stood. "It was good to see you. Truly. Even if you scolded me," James said.

They shook hands, and James added a back pat that almost but not quite turned into a hug. "I would hope this goes without saying, but please do not disclose my location to anyone, and that includes Cathryn."

"I wouldn't dare compromise your safety or your reputation, sir."

And with that little offhand reference to the dangerous Miss Wylde again, he was gone.

Chapter Fifteen

❦

THE SERIOUS business of fashioning the little tissue paper roses which, they decided, would be strung on thread and festooned across the backs of chairs, and stuffed into urns that would occupy either end of the refreshments table and along the walls of the room, continued in the sitting room that night. The resident gentlemen of the house—Captain Hardy, Lord Bolt, and Mr. Delacorte—were at present building said refreshments table from lumber left over from the stage. The table would be draped with a tablecloth elevated to elegance by more garlands. The duke was out tonight.

All twenty of the questionable handkerchiefs had been embroidered with TGPOTT, the initials of The Grand Palace on the Thames, and the fishnets—dyed in indigo in vats in the new Triton Group warehouse—had been fetched back home. The ladies had spent the afternoon painstakingly affixing to them their stars of various sizes at different lengths.

And then Captain Hardy and Lord Bolt and Mr. Delacorte had gallantly scaled ladders for the heavy work of suspending and draping them from the ceiling while the ladies stood below, supervising, criticizing, critiquing, bickering, pondering, and instructing.

Within two hours, the goodwill of Captain Hardy and Lord Bolt was as full of holes as the fishing nets.

"I think," Captain Hardy said carefully, when he'd descended, "we need to make hiring footmen a priority."

Lucien nodded slowly in agreement.

They both received copious amounts of fussing, sympathy, and gratitude from all of the ladies for their efforts. In truth, attempting to hire even one proper footman remained a trial. One prospect had stolen a spoon. Another had swiped his hand across Angelique's bottom. Good footmen could work nearly anywhere, and Angelique and Delilah offered ordinary wages, excellent food, lots of work, and a location by the docks. The search continued, attended with passionate interest by all the maids employed there.

"Oh, *look*, everyone," Delilah breathed, and pointed up.

They all stood beneath their handiwork, heads tipped back, and experienced awe at their ingenuity.

The nets had each taken a slightly different amount of dye, and layered and swagged, the effect was surprisingly beautiful. It was, indeed, like looking up at a cloud-hazed midnight sky. The stars they'd carefully constructed twisted gently, twinkling in the low light of a setting sun pouring in through the windows.

Mariana slowly paced the ballroom to where she'd stood and kissed the duke for the first time. She gazed up to find one of the largest stars dangling over her head. She wondered if it was the Star of Damocles, or the sort she ought to wish on.

Now all they needed was a moon. It seemed, suddenly, the most important part of the stage decorations, the thing that would illuminate her ethereally from behind while she sang onstage. But no one yet had any (good) ideas about how to craft one.

Because of the net raising, or as they preferred to think of it, sky raising, Dot had got hold of the newspaper late today, and was making up for lost time by reading the gossip aloud while all the ladies made folded roses in the sitting room.

"Oh, look. Here's a little bit in the gossip columns called 'The Disappearing Duke.'"

"Oh, wouldn't that be an exciting story, Miss Wylde! Maybe he's in the *attic* . . ." Mrs. Pariseau suggested slyly.

"Because he's trying to get some privacy to write a book?" Mariana said.

They all giggled.

"Can you imagine? The Disappearing Duke. You could turn it into a song, Miss Wylde."

Mariana laughed. Then she affected an ominous baritone and a sea-chanty cadence. "Oh, the duke disappeared one dark winter day—"

Dot gasped so suddenly and violently that Mariana clapped a hand over her heart.

"Sorry, Dot. I didn't mean to frighten you! I hadn't even gotten to the scary part of the song yet!"

"Sorry to frighten *you*, Miss Wylde. But oh, my goodness! They're talking about *our* duke! The Duke of Valkirk. On the gossip page!"

The dread—the premonition—was so instant and leaden it gave her vertigo.

She prayed no one had said a word about her. How would anyone know? She hadn't met anyone during her trips to his room, apart from Gordon the cat, who seemed pleased to see her.

The august and valorous Duke of Valkirk, lately a coveted presence at the best tables in the ton—notably, the ones set with the monogrammed silver and the prettiest daughters—has suddenly vanished. No one has seen him for dinner for nigh on a fortnight. Could it be that he's decided he wants to look across at a certain pair of celebrated brown eyes forever? The on dit is that his last supper with the family of a certain Lady G will be his last supper as a single man.

Her ears rang as though she was a tea tray and had been unceremoniously dropped from a great height, by, perhaps, Dot.

She suddenly couldn't quite feel her limbs.

"Oh, my goodness. So many new words in this

one, but then, that fits, don't it, Miss Wylde, as he's teaching you words."

"Doesn't it," Angelique, who was the person responsible for so many of Dot's new words, corrected her absently.

"Doesn't it," Dot repeated, dutifully. "What is 'valorous,' by the way?"

"Brave," Mariana said shortly. "Like valor."

"And why did they call him 'august'? He's a bit more like December, if I had to pick a month," Dot said.

Stop talking, Mariana thought suddenly. *I cannot bear any sights or sounds or anything touching my senses right now.*

"It means esteemed. And . . . wise and respected," Delilah told her.

"Or old," Mariana said curtly.

Delilah shot her a glance. It was the word Delilah had been diplomatically skirting.

He wasn't, really. The gossip columns just never quite got things right.

"Ah," Dot said happily, as if she'd just taken a long drink of something delicious, absorbing more words and more meanings.

Mariana realized she hadn't moved. She looked at the half-made flower in her hand as if she'd never seen such a thing before.

It was almost funny how instantly and dangerously everything had stopped mattering. How instantly different reality seemed. But it was like waking up from a dream via a splash of cold water to the face.

She imagined this young Lady G, a girl likely not yet twenty. The townhouse with marble floors and ceilings twice the height of the duke from which chandeliers dripping with crystals hung. A long table set with a linen cloth and bristling with things that gleamed and glinted, candlesticks and tureens and china. She'd be pristinely lovely and lissome, her hair done up by a maid, outfitted in a virginally white gossamer gown. She'd be gazing across at the duke by candlelight with her famous eyes. He'd gaze across at her with his own beautiful eyes.

Why wouldn't he? Why shouldn't he?

He wasn't "our" duke.

And he most certainly wasn't *her* duke.

And here she was at twenty-five years old. Last night as she'd slowly lowered herself onto his cock, his hands sliding along her back, her nipples chafing his chest, she'd leaned in to lick a bead of sweat from his collarbone. That's who *she* was. A brazen hussy who knew exactly how to use her hands and mouth to make him growl hoarse oaths of pleasure.

His hair had stood up every which way because her hands had rummaged through it while they were kissing. And his eyes had softly burned into her, and that little smile, that acknowledgment of the world they created comprised of just the two of them. She lived for that, she realized. He loved to watch her, she knew. He loved to give her pleasure, too.

And now she sat in this room full of happy chatter, wearing a dress with a spot on the hem and one on the bodice that was small but stubborn, feeling a trifle less than fresh from all the work today, though she always washed as best she could in the basin in her room. She'd already unpicked all the stitches and turned it outside in one, to keep the fabric fresh. A new dress was out of the question until she was paid to play a lobster (or a mermaid!) in Paris.

It was a madness, the lust. She'd resisted, hadn't she? A little?

Had she?

It seemed, right now, through the haze of memory, that resisting had simply not been an option, for either of them. After all, she'd shown up at his door with a candle.

What was the word for a woman like that? The *ton*—the world—did need their words and labels. She was worried the right word began with a "w" and ended with an "e." Or an "h" with a "t." Maybe they'd gotten it right from the beginning. Maybe they saw her more clearly than she saw herself.

If the duke married this girl, who was no doubt a sheltered virgin, she'd be treated just like the crystal on that imaginary table. As a precious, breakable thing who would never have to endure the challenge of a spot on her hem. Because for a duke, there was the woman you married.

And then the woman who would do nearly anything for him in the dark.

They could never be the same woman.

She'd known that, of course.

Hadn't she?

"Oh, Your Grace! Good evening!" Mrs. Pariseau called. "I don't suppose you'd like to help make paper roses?"

Mariana looked up with a start.

There he stood in the doorway, coat draped over an arm, hat in his hand. Looking every inch of what he was. Even now her body felt weak at the sight of him.

For the first time, however, she felt small and tawdry.

Her pride had taken a ringing blow. Surely that was all.

She didn't think it was fatal.

But she needed to be alone.

She turned her head away and opened her fist, amazed that she'd squeezed the little paper rose she'd been working on. It was now ragged and limp.

"I just had a meeting with my Man of Affairs about a roof repair. Paper roses would be thrilling in comparison."

She was certain he was puzzled by why she hadn't turned. She knew his face brightened when he saw hers. She was petty enough to deny him that much.

"Your Grace, we were just reading about you on page six of the *London Times*."

His face went stony. "Surely you're joking."

Dot, alarmed by his expression, silently shook her head. She held the newspaper out to him.

Mariana watched his face go thunderous.

Then carefully, studiedly, coldly blank.

He lifted his head slowly and met Mariana's eyes.

"Welcome to page six, Your Grace," Mariana said lightly. "Now we've something in common."

"Well, that, and Italian," Mrs. Pariseau said happily.

JAMES LAY MOTIONLESS on his bed. He was fully clothed, and apart from the dying fire, which he could not be bothered to get up and poke, it was dark. It was two o'clock in the morning. He'd spent the entire evening alone, waiting in an absurd agony of suspense. Starting at every sound. Every nerve on alert with hope and dread. Watching that tiny space between the door and his floor for the flash of a satin slipper.

She never came.

He was seething.

And he was in pain.

Galworthy? Galworthy's wife? His daughter? Who had done it, sent that lying little snippet of gossip to the newspaper? It was difficult to imagine Galworthy doing it, but perhaps he was desperate to marry off his daughter. Perhaps something was amiss with his finances and he needed the settlements badly, and had thus concocted a ploy to corner the oh so honorable Duke of Valkirk into a marriage.

It was almost funny that anyone, *anyone* thought that was possible.

A very bad mistake, indeed.

Perhaps one of Galworthy's servants had sub-
mitted the gossip item for money. Perhaps the
daughter herself had done it, hoping to hasten an
attachment along, or because she craved attention, or thought the attention would bring a better
match if the duke decided she was not for him.

The risk was that it exposed Galworthy's daughter to the scrutiny of *ton* gossips, and the duke to
embarrassment or accusations of faithlessness
when he'd made no such promise and had no such
intentions, certainly not now. He did not think a
few lines of printed gossip could ever embarrass
him. But they could and did appall him. A little
gossip about him merely wedged the way open for
more of it; and more of it would collect like bar-
nacles on the hull of his legacy. He had fought for
what he had now—the influence, the wealth, the
reach, the inviolable reputation—and it belonged
not only to him. It belonged to his son and to his
descendants.

And he, like his son said, belonged to the whole
country.

He would be damned if anyone would so cheaply
and willfully tarnish who he was.

He could not be embarrassed into marrying a
girl. But the gossip *could* potentially embarrass his
son and his new young wife. And while his son
ought to have thicker skin, James didn't care. He
would do anything to protect him, regardless.

He understood something now, with a resignation that made him weak and wondering. He
frankly wanted to call out whoever had put that

expression on Mariana's face—that pale emptiness, as though she was bleeding from the inside—and meet them on a field of combat, and mow them down.

But he supposed he'd be calling out himself, too. He was as much the culprit.

In his frustration, the pendulum of his thoughts swung violently and furiously in the opposite direction: *She's just an opera singer. I am a duke. How dare she make me suffer? How dare she make me wait? I could have any woman in my bed, if I chose. I could marry any beautiful girl in England.*

He knew the truth of it: if their roles were reversed, he would not have been able to stay away from her for two days.

And this meant she, incomprehensibly, was stronger than he was.

What little alliteration would they choose to use if somehow their affair was discovered? "Hero in harlot's bed." "Valkirk sinks his dirk in disgraced diva." The Rowlandson illustrations would be merciless and lurid; he could imagine them for sale at Ackermann's, with part of the populace laughing and pointing, and others crushingly disappointed and confused. There would be broadsides. Mocking pub songs. And that would be part of his legacy, too. In fact, he imagined that every part of his legacy, every assumption about who he was as a man, would be pored over and questioned, because of a woman who thought he was amusing. Whose face went soft and lit like a lamp every time she saw him. Who, when she opened her arms to him, made him feel as though he was coming home.

A girl who'd taken other lovers, kissed other men, made love with astonishing skill and sensual abandon, enjoyed champagne a little too much, hadn't quite hated her visit to a gaming hell, and who was trying to claim greatness of her own. She thought it would be safer at the top.

They could not be discovered. For his sake, and for hers.

So perhaps this gossip item was a mercy. A splash of water one threw over rutting dogs to get them to stop.

Mainly the little gossip item exposed another reality they both must face, however: there would come a day when he would make another match. He saw this as an inevitability.

And there would come a day, very soon, when Mariana was gone.

He wasn't certain how to fix this for her, or if he should. He supposed the two of them would have preferred not to face anything like reality until she'd left for Paris.

Because, as she'd said before, some people preferred their dreams to their waking life.

She'd been right about something else, too. That understanding could be found in contrasts.

As he lay there in that empty room, he had a much better understanding of loneliness, because with her he had, for perhaps the first time ever, been so blessedly, blissfully not alone.

* * *

Dear Mama,

*I hope this finds you well. I hope you
have not been worried about me. I think you'll
be pleased to learn that I've decided to join a
convent. It's the best place for someone like me,
and I think I can put my singing skills to
good use there.*

AT LEAST THIS was a letter her mother might not
be appalled to receive. After all, her mother had
always thought she was destined for great things.

She didn't write it, of course. She still hadn't
written, let alone sent, anything after those first
few words she'd written the day after she'd arrived.

Mariana had begun to believe she might make
a fine nun.

Would a convent have her? They did do a lot of
singing in convents, did they not?

And . . . spent a lot of time on their knees?

This was apparently who she was: a woman who
made jokes to herself featuring fellatio and nuns,
in order to make herself feel better about adopting
that position in the duke's bedroom after dark.

She'd adopted a lot of other positions there, too,
granted.

But surely if anyone was qualified for martyr-
dom, she was, after occupying the sitting room with
everyone else as well as the duke, who was not doing anything but quietly being a duke and making

no progress on his memoirs. And sitting at the same dinner table at which the duke sat, eating. She needed to eat, after all. She could not waste away to nothing before she redeemed herself by singing in front of—ten, was it, at last count, paid attendees?— and attempted to earn her room and board, not to mention recover a little of her pride in the process.

Playing a singing lobster ought to shave her pride down to a nub. But she was going to be so spectacular that the singer playing the mermaid would expire from envy, and in her fantasies, Mariana would then send her sympathy flowers, take over the part, and become a legend.

The pleasant buzz of plans for decorating the ballroom for the Night of the Nightingale continued, and she could shelter herself within that. There was no need to even glance his way.

He certainly glanced *her* way. How she knew this, she couldn't say. She merely felt it.

So she could do these things, bravely enough.

But it was more than she could ask of herself at the moment to sit across from him, alone, for Italian lessons. Or to speak to him. Or to look at him straight on. Though, like a feature of a landscape, say, a mountain, she could always feel his presence even when he was nowhere within her line of vision. She had a terrible suspicion that he would be a feature of her landscape for the rest of her life.

She didn't know if by distancing herself she was punishing him, though she was certain that was the end result. She was neither gladdened by nor displeased by the notion. She didn't know whether she was punishing herself, because she thought she deserved it for behaving like a harlot when she'd initially been so indignant to be called one.

Or if it was merely an act of self-preservation. A way of backing up slowly from the edge of devastation. Allowing herself space for the dust to settle after the initial shock, which should not have been a shock. She would see what feeling, what instinct, prevailed then.

She said to Dot the following day, "Would you please tell the duke that I have a headache, and that I fear I must beg off lessons?"

"Oh, dear. Do you need a tisane, Miss Wylde? Helga makes them. They could raise the dead."

"I think I . . . I think I merely sang too loud in the ballroom, and my brain needs a rest. But don't say that to the duke," she added hurriedly.

Dot studied her, brow furrowed. "Too much emotion," Dot suggested. More wisely than she realized.

"Yes, that's it."

When she begged off again for similar reasons the following day, Mr. Delacorte offered her a powder from his case of samples.

"Works a treat," he confided in a low voice, "but it's been known to cause the odd effect or two. I know a bloke who took it and had a vision of the Knights of the Round Table riding unicorns through Pall Mall," he told her. "Cured his *mal de tête*, however."

"While that sounds exciting indeed," she told him, "I think I just need a bit of a rest."

She could tell the sisters of the convent she was

contemplating entering that she was learning about sacrifice, too.

The last two nights—after dark, that was—had seemed resoundingly empty, cold and dark. Her little room, which she quite liked, suddenly seemed strange, and—not necessarily unfriendly—but foreign. As though everything in it was merely a prop onstage. It was so odd to realize how her feelings about the duke had flowed into and colored her feelings about everything else. Had given them outsized life and dimension.

Dear Mama,

I hope this finds you well. I regret to tell you that I knew better and I should not have done, but I imagined it anyway. Laughter and seashore walks and a family around the breakfast table with him passing the fried bread around. And finally waking up next to him every day with the sun shining through the curtains on our faces. I should not have done, because I feel a little like I have just watched all those people die.

The unfinished letter to her mother remained on her desk, and it looked just the same. It had even been dusted by the maids. It was now several weeks later than she normally sent off a letter.

She could, in theory, afford to buy another sheet of foolscap or some other size of paper now if she wanted to send a letter to her mother. After all, she had those seven pounds that Giancarlo had given to her. But she would need to pay for travel to Dover, and then pay for lodging at an inn for a night, and pay for her passage to Paris from there, as well as some food to keep her alive. She'd no idea if she'd come away a slightly richer woman after the Night of the Nightingale. She would not leave without paying the ladies of The Grand Palace on the Thames at least a little something.

Perhaps they could all work out a future bargain or trade of some sort. They were women of business.

What this all meant was that she now was officially avoiding writing a letter to her mother.

In truth, she *had* also spent more than a little time next to her bed on her knees, hands clasped. She didn't know what to pray for anymore, specifically. All of the things she wanted seemed inextricably entwined with the things she didn't.

Her prayers were more after the fashion of a thanks for current blessings, a request for blessings for everyone she knew, followed by, "I'm listening, if you've any ideas, God."

By the third day she knew she would have to face him again, alone.

AT THREE O'CLOCK, she paused in the doorway of his anteroom.

The window lit him from behind, and his face was turned toward it. He didn't appear to be working on much of anything. His pen was in his hand, but his hand wasn't moving.

The same stack of foolscap remained near his elbow. It didn't look any taller.

"*Buonasera*, Your Grace." She said it as politely and lightly as she could, which was no mean feat when she was dragging her spirit about like a millstone.

She could swear he'd stopped breathing when he heard her voice.

He pivoted abruptly.

For a long moment, they merely regarded each other from that distance.

"*Buonasera*, Miss Wylde," he finally said just as politely. His voice was hoarse. "Won't you please come in?"

Her heart was beating a little too quickly as she ventured forward.

Oh, what the very sight of him did to her breathing. What a sacrifice it had been to deny herself the sight of him, even if he was fully clothed.

As she came closer, she saw that he looked gorgeous, a bit hard done by, and fully his age.

There were shadows beneath his eyes. His hair was standing up a little, as if he'd just pushed it back with an impatient hand.

For that matter, she doubted she was looking as fresh and rosy as the eighteen-year-old or so daughter of an earl. She hadn't slept much, either. All the exercise she'd been getting at night had helped her sleep, apparently.

When she wasn't riding or being ridden by a duke, it seemed she worried about her future.

Mainly she'd lain awake with an ache so resonant it was a shock she didn't at all times hum sorrowfully, like a woodwind.

She pulled out the chair slowly and settled in.

He had not prepared her station. There was, in fact, nothing of his usual crisp air of taking everything in hand.

He looked as though he'd fought a battle with himself and lost.

He looked the way she'd never before seen him. Almost defeated.

"I am glad to see you," he said finally. His voice was a bit raspy. As if they might be the first words he'd said out loud to a human today.

"That is kind of you to say."

She stubbornly refused to return the sentiment in kind.

Her soul still felt sore sitting here before him. Like an empty socket, with the wind whistling through it.

She wanted him to know that she would prevail, no matter what.

"Has your . . . health improved?" he asked.

"Yes, thank you," she said quietly. "It was my *testa*," she added. She pointed. Well, her head was partially involved. She was not going to be a diva and point to her heart. She was English, not Italian.

"Ah. Did you speak to Mr. Delacorte about remedies?"

"He gave me a powder. I hesitated to try it, as he said it both cured headaches and sometimes caused visions."

"Ah, but you like dreams, Miss Wylde."

She hesitated.

Her throat felt tight. "Not always," she said.

He said nothing. He'd clearly been miserable. Which in truth gave her no pleasure.

"Would you like me to leave you to your work, Your Grace?"

"No," he said so sharply she blinked.

He took a breath. "That is . . . please stay. We'll have a lesson."

He retrieved a sheet of foolscap for her and laid a quill next to it.

After that, neither one of them moved or said anything. She wished she had prepared something specific, something witty and urbane or acerbic, to say. Something a more sophisticated, jaded woman might say. Something like, *How do you say, "Congratulations on your upcoming nuptials, Your Grace," in Italian?*

He cleared his throat. "I thought of an Italian phrase you might wish to know, Miss Wylde."

Her heart lurched.

"It's . . . *Non credere ai pettegolezzi. Il pettegolezzo non è vero.*"

She knew *vero*. Truth.

He took a breath. "Don't believe the gossip. The gossip isn't true."

She stared at him. She could feel her breathing deepening and quickening.

She was not going to cry. She willed herself not to do it.

She saw the increasing light in her own face reflected in his own. But there was something she needed to know. Something she needed to hear him say aloud.

"But one day it will be," she said. Carefully. Evenly.

The silence was long.

"It . . . seems likely," he said finally, just as carefully. Very gently. His voice was still hoarse.

She held herself very still, to prevent the pain, which seemed to congregate at the very center of her, from touching any other part of her.

"But if it seems to the *ton* that I've disappeared, it's because I find . . ." He paused, and turned toward the window again. He pressed his lips together, then turned back to look at her and said gingerly, as though he were picking his way through unstable, unfamiliar terrain, ". . . that I do not want to be anywhere other than here. I . . . I cannot imagine wanting to be anywhere other than here."

She said nothing.

She just breathed.

Breathed the beautiful air in which those words had been uttered.

They were not a declaration.

She could not expect one.

But she knew, for now, they would do.

HE DREW WHAT felt like his first full breath in two days when he saw the flash of her slippers at the door, which he opened immediately.

He took the candle gently from her, and closed the door behind her. He settled the candle on the table.

And then he reached for her, and she reached for him.

Arms folded around each other tightly, they merely held one another. He laid his cheek against the top of her head. He breathed in her hair.

She laid her cheek against his heart. She savored its thump against her skin.

It went on for a good long time, and seemed infinitely more dangerous and scandalous than immediate nudity.

The nudity happened soon enough.

Clothes were soon shed like shackles, and the tender ferocity and utter simplicity of what followed—a pounce, some deeply satisfying grappling, a swift and thorough drilling—left them both stunned and sated. Dumbstruck by their luck.

This need between them simply did not abate. It seemed to regenerate into something hungrier and more profound each time. The pleasure greater. The connection deeper. The terrain of each other's bodies more familiar, yet more richly exciting.

She lay alongside him, stroking the hair from his eyes, which were closed.

"My son came to The Grand Palace on the Thames to visit," he murmured. Her gentle hand across his forehead was bliss.

"Oh my. Did he? How lovely!"

When he didn't say anything, she added, "Or was it?"

"Mmm . . . lovely, on the whole," he said.

"How does he fare?"

"He would like me to spend a few days in Sussex with him and his wife. His wife's birthday is Sunday."

They both knew what this meant.

She was quiet. "You *must* go. If he came to you to ask, it means a good deal to him."

She knew, because he'd told her, in the meandering conversations between bouts of lovemaking, how much he regretted the time he hadn't spent with his son.

"It means . . . I shall be leaving for Sussex the day before you leave for Paris. I . . . I thought I would be here when you left."

"I know. You'll miss the Night of the Nightingale," she said wistfully.

Tell me not to go, he silently willed her.

But what would he do then if she'd said it?

He could not leave his son again. He simply wanted to be yearned for, he supposed.

"At any rate, given that we've sold almost no tickets, the crowd will be comprised of just the people who live here, their friends, and the drunk man who leans against the building now and again. I expect he'll enjoy it, though," she added. Amused. Resigned. Wistful.

He was quiet. He felt that familiar, sizzling fury at the injustice of it, of people who would deprive themselves—and in so doing, likely others, through their influence—of the elevating beauty of her voice for the nasty, unifying thrill of shunning someone. It was more about a bullying wielding of power than any outraged sense of morality. And it was also cowardice. He suspected that she, in her learning of lessons the hard way and making different choices, was ultimately more moral than that privileged lot.

"I wish it were otherwise." He meant almost literally everything.

"I've sung to smaller crowds before. I shan't mind that part, really. It's just that I wanted it to be splendid, as they've been so very kind to me here. I'm a little embarrassed. I hoped to earn a good deal of money for the ladies of The Grand Palace on the Thames. And I do wish I'd have a string quartet. They won't play for me, you see. The musicians at the theater."

Her voice had gone thick on those last words.

He couldn't speak. The notion that she would need to brace for disappointment, or feel ashamed, or pour her glorious voice into a nearly empty room made the muscles across his stomach tense.

"I would like you to be there, but I do not *need* you to be there, James. I am happier knowing you will see your son. I will stun them with splendor. And then I shall go on to play better roles, and I will look back at this and perhaps . . . laugh."

He knew she spoke truth. She'd endured before him. She would likely endure after him.

And she could, and would, leave him.

He wanted to be missed.

He turned his head to look at her. "So we've a few more days together," he said softly.

His heart thudded, waiting for her to speak what to him, in that moment, amounted almost to a vow.

The seconds he waited felt like an eternity.

"We've a few more days together," she whispered at last.

Chapter Sixteen

❧

IF NOT for Dot, the final, and arguably most important, part of the Night of the Nightingale stage decorations might never have been found.

Angelique and Helga were in the kitchen spiritedly debating whether they ought to be extravagant and have beef on Sunday, as they were, after all, hosting a duke and they could probably afford it, whilst at the same time slicing apples for tarts.

Suddenly Angelique realized they were missing one of their usual helpers.

"Have you seen Dot? She ought to have returned with the newspaper by now."

Rose, who had been promoted from the scullery to proper kitchen maid, was sleepily sifting flour. "I havna seen her," she yawned.

"She went out to get the newspaper. More than an hour ago, I'd warrant," Helga noted.

They were accustomed to hearing the news over their tea and coffee in the kitchen. And Dot liked to read the gossip aloud.

It was very early, and neither Miss Wylde nor the Duke of Valkirk appeared to be early risers, so they weren't yet about to ask whether they'd seen

Dot. Mrs. Pariseau was an early riser, and off to tea with one of her many friends in London.

She was a singular person, Dot was, but she was unfailingly reliable.

So her absence was a little worrisome.

"Shall I look in her room, Mrs. Hardy?" Rose asked. Who was not unfailingly reliable, and often looked for excuses to wander away from her post, just for the variety. Though she had a good heart and was a quick learner.

Angelique halted her apple slicing when Delilah swept into the kitchen. "Have you seen Dot, Delilah?" she said at once.

"No. Not for a few hours, I assumed she was in here with you. I did want to have a look at the newspaper." Delilah paused. "Is she missing?"

Angelique nodded slowly.

Now they were more than a little worried.

Angelique lowered her voice. "Do you suppose she eloped with the man who sold the handkerchiefs?"

She was jesting.

Mostly.

Nevertheless.

"Surprisingly, I think she's sensible about men," Delilah said.

Together they moved out of the kitchen and into the foyer, contemplating where to begin a search for her.

Mr. Delacorte was just on his way out the door with his case in his hand. He stopped abruptly

when he saw them standing beneath the chandelier, wearing concerned expressions.

They explained the cause of it.

"Let's have a good thorough look round. I'm
sure she'll turn up," he said. "I'll search from the
attic reaches of the house on down, and why don't
the two of you have a look around the Annex."

"She's afraid of ghosts," Delilah said quietly.
"She wouldn't go in the attic."

She and Angelique were somber a moment.
Each experienced a tightening clutch of worry.

"Then again, only one way to conquer a fear!"
Mr. Delacorte said cheerily.

This was a good point. One couldn't always
predict Dot logic.

Mr. Delacorte dashed gamely back upstairs,
and Delilah and Angelique made for the Annex,
swiftly, through the passage connecting the buildings, and into the corridor.

Angelique stopped sharply and placed a hand
on Delilah's arm. "Do you hear that?"

"That" was a faint keening sound.

"It's coming from the ballroom, I think," Angelique surmised.

They cautiously approached it, and this theory
was confirmed. The closer they got to the ballroom, the keening evolved into actual words. Terrifying ones.

"HELP! Heeeeellllllp! *Heeeeeellp!*"

They hiked their skirts in their hands and ran.

"HEEEELLLLP!" It was louder now.

Delilah yanked open the door, and they both burst into the room.

To discover the sky had literally fallen. The ballroom floor was a carnage of stars and nets. And in one of them something, or someone, was thrashing like a great carp.

"Heeeeelllp! It's me, Dot!"

They ran to her side and dropped to their knees. "Oh Dot! Thank God you're all right!"

"I'm not all right! I'm in a net!" She attempted to claw it away from her face and only succeeded in trapping her fingers in the gaps.

"You'll be all right in a moment," Angelique soothed. "You can stop thrashing now. How on earth did you happen to be in a net?"

"I was admiring the stars," Dot said through the holes in the net, "and then I thought, well, I think *that* one would look a little better if it was a little lower. I reached up, and I suppose I tugged too hard, and down it came, and then down everything came. Cor, was I scared!" She brightened a little. "It's a very good net, however. See how well it works!"

Attempting to free herself had diabolically only entangled her more thoroughly. Her hairpins and hair and apron strings had conspired with the net to hold her fast. Even the newspaper she'd dutifully purchased had somehow become incorporated.

"All right. Hold very still, Dot. You're making it worse," Delilah fussed.

It was ages undoing her, and a rather surgical process. Angelique was compelled to go and get a pair of scissors. In the end, Dot lost some blond hairs, and the net gained some blond hairs, but she deemed it a small price to pay for her freedom.

They got her up on her feet, and they both fussed over her and smoothed her skirts. "Poor Dot," Delilah exclaimed. "How awful for you! Are you scratched or bruised?"

Upon Dot's reflection and Delilah and Angelique's external inspection, it was discovered she was just a little dusty.

Also: more than a little blue. Some of the dye had rubbed off on her face.

Delilah had to give Angelique a little pinch to keep her from laughing when they noticed this.

"If we don't get a lot of paying guests, we can just drop the nets and shanghai the ones we have and make our money that way," Angelique said.

Delilah stifled a laugh.

"Paying guests" remained a concern. They would learn today from Lucien if they'd sold any more tickets.

"Dot, why don't you go get cleaned up. Helga needs help in the kitchen. We'll wait for Captain Hardy and Lord Bolt to return to get the nets back up."

Good God. Neither of them looked forward to asking their husbands to do that again.

They all missed Mr. Cassidy, who had found heavy work quite soothing and was happy to be paid in scones and good will.

"But I suppose it's helpful in that we know we ought not let the guests tug on the stars," Delilah said encouragingly. "We're sorry this happened to you, Dot."

"I suppose we can put it down to life's vicissitudes," Dot said blithely, and departed to get sorted out.

Both Delilah and Angelique gave a start.

"*Vicissitudes?*" Angelique whispered. "Where did she learn . . ."

Delilah shook her head, mystified.

Mr. Delacorte grinned when he saw the blue and disheveled Dot pass him on his way into the ballroom. "Good morning, Dot. Blue's your color."

"Good morning, Mr. Delacorte," she said, with dignity. "Thank you."

He surveyed the wreckage of the nets. "Oh, well, that's a pity."

"Dot was catch of the day, Mr. Delacorte," Delilah told him.

"Ha! Glad to see her safe and sound. As for me, I've been having a look round the attic," he said.

This seemed evident, as he had a cobweb in his hair, though they didn't say so yet.

"Please don't tell us you've found a ghost."

"No such luck," he said. "But you ought to come and see what I *did* find."

THEY GATHERED AROUND the sitting room at Mr. Delacorte's behest, and were silent with awe.

Mr. Delacorte had brought down from the attic a dusty stained glass window in a frame, about two feet tall and two feet wide. Against a background of deep royal blue, amber and white petals of glass had been fitted together to form a large, single, concentric circle.

"Oh my goodness. It's our *moon*," Mariana breathed.

An eager Dot had knocked on her door to tell her. Miss Wylde certainly seemed to need a lot of sleep, which was doubtless good for opera singers.

"We'll suspend it from the rafter over the stage, hang a lamp behind it. It will be beautiful," Mariana said at once.

"It has to be a good omen. It was in our own *attic*. We never would have found it if Dot hadn't been catch of the day," Angelique said.

"It was serendipitous," Dot said.

Angelique and Delilah stared at her, startled.

Dot and Mariana both glanced down and exchanged swift, secret smiles.

"You might want to have a closer look up in the attic," Mr. Delacorte said brightly, to Delilah and Angelique. "I saw a few other things up there that could be interesting."

They smiled.

"The *spiders* might want to fight you for it, though."

Their smiles vanished.

"Well, that's what husbands are for," Angelique said after a moment, wickedly.

FOUR DAYS BEFORE the Night of the Nightingale, all of the decorations were in place. The one hundred chairs retrieved from the den of iniquity, looking downright virginal with their coats of whitewash and scrubbed seats, were arrayed in two even sections with an aisle between. In the corners, bushels of paper flowers bloomed up out of huge urns. A row of green felt, purloined from battered old billiard tables and stitched, was laid down like a carpet of grass between the chairs.

They'd made a garden of the surround, lining it with pots bursting with paper roses surrounded by trailing garlands and vines.

And they hung the moon.

With a lamp situated behind, it cast a beautiful, dreamy, creamy gold light. A wall of lamps arranged in a staggered pattern on either side of the stage would light Mariana.

Who, in her simple nacre-colored satin dress flowing in Grecian lines, looked like a goddess.

It wasn't Covent Garden or the Italian Opera House. It was stunning, just the same, and they were proud.

There was a moment of silence for the beauty of what they'd accomplished, tinged with a bit of the bittersweet for Mariana, because what she deserved was a hundred tickets sold.

Eleven tickets had been sold.

Although perhaps more people would arrive the night of the performance. Especially if they sent Dot out with a bell.

(Dot still hoped.)

"I'm embarrassed," Mariana confessed. "I so hoped to return your kindness."

"We were aware of the risks. You'll be giving

us a night to remember, regardless. We have your friendship. And we would otherwise never have known how interesting Dot would have looked if she'd been born blue."

The kindness made her eyes sting.

ITALIAN LESSONS CONTINUED. Valkirk was aware that he was testing her rather relentlessly. It was as if words were weapons and fortifications he was sending with her out into the world.

She seemed to understand why he was so stern.

"Barouche," he barked.

"*Calesse,*" she replied gently.

"I need help," he demanded.

"*Aiuto,*" she told him tenderly. Her voice a thread.

He hoped she'd never need to ask for it.

Her sentences about did him in.

"*Il tuo corpo è perfetto.*"

"Your body is perfect," she'd written.

And:

"*Mi manca il duca di Valkirk.*"

"I miss the Duke of Valkirk."

He stared at those words a long time.

His throat felt tight.

He wanted to say, *Don't miss me,* because he didn't want her to suffer for even a moment.

He wanted to say, *Don't go,* but he didn't know what to say after that. He knew she must.

He did not know how to name what was between them.

The truth lay in the contrasts. If what approached

at the thought of losing her was desolation, then whatever he felt for her was precisely the opposite of that.

He had known more than one defeat in battle, but defeat was just a tool he'd used to learn to become victorious. He would never be accused of being an optimist, but he was indomitable. He'd experienced grievous losses and blows and struggled to his feet again. It was what a warrior did.

But nothing in his experience was of use to him here. Desolation was not an enemy army. It was more like a looming shadow, or a creeping mist. He couldn't grasp hold of it with logic. He couldn't conquer it with strategy. His power and influence were as nothing in the face of its inexorable approach.

But he began to think he might be able to stop it with that other tool at his disposal: money.

He wasn't yet married.

And he knew other allegedly "great" men kept mistresses.

Valkirk had always found the word "kept" distasteful in this context. One kept sheep, or horses, or pigeons, or perhaps a hothouse filled with citrus and exotic plants that ate flies, like a certain earl he knew.

Mainly because he could not imagine "keeping" Mariana any more than he could keep sunshine in a jar. And part of the magic of these few weeks had been the fact that she willingly came to him, night after night, despite the risk. Or, perhaps in part because of it. It was all good. Every bit of it.

The sweetness hid a blade, and it was this: the possibility that she might not come to him at all.

That contributed to the texture of the bliss.

And yet.

He struggled to imagine parting with her. He could not imagine a day when he did not know if she was well, or suffering from a shortage of funds, or fighting off grabby male hands, or brazening her way through a conversation full of words she hadn't yet learned.

Or suffering with a loneliness that would drive her into someone else's bed. Somehow he knew she would find no solace there. Some types of loneliness had only one cure. He was hers.

She was his.

But the notion of that was unbearable.

God help him. He just wanted to keep her.

Chapter Seventeen

⁘

THEIR LAST four nights together featured few words. Occasionally the sensual demands they made on each other in bed were nearly punishing in their ferocity, as if they were furious that life was parting them. As if in colliding, nipping, pinning, hair tugging, they could brand each other.

And other times, their hands and lips traveled every part of each other's bodies as though they could transfer the memory of each other through their fingertips right into their souls. Every texture, every curve, every bump and hollow and angle. The whorl of an ear or the space between fingers or toes, the crease of an elbow or knee, was found and caressed and loved. They played with the elasticity of desire, whipping it into a wild peak, drawing it out again until they were utterly netted in it, until the shattering release inevitably came.

Mariana knew she ought to have gotten used to goodbyes, and to paying attention only to each moment, and drawing a tall wall between the moment and anything that might follow. It was the only way she would ever be able to part with him.

She didn't want the thought of a tomorrow—of a forever—without him to steal a single second from their last moments together. When there was time, when she was alone, she would sit and, with as much pragmatism as she could muster, have a look at the condition of her heart. The way one might check to see what was left after an explosion.

Tonight he hadn't said a word, apart from her name when his release took him. She loved knowing that she was the one who could make him, in that moment, forget who he was. Take him utterly out of himself.

She felt it when his breathing went shallow, since she was using him as a pillow. It was her first clue that he was about to break the long, fraught silence.

"Mariana . . . what if you don't go to Paris?"

Her heart gave a jolt. Her languor was officially shattered, and her heart began to slam as though it were running. From or to something, she could not say.

"Stay here in London? I made a commitment to Signor Roselli. And I'll need to earn a living, of course."

She could feel his body tensing with the words he was about to say.

"I wondered if you would like to discuss a more formal arrangement."

She was afraid to breathe. Her entire being felt balanced on a wire. The moment was both exhilarating and terrifying.

"If you would . . . like to stay in London and continue to enjoy . . . our time together . . ." His words were gruff. "I can arrange for an allowance for you, and we can find an apartment to your liking, where I can"—he took a breath—"discreetly visit."

The wire snapped, and off she tumbled into the abyss.

She slowly pulled away from him. Sat up and stared as if he was a stranger.

Her hands went to her face in shock.

He sat up, too. "Mariana?"

"Oh, my God . . . all this time . . . you *did* think I was a harlot," she breathed in horror.

He visibly reeled. "What on— No. Dear God."

"You think I *aspire* to be a harlot, then? Hence the offer of money, to fund my aspiration," she countered. She could hear the increasingly dangerous brightness in her own voice.

Her lungs felt like a furnace. She suddenly could not pull in full breaths.

He was watching her warily. "I feel," he said carefully, "that the word 'harlot' as you're using it is a pejorative, that you're putting the word in my mouth, and that you're furious, but I'm not entirely certain why. And no to all of it."

Every astonishingly reasonable word he uttered was like kindling heaped upon her temper. And she didn't know what the bloody hell "pejorative" meant, but she could *surmise*.

Damn all reasonable men to hell. Damn all carefulness, all strategy, all heroes. Damn society.

Damn his ignorance of the cruelty that was his offer.

Damn her bloody heart, which he might as well have plucked out of her chest on a *spada*.

"I suppose I should consider it a compliment to my *services* that you wish to pay me for them. Your Grace."

And even as she said this, she saw herself hovering outside his door with a candle. All but quivering with desire. She had come to him. Who did that but someone determined to be a whore?

Someone in love, of course.

An idiot, madly, helplessly, hopefully in love.

An idiot who seemed destined to always, always learn things the hard way. If only she'd had a *book* on the subject ahead of time.

She could feel her heart coming apart into shards, jangling about in her chest.

"Please listen." His voice was infuriatingly steady. But she knew, because she knew the bastard now, that inwardly he was roiling. The tension around his eyes, his jaw. His hoarse breathing. He was upset, and good. She wanted everyone in the room to be upset. "What I want is to take care of you, Mariana. What I want is to take your worries away."

"I know what you want, Your Grace. *Mi vuoi scopare.* When it's convenient for you. And you're generously willing to pay me for that."

"Yes. I want to fuck you when it's convenient for me. That will never not be true," he said coldly. "On my deathbed, that will no doubt be true. It is perhaps . . . the truest thing I've ever known."

God help her, even now that bald statement just made her want to lie back and let him have his way with her.

Oh, but now *he* was angry. It was both delicious and frightening.

And he was suffering.

She was furious that it mattered to her. That she was such a fool that even now, she wanted to do something to ease his suffering.

"It would *not* be convenient for you if I was in Paris. It also would not be convenient for you if I were a famous diva, known to all, with my own money, because then you would not be able to keep it a secret. Because that's what you really want, isn't it?"

He didn't answer. She suspected that this was the first time in his life he had no idea what to say.

She knew she wasn't being entirely rational. Why didn't he know how this would destroy her?

And if she was brutally honest with herself, it wasn't the implication that she would happily take money for sex. She was fortunate life had not tested her to that extent yet.

It was hearing, definitively, that she wasn't the sort of woman he would ever marry.

And suspicions and realizations began cascading, one upon another. The momentum was such that she could not stop them, could not filter them through sense, and for a change didn't stop to consider whether it was wise to say everything she thought and felt. "You're not an impulsive man. So you must have given it some good, quality thought and decided that I'm beyond respectability. And on the heels of that, you must have decided that I couldn't possibly aspire to respectability ever again, because one just casts respectability to the wind when they're a bought and paid mistress of a duke, don't they? I'll just take my place in the demimonde. Where idiot men shoot each other over women who wait about for men to appear and fuck them."

There was a seething, fraught silence.

"It will shock you to learn," he said very, very slowly, his voice shaking with the effort of control, "that I have, foolishly, spoken without due consideration."

"No matter, James." She said this with a sort of blackly amused amazement. "I suspect these sorts of transactions are going on all over England as we speak. Now, I wonder what you thought my price should be. Did you have a starting figure in mind? I like a good negotiation, you know that. Go on, tell me about the offer so I can counter it."

"Mariana."

"Tell me."

"Mariana—"

"Tell me my *PRICE.*"

"Stop it," he ordered her in that low, slow voice that could likely stop a river from flowing.

All her reckless rage left her at once. And she was drained and trembling. Her tears blurred her vision as she stared up at him.

He had gone gray-faced.

"Mariana . . ." His voice was quiet. She could

hear in it his struggle. "I cannot change my past. I cannot change who I am and do not want to. You cannot change your past and who you are. I would not want to change one particle of you. I thought you understood this. This is how things are."

"To be clear, this money is to buy my discretion, too, is it? I'm to tiptoe about as long as you pay me to do it? Where the bloody hell is the honor in that? What kind of life is that for me?"

She could hear, she could see, his chest moving swiftly with his rough breath. Other than that, he was silent.

"Funny, isn't it?" She sniffed. "You're a bloody hero and you're used to ordering legions what to do. And your reward for that is that you're at the mercy of legions now. Brave, brave, *stupid* man who can't make himself happy. And can't you see that? Can't you see you're a *man*?"

Her voice broke. Her eyes filled and tears spilled. She covered her face with her hands, horrified by the anarchy of her emotions, heaving for breath. "Oh God. I'm sorry. I don't know why I'm . . . I haven't the right to . . ."

Because she saw it clearly. Beneath her rage was terrible, futile heartbreak. She had known precisely how it would be and *still* she felt all but murdered. How? How was it that she'd still entertained, for even a moment, the minutest possibility of a happy, improbable ending right out of an opera? That wasn't who he *was*. He'd encapsulated the problem in just a few words: he could not change who he was. She could not change who she was. This was how things were.

He'd assessed the problem and offered what he saw as the only practical solution.

And God help her, part of her thought: he cannot bear to part with me. And in that was a sort of unholy joy.

But still he would probably marry some young titled woman, and he would have kept Mariana in an apartment like a horse in a stable.

If only he had just let her go. She could have left him with her illusions intact.

James struggled to breathe. He—the hero, as she'd called him—was lost. He had no idea how to bear her pain or his own. Or how to comfort her. But he reached for her anyway. He wrapped his arms around her, because he didn't know what else to do. Holding her was the only comfort he'd truly known. Possibly the only peace he'd truly known.

Because peace was *being* known.

Once his touch had melted her. Now her every muscle stiffened, braced furiously against him.

"Mariana, please don't cry. Please don't cry." He brushed his lips across her temple, her brow, softly, softly. He kissed her cheek and tasted salt. "Sweetheart, my love, don't cry, don't cry." He had never begged for anything before in his life. He had never murmured endearments that poured from him as though his heart was indeed cut open. His throat was tight. "I cannot bear it if you cry."

But she was still weeping when she turned her lips to his. Took his face between her hands. Because God help her, he was her only comfort, too.

Half tender, half savage. The kiss was a contest. Then a war. They were out to prove that neither of them could do without the other. She dragged her hands down his chest, to his cock, took it in her hands, caressed and stroked and teased in rhythm, in time, with their deep and drugging kisses, the clash of teeth, the glide and sweep of tongues. She knew him, too: when the cords of his neck went taut, and when his breath came in ragged bursts through parted lips. His hands on her breasts, the feathery strokes, the hard thumbs across her nipples, her head falling back on a helpless sobbing catch of pleasure that made him wild. As if it was too much to bear.

She pulled him down over her. He braced himself on both arms. And then he was inside her.

And he could see her struggling to forestall it. To prove to him that he could not always conquer her so easily. Her breath gusting through parted lips. Her eyes defiant, as she denied him what he wanted. What he wanted was the satisfaction, the sheer carnal triumph, of knowing that she was in his thrall. That he could make her wild with need. He wanted to see her eyes go dark. To feel her body ripple, then thrash, in the throes of pleasure. To know he had given this to her, and that she wanted only him.

So he was slow, slow. He tortured both of them.

Sweat beaded her brow and his. He knew what she wanted and how she liked it. And he could deny her, and he saw the moment when she furiously surrendered.

"*Please* . . . James . . . you bastard . . . now . . . like that . . . Oh God oh *God* . . ." She arched up into him, begging him with her hips, her hands reaching for his hip, urging him on.

She made a fist and banged his arm with it, enduring the banking pleasure; her fist fanned and her fingers clung because she knew she was about to be all but torn from her body. She was nearly sobbing with fury that only he could give this to her. *Now and always*, he wanted to say. *Now and always.*

He unleashed himself.

His hips drummed, and their bodies collided hard. Her hips bucked to meet his, to take him deeper as he thrust swiftly. Her nails digging into his skin, her feet locked on his back. Her breath mingling with his, a storm. Her eyes black, then hazed, then closed.

And when she screamed her release, her head turned into the pillow to muffle it. Her body bowed helplessly up. He felt her pulsing around him.

"*Mariana.* Oh God . . . dear *God* . . ." He went still above her, hurled from his body and into the blackness, into that little death, lights exploding behind his eyes, his body racked with violent pleasure. He could still feel her hands digging into his shoulders. Holding him.

She kept her eyes closed.

He withdrew gently, lowered himself gingerly to lie beside her.

After a moment of silence, he whispered her name. As if he was already alone in the dark.

She said nothing.

They normally would have reached for each other, in celebration of magnificent sex and congratulations at their skill.

They lay still, side by side. Not touching.

He listened to her breathe. He could feel a hot, hollow space in his chest, as though his heart had been spaded out.

She shifted and laid an arm across her eyes, as though she couldn't bear to see him.

There were layers to this shame. He'd used this explosive hunger between them, and her own sensual nature, as weapons. He'd meant to show her what she was denying herself if she were to leave him. To show her that for all her strength and determination, she would always surrender to him. Even when she was furious and hurt.

He was ashamed that he'd still reached for her for comfort, because hurting her had hurt him.

He was ashamed he'd somehow made her feel like a whore, like a mere receptacle for his needs, when she'd always come to him freely.

And he was ashamed that he, a man who had built an entire life on knowing what to do, had done the wrong thing, out of selfishness, because of all of the losses he'd known, somehow this seemed to be the one he couldn't bear. This was the one that would level him.

He was lost.

She exhaled finally, at length. And then she sat up and moved to the edge of the bed. She bent down to pluck up her stockings. She rolled each one on, carefully, slid her dress over her head. Slowly and gracefully.

She didn't ask for his help with her laces. Deftly, she got them tied.

And once she was dressed, she quietly moved across the room, seized the candle, opened the door, and left, closing the door behind her.

She'd never looked back at him.

He lay motionless for a time. Flattened. Spent.

And suddenly he could feel a bleakness rolling toward him. A scouring emptiness in his chest.

As though he'd been swept off the jetty and hurled into the black depths.

And then there was nothing.

And now *he* was nothing.

He sat up and breathed into his hands, his shoulders heaving like bellows.

And from within that black nothingness rose wave after wave of love and fury and sorrow that he'd never dared allow expression. He did not know what to do with any of it. He could not bear it.

The man who could not be broken seized the vase and hurled it against the wall.

And saw it explode into smithereens.

Just like a temperamental opera singer.

Chapter Eighteen

❧

THERE WAS no more crying.

She felt like a husk. Awestruck by the completeness of the pain.

But, despite it all, mordantly amused: after this, she could not imagine that anything would be worth crying over.

She'd known this thing with the Duke of Valkirk would be a bloody opera. She'd *known* it was foolishness from the start. She liked to think she could not have saved herself, that she'd had no choice in the matter at all, but the truth was, she'd made a decision each time she'd stealthily visited his room, each time she kissed him, each time she took his body into hers.

She'd accepted that role, and she'd played it right through to the predictably dramatic end.

She lay awake until dawn, empty, yet somehow complete. As if every emotion she could possibly experience had been funneled through her in a month's time, so nothing could ever surprise her or hurt her again.

Most importantly, she knew now what love felt like.

She was suddenly aware of the silvery thread of outrageous luck and kindness woven through her dramas and tragedies. Fate might have made a shuttlecock of her more than once, but each time she'd been batted sky-high again. From penury to the Italian Opera House. From scandal to The Grand Palace on the Thames. From hope to heartbreak.

From heartbreak into the job of a singing lobster.

No one had *ever* been more grateful to be batted right into that job, because it meant she could be gone from England in two days, and after that, perhaps forever.

She breathed through the pain.

She imagined him lying awake next to some young woman with a title. Together and still utterly alone. His spirit going arid. Perhaps yearning for her, because of course he would.

She really didn't think she'd be easy to forget.

He deserved to live with love.

Oh God. He ought to be loved.

But he'd be comforted, naturally, by the fact that he had done his duty. That he'd done the "right" thing.

She brought her knees up to her chest restlessly. She curled in on herself to muffle the pain.

And yet. How grateful she genuinely was to know what love really was. To learn that loving, fiercely, with her whole self, was yet another of her gifts.

She *wanted* to love.

But he would be her definition of love for the rest of her days. She was certain of that, too. How could any other man possibly factor?

Well, then. So she would just go on loving him.

Perhaps he would open a window one night, and the faintest echoes of her voice from some faraway stage, singing of love and yearning and sorrow, would drift outward on a breeze. It would drift into his window, and he would feel it, and feel loved.

And tomorrow, she would look into the faces of Dot and Helga and all the maids, and she would give her all to a night they would never forget. Beauty ought not to be available only to the wealthy. They would carry that memory with them through their days like a precious thing, and perhaps their joy in it would touch someone else who would be changed or soothed or inspired.

And *this* was how she would love him for the rest of her days. Not by pining. She would send it out into the world, and her love for him would be as endless and renewing as the tides, and come back to her that way, too.

WHEN THE MAIDS crept into the duke's rooms just after dawn the following morning, they found the bed smoothly made, all of the duke's belongings missing, including the miniatures and the clock, and the duke gone.

Which was startling, as it was still dark.

In the corner was a neatly swept pile of shards from a vase.

"Looks like writing his book finally sent him crackers," they said sympathetically, and they swept it up and took it away.

He knew precisely who was in town because he had a stack of invitations to prove it.

Viscounts, earls, barons, marquesses, wealthy merchants—more than a dozen men and their wives were roused before dawn by tremblingly apologetic but determined servants who were less afraid of their employers than the Duke of Valkirk. He'd arrived before any light tinged the sky, in person, eyes burning with implacability, to thump on townhouse doors and request to be waited upon at once.

Because at the end of a night of suffering, James knew salvation meant doing the unthinkable: laying his burdens down.

And surrendering.

He'd finally met a force greater than himself.

Right. How odd that word was. "Right." So many shades of meaning. So odd, so antithetical to who he'd always thought he was—but surrendering was the right and only thing to do.

And at all of these townhouses, he was consequently greeted by variously unshaven, irritable, hungover, terrified, or burningly curious members of the elite. All of whom would appear for the unveiling of a portrait or a statue.

He didn't threaten or cajole.

He simply, finally, asked all of them for something in return.

Sergeant Massey and his wife, Emily, smiled encouragingly at Delilah and Angelique, who stood at the entrance of the ballroom behind a beautifully flower-bestrewn table. The program was due to begin in ten minutes.

They peered into the ballroom past Delilah and Angelique.

"Oh my. It's beautiful. I suspect it has lovely acoustics . . ." Mrs. Massey enthused.

"stics . . . stics . . ."

They all gave a little start at the echo. The ballroom was resoundingly empty. They were the first paying guests to arrive.

Delilah, radiant in deep red silk, and Angelique, glowing in gold, smiled at Mrs. Massey somewhat weakly.

The drunk man who usually leaned against the building two doors down (and who used to lean against The Grand Palace on the Thames, until they persuaded him otherwise) had officially been the first to arrive. He now lounged in a chair, gazing up at the ceiling and the stars. "Am I inside or outside?" he wondered aloud. "That is the question."

Suddenly a young man sporting a riot of dark curls and a modest dark suit appeared in the doorway. In his hand he gripped the neck of a cello.

Delilah and Angelique stared at him, dumbstruck.

The violinist on his heels almost collided with him when he stopped abruptly. They knew he was a violinist because *his* hand was gripping the neck of one.

Huffing on the heels of the violinist was another violinist.

Delilah craned her head to see how many stringed instruments would appear.

"Where would you like us to set up?" the first young man said briskly.

"I beg your pardon?" Angelique managed.

"Where would you like us to set up?" he repeated patiently. "We've been paid to play for Miss Wylde. We know the songs she intends to include." He fished something from his pocket. "We've a program!" he said cheerfully. "And we've played for her before at the theater. She knows us."

Angelique and Delilah stared at him wordlessly.

Then turned to regard each other in bafflement, which they attempted to disguise.

"Why don't you stand next to the pianoforte?" Delilah finally suggested. "And . . . perhaps play some Bach while we wait for our guests to arrive?"

She felt a bit as though she were commanding a character in a dream, and that there would be no telling what they would do now. Transform into dragons. Disappear in a puff of smoke.

But off they cheerily went.

"Did *we* pay for them?" Delilah asked in a low voice. "We've been so frantic these past few days, it might have slipped our minds." She was half joking.

"Never," Angelique said. "When has our budget ever slipped our minds?"

Upon tuning, the musicians at once launched into Bach's *Concerto for Two Violins* in D minor.

The night was turning out to be everything they'd dreamed. And therefore quite puzzling.

"Someone better go and tell Miss Wylde," Angelique said. "She may need to adjust her program."

They were both indescribably relieved they would not need to play pianoforte for her.

They saw Miss Wylde's little face peep out of a slit in the velvet curtains at the sound of the violins. Then immediately duck back behind it.

Then Delilah and Angelique pivoted toward the doorway again and almost gave a start.

A gentleman—for he most assuredly was—and a lady—for she most assuredly was—hovered there, each wearing evening finery and harried, wary expressions as they approached.

But when they were met by the warm, gracious smiles of two beautiful ladies, one dressed in gold silk, the other in red silk, and when they peered past them into the ballroom, their tense expressions cleared and evolved into a certain puzzled wonder.

And then relaxed into lines of pure pleasure.

"We should like two tickets to hear Miss Mariana Wylde, please. We are Lord and Lady Dovecoat," he said, briskly confident now.

"Of course," Delilah said smoothly. "Eight shillings, please. And we do thank you for coming. Here is your program. As you are among the first to arrive, you're entitled to a commemorative handkerchief, because we feel you will need it when Miss Wylde breaks your heart. We think you'd like a memento, because we feel certain you will want to remember this exclusive occasion forever."

They were visibly charmed by both this speech and the gift.

"Oh, a handkerchief, Dovecoat!" Lady Dovecoat was delighted about this. "And a broken heart! How novel! What do these initials stand for?"

"The Grand Palace on the Thames, Lady Dovecoat. We are the finest, most exclusive destination for entertainment this side of London."

Angelique had improvised, and Delilah shot her an amused, approving glance.

"Dorothy will show you to your seats," Delilah told them.

Dorothy was Dot, of course, who curtsied deeply to them, and led them to the second row and sat them three chairs in. To their evident puzzlement, her face was still, very faintly, blue from the nets, which lent her a bit of an ethereal air.

She went on to amuse herself by seating all the arriving couples by the colors the ladies wore, creating a pattern of blue, red, gold, and green stripes across the rows, sorting mauves in with the blues and pinks in with the reds, and this was often accomplished by seating one couple in the middle of an empty row, squeezing another couple onto the end, and more than once, asking another couple to move. Soon the pattern was part of the scenery and a very pretty sight that greeted all the new arrivals.

What did it mean? they murmured amongst themselves. Surely it was a *ranking* of some sort. Wasn't everything?

The cryptic and clearly deliberate arrangement

kept the aristocrats unsettled and obsessed for weeks.

Later, Mariana thought she first understood what was about to happen when she heard the first note dragged by a bow from a violin.

Her heart lurched. She'd felt that note like it had been drawn from her own heart.

She was motionless, puzzled.

Suddenly, Mrs. Pariseau, looking very handsome in a dark green silk with long fitted sleeves and a matching turban, peered through the curtain.

"Miss Wylde, are you decent?" she whispered.

"When am I ever decent?" Mariana bent to whisper back.

They both chuckled.

"A string quartet has arrived. Though the sudden Bach probably gave that away. The musicians claim they were paid to play for you. Do you know anything about it?"

While Mariana could not truthfully say she *knew* anything about it, she'd been smiling to herself since she heard the Bach. She was almost certain she *did* know how and why they were there.

He'd listened to her. He'd always listened to her. And it seemed he could make some dreams come true, after all.

She had learned her lesson about hope and portent, however. They stirred, of course; she gave them the cut direct. She would not again be swiftly encouraging something that had caused her so much pain.

"Would you like to have a word with the cellist?"

Mrs. Pariseau asked. As the cellist wasn't currently occupied.

"If you would send him over, I'll just review my list of songs with him to make certain they know what to do. Thank you."

And just like that, Mariana felt the surge of the excitement that always heralded her most transcendent evenings. She knew, in her very bones, something magical was about to happen.

The trickle of guests became, if not a torrent, then decidedly a flow. They arrived occasionally singly, most often in pairs, over and over again. Delilah and Angelique witnessed virtually the same progression of emotions on every face, all of them at last passing into the building wearing expressions of bemused, delighted anticipation. Which of course was only what the decorations deserved.

Shillings tinkled deliciously into the locked box.

And soon it was clear that not only would every seat be filled, but many members of the audience would be standing, as well.

Guests mingled and murmured, stood and craned their heads to admire the stars and draped fishnet sky and the flowers and to inspect each other, all in all quite satisfied with everything.

And yet not one of them revealed why or how they had come to be here at the last minute. Neither Delilah nor Angelique asked. They wanted everyone attending to believe this was precisely what they'd expected all along.

But they paused now and again to give each other's arms little squeezes.

Delilah gestured with her chin to her husband, who, along with Sergeant Massey and Lord Bolt, was keeping an eye on affairs to make sure things remained civil, and he came to her side.

"Do you know anything about this?" Tristan murmured to the ladies.

They shook their heads.

"I think I do," he said.

He was less amazed than he'd thought he'd be.

Because Captain Hardy knew more than a little bit about the mountains a man would move for a woman he loved. And how fragile and new even the greatest, most battered of hearts could become in the hands of the right woman.

He felt protective of his theory. He wouldn't betray the man. He let it lie for now.

Delacorte had campaigned for the role ("Who's louder than I am?" he'd insisted indignantly), but Lucien finally won the vote over who would announce the start of the performance. As Mrs. Pariseau had said more than once before, Lord Bolt had a very fine reading voice and ought to be onstage, which was what she thought of everyone who possessed a very fine reading voice.

His voice was indeed perfect for this night: resonant, refined, his pristine aristocratic English accent still a bit haunted about the edges by the French he'd been raised with and the other lands to which he'd traveled.

He strolled out onstage, stood before the curtain, and like a conjurer, raised his arms and announced:

"Ladies and gentlemen. Thank you all for coming. We are so pleased to have you with us tonight for this very special occasion. May I have your silence and attention, please. And please take your seats."

The rustling of programs and fans gradually eased, like a dying breeze.

And then Dot and Rose, each in a blue apron, a white tissue flower tucked into her hair and her belt, moved along the aisles and carefully doused every other sconce on the wall. The net effect was like watching the gradual fall of eventide.

A sigh went up when, in this darkened room, a hundred more little jeweled stars were revealed, twisting and glinting on the finest of wire from the midnight-blue-bedecked ceiling.

And then, with somber wonderment, as though he could not believe his luck and theirs, Lucien announced:

"Ladies and gentlemen . . . Miss Mariana Wylde."

The curtains shimmied smoothly aside on their runners.

To reveal a star-studded blue against which hung a huge luminous moon.

Where was Mariana?

They heard her before they saw her. A soft call. A sighing note, wavering, like a breeze moving through the trees. A call like a nightingale.

Singing, she strolled from the shadows, like a nymph called by the moonlight, a flowered wreath in her loosed hair, a nacre-colored silk gown flowing in Grecian folds from her shoulders, banded beneath her breasts with a little ribbon.

There was a collective gasp.

Then murmurs.

Then frantic shushing.

Then silence.

Then the soft, groaning sigh of a bow drawn across cello strings. Beneath it rose the siren sob of a violin. The very sounds of lovemaking.

They heralded what was about to happen to the audience.

With her voice, for the next forty minutes, Mariana made playthings of their hearts. Shredded them and tossed them aloft like confetti. Put them back together, then filled them like sails with joy. She did to their hearts all that had been done to her own in the past month by the Duke of Valkirk, and in every word, profound and mundane, she sang of him.

And in the end, she owned every heart in the room.

Handkerchiefs were soaked. Applause was thunderous. Helga's cakes were devoured, and the punch disappeared.

At intermission, every member of the audience obediently queued for an opportunity to bow over her kid-gloved hand. All the guests, unbeknownst to them, were watched like a hawk by Captain Hardy and Sergeant Massey.

"Miss Wylde, it was a privilege to meet you. A privilege, I say!" This was Viscount Dalrymple. A lowered voice. "If there's anything we can ever do to help . . ."

She made a note for the next time she might appear in the gossip columns and need a reputation burnishing.

"Miss Wylde, *what* a remarkable evening. I am Mrs. Franklin. I will of a certainty write a *glowing* notice for the newspaper," said a woman resplendent in mauve silk and pearls. A purple plume arched over her head like an alert familiar.

Not one person in the crowd said the duke's name. Oh, but she knew that this was his doing. She knew by how everyone looked at her, by that rank curiosity tinged with respect and envy—perhaps even a little awe.

And of course a certain prurient curiosity, which they would never dare to fully show to her.

Who else had the power to command recalcitrant aristocrats to attend an event at the docks en masse?

What it meant, she could not say. If it meant anything at all.

Was it a parting gift? An apology? She refused to entertain theories.

Even if she never saw him again, he'd made certain she knew she was loved.

Even if he wasn't here, she was glad she could, in this way, share her triumph with him.

Because that's precisely what it was. He had given her the audience, but the triumph was all her own.

Today a triumph.

Tomorrow a lobster.

Such was the rhythm of life.

Chapter Nineteen

❦

IT HAD been too long since James had been to this farm where he'd grown up. It looked much the same, which was precisely what he'd always loved about it. It didn't change.

A few things needed tending. The low stone walls along the walk leading to the house had been battered a bit by the weather; wildflowers were peeping through.

"You're done for, walls," he thought, amused and sympathetic. "The wildflowers will win."

They could be built up again.

But his own walls were rubble. Absolute smithereens, like the vase he'd hurled. They could not be rebuilt. Which was all to the good: he didn't want them.

He stood naked and surrendered and free.

He stood, breathing in the country air, and wondered how he'd become more a set of qualities than a person. Brick by brick, that's how it had happened. The man he was had been built up by, then bricked in by, duty and expectation and admiration and reverence and, yes, honor. And by his own pride.

He knew that what he'd felt with her was *happy*. It was not a virtue or a vice. Perhaps the condition ought not even be labeled. Because it was pure, it was everything and nothing all at once, which was how he imagined the sky above felt. He imagined it was what a baby felt when it first opened its eyes into the world outside the womb. It seemed so clear that this was the human's native state, perhaps the birthright. And that all of life was just a mission to get back to it.

These epiphanies were as disorienting as if he'd taken one of Delacorte's powders.

His every breath in their aftermath was almost painful.

It was also interesting and new.

He stood next to his son in silence, beneath a blossoming tree. The sky above had no need of cherubs trailing scarves.

He'd walked the land out over an expanse of green interrupted by contented fluffy sheep. Sky and meadow met in the purest blue and green. It was that sort of day. They were rare enough.

The sheep were healthy and fat, and the sheep-dogs were lean and lively and skilled. Earlier he'd spoken with the head shepherd, and found he was knowledgeable and conscientious. The house was in fine condition: comfortable, welcoming, warm. His son had seen to its care out of pride, not necessarily any passion for it, but James was proud of his son's diligence.

"Arthur."

"Yes, Father?"

"I'm going to ask you a question you might find unusual, but I'd like an honest answer. I shall not judge one way or another."

His son, quite naturally, looked amused and wary. "Of course. Ask away."

It was a while before James could form the words.

"Do you love your wife?"

Arthur gave a short, stunned laugh.

He studied his father's face to ascertain whether it was some sort of trap or test.

And then he fell quiet. They listened to bees humming in the partaking of pollen.

James was touched and proud that he was searching for a thoughtful answer, because he wanted to please his father.

And then he watched color move into his son's cheeks. "Yes. I would do anything to make Cathryn happy."

You're just a man, James.

She knew he loved her. She'd been asking him to choose her over his own myth, the one that was not of his making. The one built up, like a castle, over decades.

There were some in England who would consider that choice almost akin to an act of war. So many had been invested in the creation of his myth, after all. It was their castle, too. It had served them well.

So be it. He was nothing if not a warrior.

He turned to his son and said, "Thank you for

telling me. I'm glad. And," he added, "you have my permission to sell."

THE MORNING AFTER the Night of the Nightingale dawned with astonishing clarity. Mariana was surprised to see the sunrise, in fact. She hadn't slept at all; the night had flown, and it had been heady from start to finish. After all the guests had departed, and against protestations, Mariana changed into a day dress and apron and helped everyone at The Grand Palace on the Thames clean the ballroom. They'd all chattered and gossiped and reminisced happily about the evening's triumph.

She simply didn't want to be alone. She didn't want to think about James.

She'd of course collected her percentage of the profitable evening. It was modest after her room and board were deducted, but well-earned.

Those who'd attended took memories away of a charming, gracious young woman possessed of an enormous gift, and those memories—well, they might not erase her past, but they would certainly blur and dilute it, as, with luck, she gave them more beautiful memories over the years, until all they thought about when they heard the name Mariana Wylde was "beauty."

She had no illusions about the permanency of supremacy. The winds of fortune—and gossip—bent the *ton* this way and that like stalks of wheat. She needed to *become* the wind.

She'd packed her trunk with the help of Dot,

and then she'd stayed up chattering with everyone in the reception room, which was all to the good, because it prevented thoughts of James from sneaking in through chinks of silence.

She'd gone up to her room, to see it one more time.

Just past dawn, Dot appeared at her door.

"I've been down to call a hack for you, Miss Wylde. And wouldn't you know it, there was one waiting practically right outside already!"

And down they went.

"Mr. Malloy!" For that's who her hack driver indeed was. "Oh, my goodness. I'm delighted to see you. And you'll be delighted to know my straits have improved considerably since last we met! Fate must have brought us together again."

"Oh, aye, fate's what did it, not commerce," Mr. Malloy said dryly. "Still the one trunk, Miss Wylde?"

"Yes, thank you. I'll take the valise inside with me."

Because she did now have a valise, and it was stuffed full of parting gifts.

While Mr. Malloy applied himself to loading her trunk onto the hack, she turned back to the little crowd touchingly gathered in front of The Grand Palace on the Thames to wave her off.

"We shall miss you! Come and stay again please, when you're famous for different reasons!" Dot called.

"Or even if you're never famous at all!" added Mr. Delacorte, as she was helped into the hack.

". . . as if *that's* a possibility!" she called out the window, all bravado to the last. To make them laugh, because smiles and laughter were balm.

"You don't have to be famous to have worth," Mrs. Pariseau called cheerfully.

"You're famous to all of us for being a delight," the diplomatic Mrs. Hardy said firmly.

Mariana blew them a kiss. She waved a handkerchief initialed with TGPOTT. She would keep it her entire life, no matter where life shuttlecocked her next.

She had wondered. But she did not, in her heart of hearts, think he would be there, among the crowd. She was glad, truly glad, he was with his son. She thought he would eventually find some peace and solace there.

And she couldn't imagine him waving a handkerchief.

Too close to the white flag of surrender.

Through the carriage window, she saw the little crowd before the little boardinghouse laughing and dabbing their eyes, and with an ache in her chest, she watched the building for as long as it remained in sight.

Which was a long time, since it was the cleanest and shiniest building for miles.

She'd plenty to keep her occupied on her journey to Dover. She'd been made a gift of the newest book by the author of *The Ghost in the Attic*. It was called *The Ghost in the Scullery*, which Dot had promised her was just as thrilling. They'd begun reading it two nights ago in the sitting room, and

Dot had read a little bit ahead without telling anyone, and suffered great secret guilt over this.

Delilah and Angelique had given her an embroidery hoop and some pretty silk thread, so she could make a pillow to add to the collection at The Grand Palace on the Thames. She would send it back to them from Paris. Perhaps she would embroider a mermaid on it.

She could practice her Italian by reading, again, the libretto of *The Queen of the Deep*. She could look out the window at the road she had last traveled when she had gone with her family to the seaside so many years ago and marvel at the change of scene. In short, there was enough to occupy her every moment so that not one fleeting thought about James could sneak through.

She fell asleep instead.

A sleep so sudden, black, and total that when she awoke with a start, she had no idea how long she'd been asleep, or even where she was. She knew her cheek was warm when she awoke.

She turned her head sleepily toward the window.

She sat bolt upright. There were no buildings of any sort in sight. Everywhere, everywhere, were rolling green hills. Confined by low wooden fences.

She closed her eyes and opened them again, in case she was dreaming.

The view remained unchanged.

She spent a moment or two merely gawking.

But . . . was this in fact the road to Dover? At least they'd gotten an early start if they were lost.

And then she realized what had awakened her: the carriage was slowing.

And then . . . oh dear . . .

It came to a halt.

She opened the door to find Mr. Malloy's worried face peering in.

"Miss Wylde, I'd like to have a look at the shoe on one of our 'orses, if ye dinna mind. I've a bad feelin' about it . . ." He shook his head and clucked.

"Oh dear. Poor thing! Very well. I suppose if we must."

He helped her down from the hack onto the side of the road, and next to what appeared to be the beginning of another long road, perhaps leading to a house.

She turned about. Heavens, it was quiet. There were ruts on the main road, but they looked old, as though they'd been made long ago. It didn't seem as though the road was often used.

She didn't know where she was. Only if she were to describe heaven, it would look a good deal like this. Pink and white blossoms ruffling in the trees; tiny star-shaped yellow and white flowers trimming the hedgerows. Thumb-sized birds with peeping calls darting between the greenery.

A sky like a sheet of blue china.

Above her, a single cloud, like a dollop of cream, spreading softly.

The warmth.

The quiet.

The quiet was a caress.

She worried that in quiet moments, she was always going to be bound to weep, because quiet moments made her soft.

Quiet moments belonged to James.

She hated to interrupt the quiet, but it needed to be said.

"But Mr. Malloy, are you certain this is the way to Dover?"

"Well, that's the other thing, Miss Wylde." He removed his cap to scratch his head. "I thought so, but I may have taken a wrong turn a few miles back. I'll just have a look at me map, won't I?"

He reached into his coat and retrieved what looked like a sheet of parchment folded in thirds. He fanned it open.

"Well, I've a map right here, but it's in another language. I must have brought the wrong one. I canna make no sense of it, Miss. Would you have a look?"

She took it from him, gingerly. Her heart lurched in dread. Honestly, she could do with one or two uneventful hours in her life. A bit of a pause between caprices of fate.

She heaved a sigh, unfolded it, and had a look.

"Oh dear! Mr. Malloy! This isn't even a map! It's a . . . it's a . . ."

She stopped breathing.

Goose bumps spangled her arms.

It was a deed.

She stared at it.

"Oh . . . my . . . God," she breathed.

DEED OF GIFT
To Miss Mariana Wylde
the property henceforth known as Piccole Nuvole
By James Duncan Blackmore, Duke of Valkirk

Piccole Nuvole.

Little clouds.

"What on . . . what is . . . I don't under . . ."

She slowly lifted her head to find Mr. Malloy grinning at her. And then he stepped to the left.

To reveal, standing on the path before her, the Duke of Valkirk.

She stared. What *bliss* to see him in the sunlight.

For the time it took a bird to trill the first few notes of an aria, they feasted their eyes upon each other.

"Would you be so kind as to go for a walk with me, Mariana?" His voice was a little gruff.

He extended his arm.

It was a long moment before she could speak.

"I would be so kind." Her own voice was a mere thread.

She looped her arm through his.

And for a time—minutes, hours, days, epochs? They strolled without a word. Outside of time. Side by side. Along a pathway lined in a picturesque, ancient stone wall, wildflowers taking anarchic advantage of the gaps in the stone to bob over the path.

If she had actually died out there on the road

inside the hack, she was satisfied with how eternity was progressing. If she was dreaming, she would happily never wake. She would also have enjoyed the feel of his warm naked skin pressed against hers, but she would settle for this peace, this velvety contentment, the floating along on this day while her old nemesis, hope, bore her along on wings. As long as he was here.

He'd remembered about the musicians and Mr. Malloy. He'd ordered aristocrats to her event. She knew somehow he had done it.

She didn't know what was happening now. Or why, in her other trembling hand, she held a deed to a property that he seemed to have given to her.

But she would learn in due time, and something told her she now had all the time in the world.

He stopped when they came to a little wooden fence. Beyond it, pasture lands were heaped like soft, green blankets as far as her eye could see.

And scattered over them were enchanting, fluffy white sheep with sweet, long faces and ears that flickered at the sound of their approach.

She slipped her arm from his and moved along the fence. Her heart kicked inside her like a jackrabbit.

"I bought the property back from my son," he told her simply, quietly. "And I'm giving it to you. This land and everything on it should provide safety and shelter and an income for you and your mother if you choose to bring her to live with you. It's yours. If you want it."

He took a long breath and slowly released it.

"Or it can be ours . . . if you want me."

Her lungs stilled.

Her heart felt tight, like a bud. It yearned to unfurl.

She was not yet brave enough to let it. He had more to say, and she would need to hear it first.

They regarded each other in silence across a little distance. She was envious of the breeze that lifted his hair. She wanted to be touching him, too.

"I know I've bungled things badly." His voice was graveled. His breath came a little short, with nerves. With newness. "I've hurt you, and somehow in my selfishness, I've made you feel cheap, when you are . . ." He closed his eyes and shook his head. "You are so *indescribably* precious to me. Mariana, I knew I loved you before I ever touched you. I was afraid to call it that. All I knew was that I was happy. And something in me couldn't believe I would ever be allowed to keep that kind of love."

His beautiful face, saying these astonishing things, suddenly swam before her. She pushed the tears away with her fingertips.

"Am I bungling this?" he asked urgently. "I've no experience at this, Mariana."

She shook her head slowly.

"All I know is that I would rather die than hurt you ever again. All I want to do is show you how much I love you. If you would be so kind as to marry me, it would be the greatest honor of my life."

Her knees were about to give way, and he knew. He was there at once, arms around her, holding her up. She held his face in her hands, then looped her arms around his neck, met his lips with hers.

But only lightly, at first.

She had already told him with her body and with her eyes. But now, with a blessed new freedom to say whatever she liked and whatever she felt, she could say it aloud.

"I love you, too." Those words felt like a language she'd never stop learning.

His arms tightened around her. "And you will be my wife?"

"Oh, yes," she said softly. "Thank you. I think I will be so kind."

They commenced to slowly kiss each other senseless.

And when they finally took a moment to breathe, they turned to admire the green pasture and their woolly occupants. And their future.

"The sheep look like little clouds," she told him.

"Le pecore sono nostre," he said. "The sheep are ours."

Epilogue

෧෧෧

BECAUSE THE Archbishop of Canterbury, like everyone else, was in awe of the Duke of Valkirk and felt he owed him a debt of gratitude, a special license was at once granted. Mariana and James were married promptly by the local vicar, modestly and quietly beneath a bower of blossoms on a farm in Sussex. In attendance was nearly everyone who presently lived at The Grand Palace on the Thames and Valkirk's son, Arthur, and his wife, Lady Cathryn, and some observant sheep.

"With my body I thee worship, and with all my worldly goods I thee endow." The duke's voice thrummed with emotion when he said the words. He'd never fully understood how outrageously passionate they sounded, tucked in surreptitiously as they were amidst the solemnity of the rest of the vows from the Book of Common Prayer. But it was true: his body *was* hers. He would lay down his life for her. He would give her the world, if he could. Or at least, as many pairs of shiny satin slippers as she wanted.

There was nothing modest about the picnic that followed. It was supplied by Helga and the kitchen staff, paid for by the duke, and talked about with misty reverence by Mr. Delacorte for years to come.

(Mr. Delacorte had sold a few impotency cures to a viscount and a baron, respectively, during the intermission of the Night of the Nightingale.)

Angelique and Delilah and Captain Hardy and Lord Bolt were not shocked, though, when the duke informed them, quite calmly, of his impending nuptials, they did pretend to be surprised.

"One could almost have predicted it," Angelique said. "Do you suppose we're to blame?"

"I think one might say we're to thank," Captain Hardy countered.

Both he and Lucien felt protective of the duke's happiness. The unknowable man had found someone who knew and loved him. They had both experienced this sort of miracle at The Grand Palace on the Thames, and had been transformed.

"Do you suppose they broke the rules while they were there?" Delilah asked.

They were all quiet, imagining how and when it had all happened. The tiptoeing to the duke's suite in the dead of night, because that's what must have happened. The tiptoeing back again.

Then again . . . Delilah and Angelique had stolen moments with their husbands against their own rules, too.

Of course, it was possible it had been the world's most chaste affair. A meeting of hearts and minds over Italian lessons.

Looking at the two quietly besotted people, they really didn't think that was the case at all.

They would rather miss having both Mariana and the duke about, but they now counted them as friends, after a fashion. And friends could be so helpful when it came to referring new guests.

For instance, even now, unbeknownst to them, a letter was winging its way to them from a wonderful potential new guest, referred to them by Mr. and Mrs. Andrew Farraday, who had been among the first to stay at The Grand Palace on the Thames (and not married to each other at the time).

But the young woman with the French accent who would knock at the door of The Grand Palace on the Thames in about a week . . . well, she was going to prove to be quite a surprise.

"I love her," the duke told Arthur the day before the wedding ceremony, as they stood near the river together. He did not ever think he would tire of saying those three magical words in a row, but he was not and would not ever be one to gush. He'd said this firmly, unequivocally, and as a bit of a warning. "I think you will come to love her, too, and I hope this is true. Regardless, I should be grateful if you and your wife are civil and welcoming to her, regardless of your inclinations."

Arthur, understandably, was shocked into speechlessness.

His silence was lengthy but not stormy. He was clearly reflecting. The duke simply waited, quietly, and allowed him the time to do it.

And upon reflection, Arthur found he was not shocked, after all. "I knew it was the wiles."

But he was, carefully, teasing.

The duke laughed softly. "Oh, yes. The *wiles*."

Arthur idly threw a rock into the water.

"That's why you looked different to me that day, Father. You were happy. You were in love."

Oh, for God's sake.

This silenced James immediately. He did not yet have any sort of facility for discussing such a thing with his son. But he found, oddly, he did not mind being read so clearly. He hadn't been fully known to himself, until Mariana happened along. What a strange new pleasure it was to be known by people who loved him.

"And you must miss having a wife," Arthur suggested. He was not naive. He'd known his parents had lived apart.

"Yes," James said, simply.

He looked forward to spending more time with Arthur, whom he loved and liked, but whose heart he could not claim to fully know. He regretted this deeply. Perhaps it could not have been helped, but he would make it right.

There were more reasons to celebrate: he learned that Lady Cathryn, Arthur's wife, was with child. He would be a grandfather inside the year.

And the four of them, he and Mariana, Arthur and Cathryn, shed tears of joy at the news.

"I'd have people to care for," Mariana had once said, wistfully, when she'd talked of being a cobbler's wife.

And now she would.

And at the rate he and his new wife were going, he would also be a father again before too long.

"I think Primrose and Phillip would be wonderful names for children," he teased, lying alongside her, spent and nude and blissfully happy, on his wedding night.

"Oh, I should think 'James,'" she said dreamily. "'James' is all I think all the time, really."

AFTER THE WEDDING, another message was dispatched to Paris, to regretfully inform Signor Roselli that Mariana was no longer able to play the role of the lobster. She would indeed have gone to Paris, anyhow—she loathed breaking a commitment—but James needed to stay in London for parliament, and she wouldn't dream of leaving him for even a moment.

They sent Signor Roselli a tidy little sum to soften the blow of the loss of her and to apply toward hiring a new soprano.

"I'M AFRAID I'VE some difficult news," James told his publisher two days after the wedding. "I will not be finishing my memoirs. It seems my life is not quite over yet."

His publisher, Mr. Alcock, stared at the Duke of Valkirk with a pleasant smile, and thought, *I will hang if I murder him, but would anyone blame me? Or perhaps suicide is the way to go.*

"*But,*" the duke continued, "I've written something else, and I should be grateful if you'd read it."

He'd in fact been writing a libretto.

And he'd called it *The Cobbler's Daughter.*

It was Mariana's story—*their* story—told right

up until the moment he'd given it to Mariana to read this morning.

She'd read it, and afterward she could not speak for weeping.

His publisher read it straightaway, and lowered it slowly, and thought: *Dear God, if I publish this story, I'm going to make a fortune!*

He did and he did.

As it so happened, Signor Antonio Grieco, the composer who'd written the score for *The Queen of the Deep*, was responsible for its success. He was wonderfully gifted and craved an epic tale, a canvas upon which to unleash the whole of his talents. That canvas was *The Cobbler's Daughter*.

The score he wrote was exquisite and triumphant, heartbreaking and furious, then, at last, peacefully rapturous.

Mariana would sing the lead role for a dozen or so performances. But when their third child came along—James was born two years after they were married, and Primrose and Phillip followed in quick succession after that—she happily passed the torch to another talented soprano and took parts only occasionally. She and James reveled in their family and their outrageous good fortune in finding each other, and their family, and the whole of life, sufficiently, beautifully, exquisitely operatic.

The Cobbler's Daughter would go on to sell out opera houses all over Europe intermittently for decades to come.

THE *TON* WASN'T quite sure how to take the news of the duke's marriage when it became commonly known.

Oh, they tried to have a little fun at his expense, mainly because they thought they ought to. One or two cartoons were drawn. There were a few outraged murmurs. A scathingly witty, righteous editorial. Some attempts were made at rousing controversy and indignation, but they never quite took flight.

It was just that flash ballads were rather moot, because the duke had gone and unapologetically written an entire *libretto* about his story, which rather cut the authors of bawdy songs off at the knees. Bawdy songs were only funny if their subject could be embarrassed or surprised, preferably both. It was a typical General Blackmore strategy. He'd gotten ahead of the enemy, disarming them, and they were compelled to surrender.

In fact, the Duke of Valkirk in love was quite the same as the Duke of Valkirk in war—serious, dignified, absolutely certain of the rightness of Mariana and of his decision to marry her. Ridiculousness and mockery could not get a handhold on a man like this.

He was unapologetically, quietly happy, and so was his lovely new wife. He bought her dozens of shining things to wear, shoes and gowns and hats. They gave hundreds of pounds to charity. They entertained, infrequently but charmingly, in their London townhouse. They liked to spend a lot of time in the country.

It was determined that there was no dishonor in being happy.

"This doesn't mean you can go and marry an opera singer," fathers hastened to tell their sons.

And after a pause, they often added, "At least for a first wife."

THE VERY DAY of the wedding, Mariana finally committed words to her old friend, that pored-over sheet of foolscap from The Grand Palace on the Thames, and sent the letter off to her mother.

MRS. BRIDGETT WYLDE had just returned from the well with a bucket of water when she heard the sound of carriage wheels.

She slowly lowered the bucket and paused on the threshold of her cousin's cottage.

Not much found its way accidentally down this muddy lane in this damp land, and that included London gossip and sunlight. She had begun to worry about Mariana; the letter she'd anticipated was now over three weeks late. (As, mercifully, were the London newspapers, so she remained innocent of any knowledge of Mariana's eventful month.)

This meant that carriage now coming fully into view had to be, no matter how improbable it seemed, making the journey deliberately. The cottage must indeed be its destination.

She went still, shaded her eyes with a hand, and warily watched.

It was pulled by four matched bays, coats gleaming like polished metal.

And then, when it rounded the slight curve—and she would never forget this moment—the gold leaf of the painted crest winked into view.

Oh, dear God.

Everyone in England knew that crest.

The driver pulled the horses to a halt.

Bridgett tried not to gape when a footman in full, spotless blue livery stepped down and approached her.

"Pardon the intrusion, ma'am, but I should like to speak with Mrs. Bridgett Wylde, if I may."

"I am Mrs. Bridgett Wylde," she said.

He bowed.

He bowed! To *her*.

And then he reached into his coat and retrieved what appeared to be a letter. He held it out to her. It was sealed with red wax into which was pressed that bold and intricate and unmistakable letter "V."

What was *happening*?

She did not know what this meant for her. She only knew that portent traced her spine, and her hands trembled, and everywhere on her body goose bumps rose.

But she did know she wasn't dreaming, because if she was, surely she would have imbued Scotland with a little sunshine.

The man standing before her was beaming at her as if she'd won a prize.

She slipped a trembling finger beneath the seal.

Just in time she caught the shining scrap of something that fell from the letter.

It was Mariana's cherished pink ribbon.

Her heart in her throat, Bridgett read:

Dear Mama,

I hope this finds you well. I am very well. I feel it is best to come right to the point, so you shall not worry.

I have gone and gotten married. James is everything I never dared to dream, and I love him with my whole heart. I think you will love him, too.

Here is the ribbon you gave me for my tenth birthday, so you will know this is true and that you will be very certain that it is I who write this surprising letter. I should never part with it otherwise.

We should like you to come to live with us, if you would be so kind. These footmen will help you to pack your things and bring you safely to us. The staff will treat you like a queen. My husband knows how precious you are to me.

Do you remember the first time we went to the seashore, and how beautiful the rolling green hills were, and all the little sheep?

I think you will be pleasantly surprised by one of our homes.

I love you and I cannot wait to see you.

Your devoted daughter,
Mariana Blackmore
Duchess of Valkirk

Bridgett gave a stunned cry. Half laugh, half sob. She pressed her fist to her mouth.

If she'd had doubts about whether her daughter had written the letter, the last three words had vanquished them. It was just so very, very, very like Mariana to save the best part for the end.

She'd *always* had a flair for the dramatic.

And Bridgett, though filled with joy like a thousand sunny days, was not so easily rattled. She had a steely spine, too. Just like her daughter.

"I knew she was destined for greatness," she told the footman.

And she went inside to pack her things.

*Don't miss the third book
in Julie Anne Long's
Palace of Rogues series*

I'M ONLY WICKED WITH YOU

In stores now!